Dedication and Thanks

This book is dedicated to all those who pursue toleration over conflict.

Many characters and a number of events depicted within this story are based upon the real people and events of the seventeenth century. The contents though are fictional, and the story is based upon an alternative timeline.

Many thanks to Bethan Morgan for front cover artwork and Nicky Galliers for great editing input into this updated edition. Any issues which remain are purely down to the author.

7TH NOVEMBER 1617

Tony Morgan

Introduction

Remember, Remember…

History is made on all days, but the impact from some is greater than others. The sixth of November in 1605 was one such day. Our past, present and future were altered by the Powder Treason or Gunpowder Plot. Although the terrorist Guy Fawkes was discovered, a second bomber remained hidden beneath Parliament. The building was destroyed and King James I, his sons and many others were killed.

Nine-year-old Princess Elizabeth was crowned Queen of England. During her formative years her lands were ruled by her protector, the Earl of Northumberland, and the new Secretary of State, the Earl of Suffolk. Good men, they prevented a religion-fuelled civil war by passing new laws of tolerance, allowing the people to worship in Protestant or Catholic churches.

England was beginning to prosper but in times of change there are always dissenters. Tensions with France and Spain were increasing, and although Protestant Puritans and Jesuit Catholics hated each other, they despised tolerance even more. In their eyes there could only ever be one church. And then there was Ireland…

Part One

Extract from Traditional English Rhyme - Early 17th Century

'Elizabeth is chaste
Elizabeth is chased
If not married soon
It will be a waste'

Chapter I

Everard Digby slowly began to become aware of his surroundings. He squinted open one eye and then the other. The inside of his mouth felt dry, like a condemned man's. His bed was set between two windows but the heat was stifling. Wooden shutters kept out the light but limited the air flow. He moved his head. It ached.

The time was almost noon. The previous day was a drunken blur but the past was clear. Treason and betrayal, he was guilty of both. A dozen years earlier Digby had taken part in a conspiracy. He wouldn't have baulked at killing the king but at the last moment he'd walked away, turning his back on Robert Catesby, Guy Fawkes and the others. Shortly afterwards the majority of the plotters were rounded up and killed but Digby remained unscathed. He wasn't even arrested. There was no show trial, no execution.

His role in the Gunpowder Plot remained a mystery. It was Digby's guilty secret, subsequent punishment came from within. He estranged himself from his family, got on a boat and forced himself into self-imposed exile. His existence only became bearable when fuelled by drink, life-threatening adventure or both. And a few good friends.

Naval man Thomas Button was the best of them but Button's ship was in need of a refit, so they'd returned to England. The Navy Board had promised the work would only take a few weeks. With the ship berthed in Bristol, Digby travelled to London. He'd taken a room at the Duck and Drake, an inn on the Strand near the Thames. As he tried to sit up his forehead complained. He realised he'd drunk more the night before than he'd thought or ought.

\#

Queen Elizabeth II was busy, preparing for her twenty first birthday celebrations. The date was 19th August, in the year of our Lord 1617. The Queen glanced through the mullioned windows. The gardens around Greenwich Palace were a hive of activity. Inigo Jones strutted about, as was his wont, waving his arms in the air. The architect had always been one of her mother's favourites. The nervous energy flowing through the London-bred Welshman's body was plain to see.

A sizeable army of groundsmen hurried around positioning the output of Jones's imagination alongside the track. Newly laid flower beds and topiary ran from the gates which separated the inner and outer grounds to the steps at the palace entrance. Later in the day the route would be followed by the finest livery and coaches as they delivered more than two hundred guests to the festivities.

Under the direction of Jones and his assistants, men dressed in green robes lifted, moved and positioned heavy stone troughs, each filled with colour, greenery and back-breaking soil. The previous evening they'd worked late into the night to complete a lavish transformation of the interior rooms of the palace. Jones's focus had been on the entrance hallway, banqueting room and the great hall which the guests would pass through and congregate in.

The architect's extensive knowledge of theatre design had been put to good use. The rooms represented aspects of the English countryside. Rambling roses and honeysuckles lined the walls and filled the building with marvellous colours and scent. Strawberry plants and raspberry bushes had been engineered to fruit late in the season. Each was now covered with a mass of ripening red or purple berries. The corners and doorways were adorned with potted plum trees, laden with their mauve fruit.

The centrepiece of each room was a great English bough. An oak tree stood in the banqueting hall, whilst a magnificent horse chestnut filled the central section of the great hall ready for the evening's music and dancing. The trees had been carefully dug up and pruned to limit their height and spread. Selected roots had been retained, flattened and placed in soil and water. In a few days the trees would inevitably die but for now they looked magnificent.

In his mind Jones's design combined the power and awe of God and nature with the beauty and wisdom of the English monarch. To the Queen Mother's mind, it was all this and more. Anne of Denmark stood at the base of the palace steps. She beamed at Jones and his plethora of helpers. The banquet and musical celebration for her daughter's twenty-first birthday was going to be another triumph.

In recent years Anne's life had become increasingly dominated by two callings. The first was her passion for music, the arts and the finer things in life. The second was her love for her daughters Elizabeth and Mary. She'd lost too many children not to dote on the two she had left. Most of her offspring had died of natural causes but not her two sons Henry and Charles. The princes had been murdered, along with their father King James and many others in the bombing of Parliament on sixth November 1605. The events of the day were never far from her thoughts. Neither was the popular nursery rhyme. *'Remember, remember the sixth of November. Gunpowder, destruction, the lot. We see no reasons, there are no reasons that day should be forgot.'*

Queen Elizabeth looked down at her mother fondly. She wondered why the smile Anne had been wearing had left her face for a moment but her thoughts were quickly interrupted by her best friend and leading lady-in-waiting Anne Dudley. Anne politely drew the Queen back from the window and gestured for her to sit on the cushioned bench.

Elizabeth carefully positioned herself on the seat, folding the layers of her gown as she did so. Anne and the other ladies present knew better than to attempt to help her. Eventually she sat sufficiently still for her dressers to wire a collection of white pearls into her hair. Set against the patterned lace of her stiffened high collar the pearls appeared to emit a light all of their own.

'You look stunning,' said Anne. The hairdressers and other ladies-in-waiting left the room and the two young women were now alone. 'And so does the palace. I can smell the honeysuckle from up here and it's not even evening time yet.'

'I know. It's a gorgeous fragrance.' agreed Elizabeth. 'And I'm so glad we're on our own at last. Now we can talk freely without worrying about gossip and etiquette. I can't believe its my birthday already. The last year has passed by so quickly.'

'It has,' said Anne. 'How do you feel about being twenty-one?'

'Not very different to being twenty if I'm honest. I'm not a spinster yet, you know.'

Anne smiled sympathetically. Although she knew it annoyed Elizabeth, the importance of her future successful marriage was never far away from conversations in Greenwich. 'Do you think he'll be here tonight?' she asked.

'Who?' asked Elizabeth.

'The *one* of course,' Anne replied 'Your future husband. He's going to be someone special to measure up to the expectations of my lords Suffolk and Northumberland.'

'And those of my mother,' added Elizabeth.

'And most of all your own,' said Anne, 'I know you're a woman of high standards.'

8

Elizabeth shook her head. She enjoyed the gentle teasing from her friend but felt they should be discussing weightier topics.

'Do we always have to talk so much about my impending marriage?' she asked. 'Can we not converse about science instead? Astronomy for instance. Great discoveries are being made across Europe but the worthy men who make them are being persecuted for their trouble.'

'Have you received a reply to your letter ?' asked Anne.

'Which one?' replied Elizabeth. She wrote many letters, as her father had before her. 'I've written twice to the Roman Inquisition but not received a single reply. I fear they don't take me seriously enough. I will change their minds. In time they will listen but for now I must wait for them to lift a quill.'

She paused a moment before continuing. 'Oh Anne, their approach is madness. They think Rome and the Earth is the centre of our universe when the great European scholars of our day have proven otherwise. I'm the leader of the Church of England but I'm not arrogant enough to think that the planets rotate around Westminster Abbey or St Paul's or myself. The conclusion should be clear, examine the facts, do not close your eyes to them.'

'Perhaps we should keep this discussion to ourselves for now,' said Anne. 'You'll be giving the Earl of Northumberland a fit if you talk like this outside these rooms.'

Elizabeth put on her thoughtful face. She looked at the pearls in the mirror. The Queen moved her head gracefully from side to side and observed how they appeared to leave a trail of light to show where they'd been.

'Old Northy's alright,' she said. 'He may be a little traditional at times but he believes in science as much as I do. Wasn't it his passion for learning which ensured we both received such a great education?' Elizabeth looked at her friend for a moment. 'Why educate us if we're not permitted to use this knowledge to expand our minds further?'

'Of course you're correct but you're also a queen,' replied Anne, 'I know you never forget this but neither does Lord Northumberland, nor the Earl of Suffolk, nor the Queen Mother. They all want what is best for you...'

'As long as it's best for the country too,' interjected Elizabeth. 'And that means finding a suitable husband for me to bed down and make babies with as soon as possible. Don't worry, there'll be plenty of candidates around tonight. Perhaps even *the one* as you call him.'

9

Still sitting on the stool Elizabeth admired herself in the full length mirror. She was young and attractive but not beautiful in the way Anne Dudley was. Men looked at the two women in different ways. Was it because of their looks or their status, she wondered? The smile in the mirror began to leave her face.

'Do you have any new favourites?' asked Anne. 'Last night when you met my lords Suffolk and Northumberland did they have any countries they wanted you to target in particular?'

'We didn't discuss suitors,' replied Elizabeth, admonishing her friend. 'If you must know we talked about my plans to send a peace envoy to Ireland. It has taken some time but I've finally persuaded the two earls my choice for the role is sound. I can hardly believe their reluctance in the matter.' She laughed dismissively. 'It's not as if I need their approval. We shall meet the man for the first time next week.'

'I don't think they'll want you to marry anybody Irish,' said Anne quickly.

'No, indeed.' Elizabeth's face softened. 'Nor anyone French for that matter. At least not now King Louis has married his Spanish princess. I understand their union is already causing problems. Northumberland says our treaty with Spain is strong and worth too much economically for the Spanish to pull out of, but Suffolk is worried in case Louis attempts to turn Spain against us.'

'Do you think you've had a lucky escape?'

'Yes, of course I do,' laughed Elizabeth. 'Very much so. Before the betrothal, Northumberland and Suffolk spent too much time trying to match me up with King Louis for my liking. For heaven's sake he's only fifteen. They may have wanted to get into bed with the French but I was the one who was going to have to physically do it. Have you heard the stories about the state of his teeth? Imagine having to kiss that!'

Anne placed her hand over her mouth in mock surprise at Elizabeth's words. After a few moments she glanced at the second mirror at the far side of the room. With a quick movement of her fingers she nervously straightened her hair.

'What about Frederick of Palatine? He'll be here tonight, won't he?' she asked.

Elizabeth sighed. 'Yes, Freddie will be here. You know I like him. He's brave and charming and makes me laugh. What's more, unlike Louis he's not a boy, he's a fully grown and well proportioned man. I'm sure we could...' She hesitated for a moment as if to select the right words. 'I'm sure we could do business together if you know what I mean.'

10

'I think I do,' replied Anne.

'No, I didn't mean like that. Well, perhaps I did… Anyway Freddie is unfortunately a most unsuitable suitor,' said Elizabeth. She took a breath. 'Palatine is just a small state on the banks of the river Rhine. It's not even a proper country. Never mind Northumberland and Suffolk, my mother would have tremors at the idea of me entering into a union with such a minor entity. I like Freddie a great deal but he's too far down the pecking order I'm afraid. Surely he can't believe the Queen of England could marry a prince from such a minor German state?'

Anne ceased playing nervously with her lace collar. 'That's a pity,' she said.

'It is,' replied Elizabeth. There was a wistful look on her face as she nodded in agreement. 'Another time… another place… another life… Perhaps Freddie could have been the one. We may have been happy together but as you say I'm queen of these lands and I have my royal responsibilities to think of.'

Anne said nothing after this. Elizabeth paused for a moment before continuing. 'Don't worry. I'll find *the one*. I won't become a spinster like Elizabeth Tudor before me. I just want to be given sufficient time to make the right choice. If I can't marry for love I should at least be able to marry for like. But alas no, Frederick of Palatine can't be *the one*.'

Elizabeth's eyes stared into the depths of the main mirror. Behind her, Anne Dudley breathed a long and deep sigh of relief.

Chapter II

The music and dancing was well underway when Sir Everard Digby arrived at Greenwich Palace. Fleet of foot couples whirled around the dance floor celebrating the Queen of England's birthday. Floorboards creaked and bounced beneath the weight of their bodies. The doublets and dresses the dancers were wearing filled the air. People were happy.

Digby wasn't sure if it was the scent of rosewater or human perspiration which was making his nose twitch. At least he didn't sneeze. Once upon a time he'd have been delighted to receive a royal invitation. These days he preferred the quiet life. When in England, if it was possible, he shunned the court and avoided attention. Since his return with Button his social engagements had mostly been in taverns, drinking with friends he'd made in the Americas.

The morning and early afternoon had been spent sleeping off the effects of the evening before. Digby had deliberately missed the banquet. The thought of having to sit down and dine with a bunch of strangers and, worst of all, make polite conversation with them, was more than his headache could bear. Inevitably someone would ask him about the painting and he didn't want to talk about it. But an invitation from the Queen Mother was not to be ignored. So here he was at the evening party showing his face for etiquette's sake.

As he looked around for Thomas Button, Digby reflected he'd lived his life in two parts, separated by an error of judgement in between. Perhaps it was time to integrate back into English society? No, he thought. He'd grown too accustomed to the way things were. Life as an outsider suited him more than a position in the royal court.

It was a shame Button wasn't there. The Welsh sea captain was a man whose company Digby enjoyed immensely. They'd been through so much together. Button never complained and he knew how to drink and tell a joke. Sailors were like that. Unfortunately Digby's friend was nowhere to be seen which meant the evening was likely to be a dull one.

At least the wine was good. In fact it was very good. From France no doubt. The French knew how to make good wine. If the physicians said wine was better for a man's health than ale or cider, who was he to disagree, thought Digby. Taking their advice to heart, he supped a deep draught of the blood red liquid.

A swathe of the nation's finest were out that evening. Each was determined and dressed to demonstrate their fame and fortune. On top of the nobility and Parliamentarians, Digby couldn't help but notice the new type of urban luminary. Half the room appeared to be populated by writers, composers and architects. Most were accompanied by their wives or young ladies. A few stood apart talking solely to their male friends.

If the Queen celebrates her birthday like this again next year, thought Digby, they could be joined by the foremost scientific thinkers from across Europe. He'd heard many amongst them were keen to escape the Inquisition and religious persecution on the continent. Rumours were rife that Elizabeth planned to give them sanctuary and a new home in England.

For now she'd have to make do with the presence of the artisans, many of whom earned their living due to the patronage of the Queen Mother. It was said Anne of Denmark missed Shakespeare badly. Despite the bard's death two years earlier at the hands of a mob of Puritan extremists, London still felt his influence. The city had become a centre for cultural change. Women acted upon the stage almost as much as men. A number of female thespians were becoming increasingly famous, encouraged by Anne's support and the leading roles Shakespeare had written for them.

Shakespeare of course hadn't been the only writer in England. As if in response, a beaming Ben Jonson, the King of the Masques, caught Digby's eye. Jonson lifted a tankard and winked at him from across the busy room. Digby nodded back. They'd met a couple of times in recent weeks, stumbling across each other in various London taverns. Jonson liked a drink as much as the next man and more than some. Digby raised his goblet to his lips and threw back his head. The liquid slid down his throat all too easily,

He realised he was becoming a little merry. Absentmindedly he watched Jonson deliver a master class in meet and greet across the way. Old friends were embraced. Cheeks were kissed. Hands were shaken with fawning members of the minor nobility as a small crowd lined up to engage him at the edge of the dance floor. Eventually the writer was lost from Digby's sight, hidden behind the leaves of the doomed but magnificent chestnut tree at the centre of the hall.

Last but not least came the international contingent. As he walked around them Digby could see the best tables had been reserved for the ambassadors, their wives and junior members of the royal families of Europe. A state of princes lined the walls. Each was under careful instruction from their advisors to do anything possible to catch the eye, and anything else, of the Queen of England, Wales, Scotland and Ireland.

Elizabeth was undoubtedly the most eligible woman in the known world but how long could she keep this exalted position, wondered Digby. Like many others, he believed the Queen had little choice but to marry strategically for the benefit of the nation. Whoever the new king would be, it was likely he'd swiftly become the real holder of executive power. Elizabeth's role would change from policy maker to wife of the king and mother to his heirs. It was the way things were, thought Digby. She must be expecting this.

The royal table was strategically positioned at the head of the hall. A subtle rise in the floor ensured the sovereign could look down upon her subjects and view every part of the room, or at least the ones not hidden by foliage. Elizabeth was dressed magnificently. Although she wasn't wearing her crown, the English royal jewels were around her neck. A stunning set of pearls adorned her hair.

The Queen sat in the middle of the finest oak table Digby had ever seen. She appeared to be watching the dancing with interest but despite her gaze he believed her mind was elsewhere. Perhaps she already knew who the favoured suitor was. Perhaps he was in that very room. Whatever would happen, Digby wished her well. The new tolerance laws the Queen had encouraged were a good thing. It would be a tragedy for England if any new King attempted to roll them back, and in doing so create the conditions for another man like Robert Catesby to step forward.

Alongside Elizabeth, her mother was beaming from ear to ear. After a moment Digby realised Anne of Denmark hadn't stopped smiling since he'd arrived at the palace. For a moment he even thought he'd caught her eye. He grinned at this but wasn't egotistical enough to believe the two things were connected.

His assumption was correct. At that moment it was the music and dancing that was captivating Anne. The Queen Mother had spent so much time over the years auditioning and selecting musicians for her royal consort group. The chosen players were renowned for their excellence. If they were often good, tonight they were brilliant. Anne believed this was the performance of their lives. She smiled across the room at her favoured composer, Nicholas Lanier. He'd written a number of new compositions especially for the evening.

Led by a lute, the instruments included a bandora, cittern and two violins. At times they were accompanied by the magical sounds of a flute. The musicians played their instruments hard and loud so they could be heard through the plant foliage by the dancers and revellers on the far side of the room. A few older people sitting nearer to the orchestra's location moaned they couldn't hear themselves think. Luckily nobody heard their complaints.

Servants walked around constantly filling and refilling tankards and goblets. Digby was sure the food at the banquet would have been equally free flowing. Wandering around the party side-lines he wondered at the sheer cost of the event. A fortune spent entertaining the rich, whilst a few miles up the river paupers begged on the streets. Since his time in the Americas inequality saddened him. It appeared out of kilter with the world he believed Elizabeth sought to create. Idly he speculated the Queen Mother was likely to blame. After all she had a certain reputation.

The fact that this sudden melancholy had come over him was no surprise. The sound of the lute didn't help. Digby found the noise mournful. He wondered how anyone could dance to it. After a few moments of reflection, the grimace on his face was replaced by a resigned smile. He realised he was becoming a grumpy middle aged man.

Glancing up at the royal table, Digby admitted that Anne of Denmark might be extravagant but she was also an attractive woman. He wondered why she'd not re-married in the long years since King James's death. At least she looked happy. She had every right to be, he thought. Under her watchful eye, the arts were flourishing, Greenwich Palace looked magnificent and her daughter was attempting to change the world for the better.

Sitting on the opposite side of Elizabeth, Digby recognised her leading lady-in-waiting Anne Dudley. He knew the two women had grown up together. His mind wandered back to Coughton Court and Coombe Abbey in Warwickshire. For a moment a dark cloud dominated his thoughts as his memory replayed the final days of the first part of his life.

In 1605 Digby had been a young man, well presented, well favoured and recently knighted by the newly crowned Scottish King James. He was popular, with a wife, two fine sons and ample opportunity to move from the fringes to the centre of the royal court. And all this despite his recent conversion to Catholicism. Before the knighting ceremony, the King had told Digby that being a Catholic would no longer be a hurdle to success in England, on condition that every Catholic swore loyalty to the crown over Rome, which the majority did.

But James did not remain true to these words. Perhaps there were reasons, but slowly and surely the King and his aides turned their backs on tolerance and returned to the country to what it did best, religious persecutiom. As all this was happening, Digby's own Catholic convictions were growing, although like many he neither believed in nor condoned any violence against the King or his government.

It was around this time Digby was introduced to Robert Catesby, a man with ideas. Never before nor since had he encountered a more charismatic and natural leader of men. A younger and more idealistic Digby found his heart was swayed. He listened. He believed. Real change was coming to England. Change which would prevent further persecution to those of his faith. We just have to be patient, Catesby has said. Soon all would know the role God had selected them to play.

A large group of Catholics, Digby and Catesby amongst them, made a pilgrimage to St Winefride's Well in North Wales. One evening Catesby took Digby aside and asked him to swear an oath of secrecy. Digby was then informed what he'd been tasked to do. Catesby and his friends were to *take care of* King James in London, whilst Digby would travel to Warwickshire to ensure the safety of nine-year-old Princess Elizabeth.

A few weeks later, Digby watched from the woodland beyond as Elizabeth and her friend Anne played in the gardens of Coombe Abbey. He observed the abbey for a number of days and drew up detailed plans of how best to move in and secure the princess. His orders were to take her away to safety, so that afterwards she could be converted to God's own religion and placed on the throne.

Under the pretence of a hunting party, Digby had gathered a group of trusted men at nearby Coughton Court. They would be needed to overcome the small garrison at Coombe. The party was about to depart on their mission when Digby discovered the wider details of Catesby and the Gunpowder Plotters' plans in London. He was appalled to hear that their intention was not simply to assassinate the King but included mass and indiscriminate murder through the destruction of Parliament.

Immediately he abandoned all plans to capture Princess Elizabeth and stood his men down. In doing so he saved all their lives and his own. Catesby and the other conspirators were not so fortunate. After the arrest of Guy Fawkes, they were ruthlessly pursued by government forces. They fled north and holed up in Coughton Court, expecting to find Digby's group there to join up with but of course they were gone. The Earl of Suffolk led a full scale attack on Coughton and all inside were killed, including Catesby as he attempted to escape. Suffolk's men had appeared to have an intimate knowledge of the layout of the buildings which greatly aided their attack.

News came through to Digby's home in Northamptonshire a few days later of both this and the destruction of Parliament. King James, the princes and many others were killed. Princess Elizabeth was suddenly next in line for the throne. Suffolk and his men acted quickly and transported Elizabeth to London ahead of her eventual coronation.

Much to his relief, Digby's role never became public, but the incident affected him in many other ways. He turned to drink and his relationship with his wife broke down, but he didn't want to think about that now. After all, there was wine to drink, and the memories of 1605 were becoming hazier. Sometimes they appeared like a dream, something that had happened to somebody else a long time ago.

As he continued to watch the royal table, the Queen Mother spoke briefly to Anne Dudley. After this the Queen's friend stood up and walked to the far end of the table where she sat down again. A handsome young man accompanied by a chaperone approached and was introduced to the Queen Mother. Anne of Denmark appeared to greet the man but even from a distance Digby could see there was no real warmth in the welcome. Still the Queen Mother politely invited him to sit down between herself and her daughter so he could talk to Queen Elizabeth.

Anne Dudley watched these events unfold rather unhappily, thought Digby. He observed as the man, the first of an array of royal males hoping to impress Elizabeth that evening, engaged the Queen in conversation. Leading lady-in-waiting Dudley needn't have fretted. The discussion between Elizabeth and the hopeful suitor was all too brief.

The man was handsome, smartly attired in a fancy tunic and ruff and appeared confident at first. However, try as he might, he didn't seem to be able to make a favourable

17

impression on the Queen. On the brief occasions when their eyes met he soon found hers wandering away across the hall. With a resigned look on his face he made his excuses, stood up and left the table.

Digby received the latest top up of wine on offer to him from one of the serving women. Looking over the woman's shoulder, he thought he saw Elizabeth observing Anne, as she in turn watched the disappointed man make his way back to his table. He prepared to leave the palace altogether. Neither woman's face gave any indication of what, if anything, this meant to them.

Digby decided further staring in the direction of the royal table was probably not a good idea, so he turned his head to look the other way. Reading people's intentions was not something he was accomplished in anyway. Instead he took another drink from the refreshed goblet. Despite his own feelings on the choice of music, Digby recognised everyone else in the room seemed to be enjoying themselves. Good for them, he thought, and contented himself with the prospect of getting drunk at the royal family's expense. Once again he attempted to spot his friend Button but his luck was no better. It was a shame. Button was the life and soul of any party.

Meanwhile, not far from Digby, a Parliamentarian with a much younger wife had begun to tire of the dance. Deciding he'd had enough, he moved quickly away from the other couples, dragging his surprised and somewhat reluctant partner with him. Digby had to shift his position to avoid being bumped into by the pair as they left the dance floor and moved back to their table.

As he stepped aside, a strange sensation came over him. He felt he was being watched. Turning around slowly, he scoured the room to see if anybody was taking an interest in his whereabouts. On the far side of the hall, well away from the royal table, a pair of studded wooden doors had been wedged open to admit light and fresh air from the garden outside, much to the relief of the party goers. The table situated to the left of the entrance was occupied by the French delegation.

Most puffed tobacco pipes. Despite King James's protestations, smoking had taken off as quickly in England over the past two decades as it had across the rest of Europe. As Digby watched the French talking and smoking, he instinctively believed the table was the source of his unease.

For many reasons he didn't like the French. Many of them felt the same about him. He'd crossed swords with them in the Americas. Sometimes he'd got the better of them. Other times not. He recognised their ambitions. They wanted more than mere trade. The French considered the newly discovered lands to the north as a second "New" France. Digby loved the place and had no wish to share it with anybody but the native population and a few of his own countrymen. In any case, one France was more than enough.

Despite Digby's views, there were many similarities between England and France. Both countries had been destabilised by religious tensions. Their kings had been assassinated and succeeded by young children. When her father was killed in the blast in Westminster, Elizabeth had only been nine years old. Similarly Louis XIII was just eight when five years later his own father, King Henry IV, a Protestant converted to Catholicism for pragmatic reasons, was murdered by a Catholic extremist.

When they returned to England from the Americas, Digby and Button had been grilled in Whitehall about France's intentions in the Americas. During these sessions, Digby learned much about the intrigues of the French court. King Louis was now sixteen and was chomping at the bit to lead his country but he'd had a problem. For several years he'd been prevented from doing so by his mother, the Italian Marie de Medici. Unlike Elizabeth's mother, Anne, Marie had developed a taste for power. She continued to act as Louis's regent long after he'd reached thirteen and by rights should have taken direct control of his throne. It was Marie who directed Louis to marry the King of Spain's daughter to create a strategic alliance between the Catholic superpowers of Spain and France.

This was the move which worried Elizabeth's advisors. If the pact was successful, there was every possibility they'd be encouraged by Rome to turn their attentions towards tolerant and ungodly England. For some time the English had watched as tensions rose between Marie and Louis. Despite Suffolk's doubts, Northumberland had been optimistic France would become increasingly inward looking due to this and not grow into the threat they all feared it could be.

English hopes has been dashed when Louis, encouraged by his key advisor Charles d'Albert, made a decisive move. Within weeks he'd wrestled control of the country away from Marie. Many of her advisors, particularly the Italians, were put to the sword but Marie herself wasn't executed. Instead, Louis placed his mother into internal exile. With his place on the throne secure, Louis had become increasingly keen to further French and Catholic ambitions abroad.

Digby moved a little closer to the French table so he could see who was sitting there. He remembered a discussion he'd recently had in an ale house with Button. The Welshman had warned of trouble ahead. The continent, he said, was a tinderbox just needing the wrong person to set it alight. If this happened, he argued, religion-fuelled wars could rage across Europe for thirty, fifty or perhaps even a hundred years.

One of the things Digby admired most about Button was the way he always saw the positive side of things. Just after the Captain had predicted a future of mass death and destruction, he said it could be a profitable time for Digby and himself. The fighting and leadership experience they'd gained in the New World would place them in high demand in the old. They'd be able to name their price. Digby had shaken his head. War and conflict were evils he'd prefer to avoid. The prospect of becoming a mercenary in someone else's army filled him with dread.

As the twitchy feeling began to fade, Digby mused at the make-up of the French delegation. He was sure Suffolk's watchers would have them all under observation. It was understandable that King Louis was not amongst them. What would be the point of him attending? He already had his bride but England was important so he'd sent his right hand man, Charles d'Albert, as his personal representative.

Digby recognised d'Albert as the man sitting at the head of the French table from the descriptions made of him in Whitehall. His brown hair was shorter than most but not out of the ordinary. The beard on his chin was closely trimmed like many others but one feature set him apart. He wore a wispy moustache which extended so far it touched the stiffened lace of his collar. To Digby's mind it gave him a faintly ridiculous look.

D'Albert and the others drank, smoked and shrugged their shoulders dismissively at each other. The man to his right wore the dressings of a bishop. There appeared to be some antagonism between d'Albert and the bishop. Their eyes narrowed as they talked to each other in an animated fashion. For some reason, Digby didn't like the look of the cleric. He had his reasons for not trusting men of the cloth. Perhaps it was the bishop who'd been looking at him? Digby was deliberating whether or not to walk a little nearer when a voice spoke out to him.

'My countrymen are interesting, are they not?'

The words came from a woman. They were heavily accented. She was clearly French. As he turned to face her,

Digby thought for a moment she looked vaguely familiar. More than anything he was struck by her beauty. There was something else too. There appeared to be something significant about her. It was if their destinies were linked. He recognised the feeling. He'd felt it twice before, each time as he'd met the two women he'd loved most in his life.

Her eyes were dark, almost black. They matched her hair. This was partly tied back and held together over the top by an elaborately jewelled bow. Her dress was black also, or if not that, a very dark colour. In stark contrast the lace around her wrists and low-cut neckline was a snow-like white. He forced his eyes not to look down there.

'I'm sure they are,' replied Digby as their eyes made contact. 'But I know so very little about the French. I'm pleased though, to make your acquaintance.'

Their eyes separated as Digby bowed. The woman smiled.

'Come now, Monsieur Digby, it is my understanding you know a great deal about us.'

'You know my name already. Splendid! But of course you have me at a disadvantage,' replied Digby. 'How should I address you?'

'Names are not important. No, they are not,' she said quickly wagging the index finger of her right hand to prevent any disagreement. 'For now, let us say I am simply a woman with an interest in you, an admirer from afar if you like, but I would like to get to you know you a little better, in a manner which is more, how should I say this, up close and personal.'

For once Digby was lost for words. What could he say to that?

'Should we dance perhaps?' he asked, after a few moments of silence had passed between them.

'No, I don't think that would be a proper thing to do, at least until we've spent some time together. Perhaps we should plan to become engaged to be married but that would not be proper either, would it? I believe you already have a wife in England and perhaps another less official one in the Americas? You really are the most interesting man. I have made it my business to find out all about you.'

She smiled at the obvious discomfort and uncertainty she saw in Digby's face. He sighed.

'You really do know an awful lot about me, don't you?' he said. 'My relationships with the fairer sex are indeed, how should I say this, a little complicated.'

21

'Don't worry, Monsieur Digby, I understand. Love is never easy. Let's ensure what happens between us is not so very *complicated*. Let's keep things as simple as possible.'

Their eyes met again. This time they maintained contact.

'In a little while,' she continued, 'I plan to go for a walk in the grounds. Everyone says the scent in the walled garden is lovely in the evenings at this time of year. Perhaps you could walk out ahead of me and perhaps we might meet by chance at the entrance of the labyrinth? We could look up at the stars, talk and get to know each other, away from prying eyes. I feel crowded rooms like this make us both feel uncomfortable. We are people of the open air, are we not?'

Her eyes left Digby's and gave a sweep around the room. The French bishop turned his head quickly towards d'Albert when he saw her looking towards him but Digby didn't see this. He was still looking at the Frenchwoman.

'Perhaps,' he replied, 'perhaps, perhaps, perhaps indeed.' He emptied the last few drops of wine from his goblet and bowed to the beautiful woman for a second time. 'Please excuse me. I feel a sudden urge to go outside for an evening stroll. How lovely it was to have met you. I do hope we meet again soon. Good day to you, mademoiselle.'

Digby hesitated for a moment but when it appeared he was not going to receive a hand to kiss, he turned away and walked off towards the garden.

The Frenchwoman watched Digby go. When he'd left the room, she whispered under her breath, 'Madame not mademoiselle.' She extended her left arm so that her hand protruded fully from beneath the sleeve of her dress. She looked at the gimmel ring on her wedding finger and wondered once more at the intimate pattern of the two clasped hands and single heart. The ring remained on her finger, though the husband who'd given it her was dead.

The room was becoming increasingly hot and busy. A walk into the gardens would be welcome. She circumnavigated a third of the hall, smiling at the dancing couples as she did so. When she finally reached the French party she nodded at the bishop but continued to walk on. As she reached the door, she stopped and enjoyed the breeze on her face. Digby was already some distance ahead. The Englishman strolled quickly across the grass towards the maze.

Chapter III

Digby was soon out of earshot of the other guests who'd wandered outside to enjoy the cooler air. There was a marked difference in temperature between the banqueting rooms and the gardens. As a soldier nodded in his direction, Digby nodded back and continued on beyond the inner cordon of sentries.

With September approaching it was no surprise the evening light has begun to fade. The first stars were already visible. Digby felt the dampness of the newly forming dew on the grass beneath his feet. A light sheen of mist marked the position of the River Thames beyond. As he neared the maze, the flow of the river muted the noise of the party across the way. The fountains within the hedgerows added to the effect of isolation. Digby had the whole area to himself. It was difficult to imagine a royal celebration was taking place only a few yards away.

He sighed. Did this woman wish to talk to him about important matters, or was she after something else? Surely she hadn't brazenly propositioned him in the hall? He was a little drunk but that's how it had appeared. The Frenchwoman was so unlike the two great loves of his life. The first had been his wife, his childhood sweetheart. The second he'd met in the Americas. Their backgrounds were so different, yet in some ways the two women were similar. Was he about to fall in love for a third time?

He imagined standing at the centre of the maze under the stars and passionately kissing the Frenchwoman. The idea was appealing but it appeared too good to be true. The thought triggered a tiny alarm at the back of his mind but he ignored it. She couldn't have picked a better spot for such a secret liaison, he thought. The area in front of the privet maze was deserted. They couldn't be seen by any of the palace guards or guests. The surrounding hedgerows were seven feet tall.

Digby wandered into the funnel at the entrance to the maze. Mirror glass has been placed on either side of the first corner, so the Queen and her guests could admire their appearance as they entered the labyrinth and again as they left its twisted avenues. He glanced at the looking glass on his right. There was sufficient visibility for him to pat down his hair and smooth his beard.

The second warning bell rang more loudly than the first, triggered by the reflection of a sharp blade. Seeing the metal glint in the corner of the mirror, Digby swung around and stepped back. The flailing arm missed his face by an inch. Digby's would-be attacker was young and powerful but he no longer had surprise on his side.

Digby peered into the assailant's face, and saw a fanatical zeal staring back. The man was dressed in the same gardener's clothes as those who worked for Inigo Jones. The younger man thought his fanaticism was his strength, but Digby recognised a weakness he could exploit, if only he could live long enough to try. The attacker lurched forward once more. The older man used his fighting experience to dodge the blade. The two men weaved and parried for a few moments, each looking for an angle to attack.

They circled each other, and a face-off began. Digby threw a punch but it struck fresh air. The attacker kicked out, but his target shifted away. Digby grabbed the youth's foot. A dagger forced him back. He caught a sideways glance in the mirror. He felt he'd put too much weight on these last few weeks.

The zealot came at him again. This time Digby feinted to the left before throwing his body to the right. He charged at the dagger-man. They both went down. The two men wrestled on the wet grass, as both sought to gain control over the other man. The attacker gripped his knife. Digby punched him. He slid his right knee forward and pinned the wrist which held the knife to the ground. It was time, Digby thought, to put his extra weight to very good use.

The dagger-man thrashed around but Digby had him tight. In desperation the youth tried to bite Digby's arm. Taking umbrage at this Digby swung his other knee downward. A crunch was followed by a wince of pain - the attacker was hurt. He wrapped his ankles around Digby's leg to try to prevent any further blows.

Although the two men continued to struggle, eventually they reached an impasse. The zealot attempted to liberate himself from Digby's grip but couldn't break free. The one man's strengths negated the other's. Digby's mind wandered. He'd imagined coming out here to enjoy a roll in the grass but not like this. Perhaps the Frenchwoman or another guest would arrive soon, witness the scene and call for help?

The fight was interrupted shortly afterwards but it wasn't her. Another man entered the labyrinth. This one was also dressed in gardener's apparel. The newcomer stared at the figures on the ground, as if wondering what to do next. After a few seconds he made a decision and edged towards them. Digby thought the man was considering the most effective means of intervention, with least risk to himself. The apparent hesitation offered little reassurance. Neither did the size of his knife.

The second gardener smiled. Even in the dying daylight Digby could see the man standing before him was older than the zealot, nearer his own age. His teeth were yellow, uneven and incomplete. He looked like a street fighter. The man wiped his nose with the sleeve of his tunic and broadened his smile.

Digby watched the second assailant come for him but he couldn't loosen his grip on the other. The situation didn't look good. The gap-toothed man switched the grip on his knife to make stabbing downwards easier. There was no glance in the mirror. He knew what he looked like. But if he had, he'd have seen the spade swing towards him.

There was a crack. The bruiser took the blow squarely in the side of his face. The force would have killed many other men. This one lurched and staggered sideways, but somehow remained on his feet. He was a fighter after all. For a few seconds he closed his eyes. The knife slipped from his grasp. He shook his head, emitted a growl and took a wild swing.

The hands which held the spade were calloused. The newcomer had known hard work but he was dressed in a gentleman's tunic and doublet. The punch missed. The street fighting gardener took a step forwards. There was a snarl on his face. He growled again. The spade came back towards him, as a warning. This time it was meant to miss, but not by much. Rusty iron cut through the air like the swing of a sword. The street fighter grunted. It was difficult to see his chin for blood. He spat out a tooth, he could ill afford to lose. There weren't that many left.

By the time the spade was swung a third time he'd had enough. He took a step back. When the spade-wielder followed, he scrambled in the opposite direction. The darkness of the maze was behind them. Digby and the zealot were still on the ground. The bloodied man paused, booted Digby in the ribs and then ran off.

Digby grimaced. It was enough for the zealot. He jerked his body violently, shook the older man from his body and turned towards him, the dagger still in his hand. The spade wielding gentleman moved quickly forward and took an agricultural swipe at the youngster. Solid iron moved within inches of the zealot's nose. He stepped back a pace. If the next swing hit him he'd lose his face.

He'll run, thought Digby, if he's got any sense. Their eyes met. Digby felt hatred. For the first time he looked properly at his attacker. His skin was pale. The dark eyes were pitted with blackness. His hair was black also and he wore no beard. With a look of contempt the youth turned and fled into the labyrinth.

From his spot on the ground, Digby gazed into the mirror. In the dying light he saw a sorry-looking fellow glancing back. His face was sweaty and covered in grass.

The man with the spade now stood over him. He was strong, mean and angry-looking. Digby was defenceless. One strike with the gardener's implement and he'd be dead. For a few moments the well dressed man continued to swing the spade from side to side, watching to see if Digby's attackers returned. When this didn't happen, he drove the spade deeply down with his boot. The blade split the grass and slid into the soil, a little too close for comfort to Digby's head.

A hand stretched down and hauled Digby up. Once standing, Digby steadied himself. He patted the left side of his torso. The ribs were sore but unbroken. The other man began to laugh, increasingly loudly. Digby joined in. It hurt but he couldn't help himself. Button's laughter was always infectious, a little like smallpox. The stupid Welsh bastard, thought Digby. He sees the funny side in everything.

'What brings you out 'ere into the maze at this time of the evening then?' asked Button.

'A lady,' replied Digby.

Button shook his head. 'Then I'm afraid you're starting to lose your touch, my friend, because you may have been 'aving a cwtch and a cuddle but that was not a lady, believe me.'

Digby dusted himself down. He removed some of the grass but even in the dimmest light it was obvious his best evening clothes were a mess. His appearance didn't look fit enough to re-enter the royal hall any time soon.

'No,' replied Digby, sighing. 'You're right of course. I bumped into that young fellow and his friend by accident but I did come out here to meet a lady, I can promise you that.'

'Some lady, if she wants to meet a man like you between two 'edges on a dark night like this.'

'It wasn't quite dark when we arranged it, but it's a good point, well made. What about you? What do I have to thank for bringing you out here to my rescue?'

'No need for thanks, my English friend, it was all down to my little Welsh bladder.' Button's laugh was quieter this time, a little self-deprecating. 'Wine, ale and mead are a challenging combination for a man of my years,' he added. 'There was a time when I could last hours before breaking the seal but these days I pee on the privet much more often than I used to, if I'm 'onest with you.'

He looked in the direction of the interior of the labyrinth. 'Do you think we should go in there after 'em?'

'No,' replied Digby. 'They'll have hacked their way out by now and be gone. We could call the guards and kick up a fuss but I'd prefer a quiet getaway if you don't mind?'

'I understand,' said Button. 'It's not easy when you've been stood up by a woman and we wouldn't want her 'usband asking any questions, would we? Do you think he sent those lads out 'ere after you?'

'It's not like that,' protested Digby with a wry smile on his face. 'She was gorgeous. You should have seen her, and it was her idea to come out here in the first place, not mine. She's part of the French delegation. Did you see them sitting there near the doors by the garden in the great hall?'

'French indeed? Bloody 'ell! I may have seen 'er now you come to mention it. Dark hair, smouldering beauty, was she? She was talking to a Frenchie of the Catholic cloth by the doors when I came out. I don't know, Digby, I can't leave you for a few moments before you're trying to 'ave it away with a mysterious Frenchwoman or picking a fight with the Queen's gardeners. Either way, you could cause a diplomatic incident. And if those boys 'ad done you in I'd 'ave 'ad to pay for your funeral too. Now, do you want that on your conscience?'

Button paused for breath. 'You're not in a state to go back inside anyway,' he said, 'so I suggest we pop over to the stables. I'll sort out a carriage and you can come back to my lodgings and we can crack open a keg or two. What do you think?'

'It sounds like a plan,' said Digby. He ceased rubbing his tunic. His attempts to remove the grass stains had been in vain. The idea of slipping off quietly and sharing a drink with Button was more appealing than attempting to explain how he'd got himself into such a mess.

'I know the French don't like you,' said Button with a curious look on his face as they walked back across the lawns. 'They don't like me much either but would they risk trying to do you in 'ere in Greenwich Palace? And at the Queen's birthday

27

party at that? Those two chaps were dressed like gardeners. Maybe you criticised their hedge trimming skills or something?'

'I haven't a clue,' replied Digby.

'That's the first sensible thing you've said all day.' With this Button shoved Digby in the back and pushed him onwards in the direction of the palace stables.

Chapter IV

Digby had a sore head to go with his ribs when Button woke him. He'd dreamt of being in a fight with Abacuk Pricket, the navigator from Henry Hudson's ship the Discovery. Pricket had been charged with murder and mutiny when the Discovery returned to England minus its captain in 1611. Led by their navigator, the surviving crewmen had claimed Hudson was a bully and a traitor, unfit for the task of finding the mythical North West Passage. They claimed they'd bundled him, his son and seven others safely into a rowing boat. There had been no murder. Digby and Button were subsequently despatched, on what was to become their most famous mission, to find Hudson dead or alive. Eventually they discovered the truth.

Button reached over the bed and pushed open the wooden shutters. Bright sunshine glared onto his friend's face. As Digby regained consciousness, Button said he looked a sorry state but at least he knew how to drink. Memories of the night, day and second night before began to filter back through Digby's mind.

The two men had put the world to rights but Digby was paying for it now. It was the worst hangover he could remember since the last one. How much had they drunk? His head ached and his ribs reminded him of the fight two evenings before. As he sat up he related his dream, or at least the parts he could remember, to Button.

'Pricket? A nasty piece of work 'e was, alright,' said Button. 'But 'e can't do you any 'arm now, can he? And don't forget that trip was the making of both of us.'

As Digby washed his face using water from the bowl on the window sill, he noticed Button was wearing a new set of clothes and looking very smart indeed. For a few minutes the two friends recalled highlights from their mission to rescue the survivors of the Discovery Mutiny. They'd taken the ringleader Pricket on Button's boat with the man constantly shackled in chains. He wouldn't have travelled back to the Americas voluntarily. Once they arrived they searched the coastline of the bay where Pricket claimed Hudson and the others had been left alive. Button scoured the shore and waters for weeks in vain. It was only when he re-directed the search further north that they had their first stroke of luck. Wooden planks were spotted on a nearby shore, which could have been the partial remains of a rowing boat

Five miles further up the rocky coast the two rescue ships discovered a wide river inlet. Alongside this stood a tall wooden cross constructed from a dozen sizeable saplings, strapped together with ship's rigging. Such was the height and prominence of the construction it was clearly designed to be visible offshore. Beneath the cross lay a hefty pile of rocks fashioned into the shape of an arrow. The head of the arrow pointed inland, heading upriver.

Button selected a group of his best men. Each was given a double shot of rum and told to prepare for a hazardous journey. The next morning they stocked a longboat with a few weeks' provisions. Button left his first officer in charge of the warship. On the incoming tide, the party which included Digby, headed upstream. After two uneventful weeks of searching the men encountered a native fishing canoe. Although lacking a common language to communicate with, the tribesmen weren't hostile and appeared excited to encounter foreign visitors. The men led Button's crew along a narrow tributary until they eventually reached a nondescript village where one of the most famous moments in exploration history then took place.

Rounding the final bend, they spotted Hudson's son on the river bank. The boy leapt into the air when he saw them and ran around shouting loudly. A flurry of excitement was emitted from the encampment beyond. A dozen local people and an Englishman ran quickly to the edge of the water. A second native canoe was launched.

Button stood tall on the bow of his boat as it drew parallel with the tribal kayak. The native oarsman smiled up at him. In front of the man stood the eagerly searched-for sea captain Henry Hudson. The historic moment happened.

As the two men, the lost explorer Hudson and his rescuer Button, met for the first time they reached out and shook hands across the water. A hearty cheer went up from the crew behind Button and from the men and women on the riverbank. Little did any of them know that the moment would later be captured for all eternity in one of the most famous paintings of all time; the twelve foot high masterpiece which led to long-lasting fame and fortune for its artist Nicholas Hilliard. But work on that would not start for another nine months when the Queen would personally commission Hilliard to record the scene on a huge canvas at his studio in the back of his town house in London.

Although Hilliard was a favourite of the Stuart royal family and well known for his portraits, he'd never once visited the Americas. Despite this, experts and laymen alike have complemented him down the years on the incredible accuracy of his painting, which was to become one of the most iconic images of British and American history. The colours, the lighting, fauna and flora, sailors and tribes people were captured as if he was there. There was only one slight mistake.

The sea captain Thomas Button, the man who'd discovered and shaken hands with Hudson, was painted sitting down and looking away so only the back of his head was visible. Instead, Button's place at the bow of his boat had been taken by his best friend. Although it may not be true for expert historians, virtually everybody else believed that the man who led the rescue of Henry Hudson was in fact Sir Everard Digby.

This had not gone down very well with Button, although he didn't blame his friend. Two years ago when they were last in England, Button had met Hilliard in a social gathering and demanded to know why he'd been omitted from the picture. An embarrassed Hilliard had apologised profusely. It was most regrettable, he explained, but when the Queen commissioned him to paint the picture he'd never once met Button and had no likeness of him to work with. In contrast, he'd made Digby's acquaintance several times around the time of his knighting by King James. When he was informed of Digby's presence at the scene, it appeared he'd found the ideal solution to his problem but in doing so he'd robbed Button of his rightful place in history.

'You're still upset about that picture, aren't you?' asked Digby.

'Not at all, bach. Not bloody at all.' Button was beaming.

'I don't believe that for a moment, but what is it?' asked Digby. 'Why are you so insufferably happy, Captain Button?'

'Captain, my arse,' replied Button, even more cheerfully. He'd wanted Digby to ask, and now he was going to tell him. 'Whilst you slept your hangover off, I was called into a meeting with the Navy Board. The good news is they now seem to have sorted themselves out. For a while they were too busy taking back-handers but thank goodness the Earl of Suffolk was a naval man. What a difference he's made by placing Johnny Coke in charge. At last we've now got somebody who knows what they're talking about. The Board is investing in real ships now. I've just come back from seeing Coke and the Marquis of Buckingham and wanted you to be first to know, you being the famous 'ero from Hilliard's painting and all that.'

'Know what?'

'The bloody idiots 'ave only just gone and promoted me to admiral, 'aven't they? Me, a boy from the Vale of Glamorgan! What do you think of that? Admiral Thomas Dutton. I thought I might get you out of your bed and take you for a few beers to celebrate. Hair of the dog and all that.'

Digby's insides contracted in protest at the thought of more strong drink. He needed some time to recover from the last session but he was delighted for his friend. He stood up a little uncertainly and shook Button's hand warmly. In turn, Button enveloped the Englishman in a bear hug before releasing him quickly when he thought he might be sick on his new outfit.

'Not on these clothes, boy,' said Button as Digby sat back down on the bed. 'I'll be 'anging up my old stuff and sending it 'ome to Wales. On second thoughts, I can see you're not quite ready for another ale at the moment. Don't worry. I know where a few of the lads will bem so I'll tap 'em up instead. What are your plans for the rest of the day?'

Digby considered a moment before answering. 'Well, my intention was to spend a few days in Buckinghamshire with the boys but Mary doesn't wish me to go before Tuesday. She's arranged to visit her sister in Northampton, so she won't have to see me.'

'Still not talking to you, is she, even after all this time?'

'It appears not,' replied Digby, his voice tinged with sadness. 'I'd hoped when we returned to the country she may have seen the world differently but it is clear from her letter she does not.'

'It's a bugger alright but you can 'ardly blame her, can you? It was you who pushed her away first.' Button's smile had gone. He knew how his friend had been hurt by his wife's continued refusal to meet. They'd been childhood sweethearts. The perfect couple. At a time of arranged marriages theirs, twenty years previously, had been one based upon genuine love.

At the time Digby had thought it would last forever. He still felt something for Mary, and in her letter she wrote she still loved him but she could no longer bring herself to see or talk to him. Everything had gone wrong in those drink-fuelled days in the winter of 1605 and 6. He wasn't proud of how he'd behaved.

'No,' replied Digby to Button. 'But you know what happened, and why I turned to the bottle. For a few months I just couldn't cope.'

'I know,' replied Button. On a dark night during a storm half way across the Atlantic Ocean, Digby had confessed his role and subsequent last minute exit from the Gunpowder Plot to Button, along with the guilt he felt about the death of his friends. It was a dangerous secret to share and he'd never told anyone else other than Mary.

'Well, it was from then. I drank to excess. I said and did things. Mary refuses to speak to me now, so how can I make amends?'

The conversation was halted by a rap on Digby's bedroom door. Button opened it and found a messenger outside. He passed a sealed note to the two men in the room and left. It was addressed to Digby, who opened and read it. He was being summoned by the Earl of Suffolk to attend a meeting in Whitehall the next morning. He must ensure he arrived in good time for the meeting at ten and wear nothing but his finest clothes.

'Perhaps they're going to make an admiral out of you too?' beamed Button, once Digby relayed what he'd read.

'Unlikely, my friend. I'm not even a proper naval officer,' said Digby intrigued.

'Then they're probably going to give you a medal or something,' said Button. 'I bet it's something to do with that bloody picture. Make sure you tell 'em it should have been me! Anyway, I'm off for a skin full of ale.'

With this Button left his friend alone. Lying back on the bed Digby wondered why Suffolk wanted him to go to Whitehall. Perhaps they needed more information about the French? Whatever it was, it could wait. He pulled the shutter back over the window, closed his eyes and went back to sleep. Thankfully, this time he didn't dream.

Chapter V

Elizabeth sat at the fine oak desk in her private rooms in Whitehall Palace, as her predecessors had done before her. Writing was one of the few traits she'd inherited from her father. Where King James had penned treatises on the divine right of monarchs and the ills of tobacco smoking, Queen Elizabeth wrote letters demanding change. As monarch of England, Wales, Scotland and Ireland, she wanted to use her influence to make a difference.

When Elizabeth wanted to change the policies of other rulers or churches in Europe there were several actions she could take. The Queen could declare war and send an army, although this was becoming increasingly costly. She could summon an ambassador and rant in his face. Most didn't like this, it showed in their eyes but perhaps they laughed at her when they got back to their official residences because little seemed to change. The third approach was to write a missive to the relevant leader. Again, all too often this made little difference but the process at least made Elizabeth feel better and highlighted the enlightened status she felt she'd brought to her own lands. Was it not better to despatch a letter than send men to be killed?

Her latest correspondence was laid out in front of her on the surface of the desk. Although the representatives of the Roman Inquisition hadn't yet replied to her previous letters and perhaps never would, Elizabeth didn't mean to give up. She pored over the paragraphs she'd spent several hours writing, editing and re-wording, to ensure the tone was right.

Dear Sirs,

I note I have not received a reply to my earlier correspondence, which included a series of rational arguments which I urge you to review and consider.

If the Inquisition continues to conclude the heliocentric theories outlined by the most eminent thinkers of Europe, such as Copernicus, to be "foolish and absurd" and "formally heretical" without examining the evidence proffered by the scientific community, the Inquisition risks undermining the good name and standing of the Catholic Church itself. It would be quite wrong if such an approach led directly or indirectly to further persecution of those who seek only to explore the physical truths of the world we live in.

Surely it is God's will, rather than a sin, that man should study, discover and explain the wonders and mysteries of His universe? Persecution on grounds of religious beliefs has been outlawed in the lands of England, Wales, Scotland and Ireland. If the Inquisition insists on outlawing and imprisoning the forward thinking scientists of Europe, on the basis of their thoughts and words rather than their deeds and actions, if and when these scientists flee such tyrannical behaviour, they will find a welcoming and understanding home in the British Isles.

I urge you to review the Inquisition's findings and re-consider your approach.

Yours in good faith,

Elizabeth S, Queen of England, Wales Scotland and Ireland.

Were the sentences too long? Should she make a more direct threat of action? If so, what form should it take? Would Parliament and the country support her? She didn't think so. After all, she wasn't asking them to support a holy war, gain territory or even defend the country's borders. Elizabeth purely wished to support scientific advancement and freedom of speech.

Were these things people would fight for? Even if they did, did Elizabeth herself have the stomach to send men die when the rest of Europe was already beginning to tear itself apart for no good reason? No. She picked up the manuscript and tore it into long strips.

Anyway, there were troubles closer to home, such as Ireland. Like her forbears, Elizabeth had less of a personal stake in what until recently had been thought of as her third kingdom. The newly announced elevation of the status of Wales had of course relegated Ireland down to fourth. She'd been born in Scotland and lived most of her life in England but Ireland, like Wales, was one of her lands too, if a more troubled place.

Six months ago she'd decided to learn more about the island. She wanted to know why the Irish population lived in a state of almost constant rebellion. She'd wished to visit the country but had received a categorical 'No' from her advisors when raising the idea. It was too dangerous, they said. Ireland was a troubled place. Perhaps in time a state visit could be possible but not at present.

She'd dug deeper. It hadn't been easy. The primary channels of information into her were controlled by others. She

35

trusted the two earls and considered they meant well but even they had their own agendas. Thankfully, when it was necessary Elizabeth could be ingenious. She found ways to get things done.

Over time she'd discovered what was really happening in Ireland. The word 'plantation' came up again and again. Lands and power were being confiscated from the indigenous Catholic population and handed over to Protestant settlers from her other three kingdoms. The Queen read a great deal about the Nine Years' War fought between the English and Irish around the turn of the century. Led by the chieftains Tyrone and Tyrconnell, the Irish had fought for an end to English rule. Although the war had ended in Irish defeat, the cost to the English had been high and the terms offered to the rebels were generous.

The timing had helped. Her father, King James, had just acceded to the English throne. He inherited a country suffering from poor harvests, plague and near bankruptcy. Discovering he could ill afford to prolong the Irish war, the King pardoned the surviving Irish leaders and agreed to return many of their estates, on condition they adhered to English law and swore loyalty to his, now Elizabeth's, crown.

But the Irish had found the peace difficult. Two years after James' death, the earls of Tyrone and Tyrconnell had left Ireland in a boat with their closest family members and supporters. Their plan was reach to Spain to gain support for a new war to rid Ireland of the English once and for all but things didn't go to plan. After being shipwrecked on the French coast, they found the Spanish desired peace with England for economic reasons. The Irish earls travelled to Rome, where they remained in exile until their deaths.

With their Queen still a young girl, Suffolk and Northumberland had worked hard to ensure peace and religious tolerance on the mainland but were too stretched to also address the troubles across the water. The polices of plantation started under King James continued. Newcomers to the island of Ireland were handed the best of everything – land, jobs and food. Economic conditions for the Gaelic population became increasingly bleak. With no figureheads left to rally them, the impacts only deepened, especially in the northern heartlands of Ulster. Tensions remained high.

Ireland, mused Elizabeth. The most troubled and divided part of her land. Her government had outlawed persecution on religious grounds but across the Irish Sea the topics of language, culture and ethnicity were as much an issue as religion. The Queen had determined to do something about it, something positive, something different. How could she criticise the hateful policies of the Inquisition across Europe if she allowed persecution to flourish unchallenged at home?

#

Digby was more than a little surprised. When he'd been summoned to Whitehall he hadn't expected to attend a meeting with Secretary of State Suffolk, the Earl of Northumberland, other government members and Queen Elizabeth, herself. Suffolk started the meeting with a short briefing, during which Digby's surprise morphed into confusion. He began to wonder if he'd been invited by accident. Maybe they thought he was somebody else, Button even. Or was this somebody's idea of a joke? The focus was on Ireland, a subject Digby knew very little about.

Close up, he noted, Elizabeth was a thoughtful woman and young enough to be his daughter. He was getting old. Of course the age gap had been the same them when he'd been ordered by Robert Catesby to kidnap the nine-year-old princess a dozen years earlier. It was a sobering thought. Digby felt a little hot under his ruff. Thank God the Queen knew nothing of this. If the information was made public he'd face a trip to the Tower, a charge of treason and a one way visit to the gallows.

Digby realised his mind had drifted off topic. He'd lost all. track of the conversation over the last few minutes. The discussions had opened up and Suffolk was now inviting other attendees to share their points of view. Several appeared to favour the status quo, continuation and even acceleration of plantation in Ireland. Others argued against this. Digby couldn't help but wonder if some of those present said the words they believed would most please the Queen. So far Her Majesty hadn't spoken at all, although her face had given away her feelings. This Queen was no card player, thought Digby. Her eyes tightened considerably as Suffolk outlined the challenges facing any attempt to bring about lasting peace in Ireland.

'What do you think, Sir Everard?' asked Northumberland when everybody else had shared their thoughts on the matter.

Digby was taken aback but realised he couldn't play dumb. The other attendees, including the Queen, now stared in his direction. The invitation hadn't been a mistake after all. They knew who he was and for some reason wanted his opinion.

'I must confess to knowing little about Ireland, particularly recent history,' said Digby, 'I've spent the majority of the last ten years overseas.'

'We know all about that man,' said Suffolk impatiently. 'We've seen the painting.'

A few people laughed. Virtually all smiled, even the Queen, who'd appeared to be deep in thought.

'Nevertheless we would value your opinion,' Suffolk added.

'Well,' said Digby. 'I agree with some of the points already made.' He was careful not to say which ones, to not offend either side. 'But if we truly wish for peace and prosperity in Ireland there has to be something in it for both sides and a binding together of the two populations.' Where did that come from, he wondered.

'Here, here!' The Queen beamed. 'Well said! If we continue this policy of plantation we take from the Irish but offer them nothing in return. In this situation they'll continue to harry and attack the settlers, steal and kill because they've nothing else to live for. In the coming days when war spreads across Europe - and we know it will - why wouldn't they grab the chance of an armed uprising funded by our enemies on the continent? If I were an Irishman and treated the way they have been, I would rise up too. We must give them something, some hope, but what? Continue, Sir Everard, please. You have the floor and we are listening.'

'As I say, I'm no expert on Ireland, Your Majesty.' He lowered his head before continuing. 'But I'd say start with the basics. What do the Irish need? What do all people need? Food, money, somewhere to live and work, decent land to farm, hope, and a future for their children.'

'The settlers need all these things too. If we give to the Irish, the planters will riot and they're well armed and connected. Before we know it the troubles could spread back across the water to England,' complained a man Digby didn't recognise.

'I didn't say it would be easy,' said Digby, 'It's an almost impossible situation. There's too much history already but I agree, there has to be something in it for the planters too. From what my lord Suffolk says they live in fear, afraid to leave their stockades. If they do not travel in force they're ambushed, robbed and sometimes killed. Their clear need is a peaceful future but will this happen if they continue to take the best of everything and leave the Irish with nothing?'

'If we intend to give portions of land back to the Irish, we'll need to give compensation to those who lose it. The whole thing is going to be very expensive,' argued the same man.

'I agree,' said Northumberland. 'But things are better now. Trade is good. Tax revenues are increasing. The government has more money. Surely we must try to make things work? We can't bring all the settlers back but we could make changes and ensure a more even distribution on the basis the Irish desist from their attacks, whilst we offer financial and other compensation to the affected settlers. I fear if we do not, the Irish will welcome any new alliance of France and Spain and give our enemies the opportunity to stab us in the back.'

'But would the Irish go for it?' asked Suffolk. 'In their view their land is under occupation. And who can make decisions on their behalf anyway? If only the earls hadn't flown to Rome, at least we'd have some Irish leaders to negotiate with.'

'Yes,' said Elizabeth. 'I think you are right. If we are to forge lasting peace in Ireland we need strong leaders on both sides of the divide committed to the peace process. Thank you, Secretary of State, this has been a most useful discussion but let us now bring it to a clos. The Earl of Northumberland needs time to review the options, so he can make further recommendations to this group and in time to Parliament. Are there any dissenters to this approach?'

The Queen scanned the table. Nobody spoke. She dismissed the attendees and they began to leave. As Digby attempted to stand up, Northumberland placed a firm hand on his shoulder and he remained seated. Within a minute the others had left the room, apart from Northumberland, Suffolk, Digby and the Queen. Northumberland stepped forward and closed the door.

#

There were a few moments of silence, whilst Digby wondered what on Earth was going on. It was a feeling he was getting used to.

'Well done,' said Suffolk quietly to Digby. 'I had no idea you had such strong opinions on Ireland.'

'I didn't either,' replied Digby, surprised to be still in the room. 'It's just common sense. If we aren't careful, we shall repeat the same problems in the Americas and elsewhere. This is my primary concern. The truth is I know little about Ireland, as I said.'

'A little wisdom can a go long way, Sir Everard,' smiled Elizabeth. 'You were knighted by my father. Did you know him well?'

The comment threw Digby slightly off balance. 'No, not so well, Your Majesty,' he replied. 'It was early in his reign and I was quite young in those days.'

'It would have had to have been in the early days, he didn't last long, did he?' said the Queen, not looking for a reply. 'My father knighted a lot of people when he first came down from Scotland. He was trying to buy their favour, I suppose. Did he buy yours, Sir Everard?'

It seemed a strange question.

'Only with his words, Your Majesty. I was an admirer of the King's early speeches,' said Digby.

'But not his later ones?' asked the Queen.

Digby didn't answer. He was beginning to worry he'd incriminate himself. From now on he had to choose his words carefully. Perhaps it was better to say nothing.

'Never mind,' said Elizabeth. 'Cheer up. I'm no supporter of my father's later work either. Persecution and plantation have only done harm. In contrast, the policies of toleration started by my two most trusted advisers are the best things which have ever happened to this country, but that's not why you're here. I'll wager you're wondering what this is all about, Sir Everard?'

'I would be lying if I said I was not a little confused, Your Majesty,' replied Digby.

'We have a job for you,' interjected Suffolk on the Queen's behalf.

Northumberland spoke up next. 'In a few weeks' time you're going on a trip.'

'Will I be returning to the Americas?' asked Digby hopefully.

'No,' said the Queen. 'You're going to Ireland.'

Chapter VI

After the meeting, Digby was left alone with Northumberland.

'I'm sorry, my lord,' he said, 'I'm flattered to be asked but I have no interest in travelling to Ireland. As soon as Button's ship is refitted, I'll be returning to the Americas.'

Henry Percy, the ninth Earl of Northumberland, didn't take kindly to this response. 'Do you remember what this country was like before the anti-persecution laws?' he asked.

When Digby didn't answer, Northumberland filled the void. 'Well, I do. I was born in the year of our Lord, 1564. The older Elizabeth had only been on the throne for six years by then. England was a land where Protestants suspected Catholics and Catholics feared Protestants, much as they do in Ireland today. Every now and then, things would flare up and a few people on one or both sides would be killed. Luckily for me, I was a Protestant, although some suspected otherwise. Many of my friends and family were not. I saw them harried and their lands, fortune and freedoms taken from them. Over time, things got worse. Our Lord Jesus Christ would have flinched at some of the things done in His name.'

Northumberland took a deep breath. 'When James Stuart came to power I spoke to him. He preached the policies of tolerance but as we know now he went back on his word. Perhaps he never meant what he said or maybe he was turned by the stupid plots made against him, I don't know. Either way, it killed him, and in the aftermath of his death these islands almost fell into the bloodiest of civil wars. Ever since that day, when the King, the princes, and dozens of others were murdered, Suffolk and I have worked every hour God sends us to stop this country from tearing itself apart.'

When the old man paused there was fire in his grey eyes.

'You will go to Ireland, Digby, and you will do exactly what is asked of you. Ireland is a threat to the peace of this nation. The people there speak different languages and attend different churches but by damn they pray to the same God. You will make them see sense. Do you understand me?'

Digby bowed his head in deference. He understood, but he had no intention of going to Ireland, whatever the mission. It was somebody else's problem, not his.

'I understand what you're saying, my lord,' said Digby, 'and I agree with many of the points you make but Ireland isn't for me. You need a better man, one more suited to the job.'

Northumberland grimaced. 'No, you are the perfect man for this task. We've reviewed your suitability. The Earl of Suffolk's men have assessed you. They've done their research. We know what you did in the Americas to make friends with the natives, see their point of view and make peace with their leaders. You'll do the same in Ireland.'

The older man looked away from Digby, as if determining what to say next. His face darkened.

'There is one thing I'd add,' said the Earl of Northumberland finally. 'When they look into a man's past, Suffolk's boys have a habit of finding out a few nasty surprises. Who hasn't been involved in something we come to regret? Some are simply embarrassing and make people laugh. Hilliard's painting for instance. Other revelations are more serious. Some may even lead to the hangman's noose. Do you know what I'm talking about, Digby? I'll give you a few days to consider your position. I hope you make the right choice... for the sake of yourself and your family.'

With this Northumberland stood up, pushed his chair beneath the table and walked out of the room. Digby was left in no doubt. The new regime might be better than the old in some ways but in others their methods were largely the same. Information was a precious commodity. What did Suffolk and Northumberland know about Digby's past?

#

The next day, Digby made his long planned trip to Gayhurst House in Buckinghamshire. It had been his wife's family's home rather than his, and it always would be. When he arrived he was warmly greeted by Haywood, the head serving man. They talked of the old days, more than a decade before. They'd both aged well but also lost something else - their wives. Haywood's had died three years earlier following a short illness. Digby lost his through his own actions and her revulsion of them.

He sought out his sons. It wasn't easy. Kenelm was fourteen and John twelve by now. They were no longer the boys he remembered but young men, old enough to have their own opinions. They'd not seen their father for several years and hid in the woods to avoid him. To his sons he wasn't a returning hero and famous explorer but simply the man who'd abandoned their mother, and, by extension, themselves.

When eventually he rounded them up and they spent a few hours together, the time was fraught with periods of silence. For a few moments Digby would pick out genuine interest in their faces as he told stories of his adventures. But all too soon it would be replaced by gloom as they remembered they weren't supposed to enjoy his company. It wasn't Mary's fault; she hadn't turned them against him. It came from the boys themselves, especially Kenelm. They resented their father's presence. When Digby gave presents to the boys they refused to open them, saying they'd do this later when their mother was home.

After two days, Digby could take no more. He bade farewell to Haywood and the other household staff, kissed his surly sons goodbye and reclaimed his horse from the stable block ready for the ride back to London. As he left the estate he didn't turn around. If he had, he'd have seen John running behind him with tears in his eyes, trying to catch the attention of his father to beg him not to leave him behind again.

#

When he returned to London, Digby received more bad news. Button had already been posted by the Navy Board and left the capital for goodness knows where. Thomas Button was the one man in the world Digby could open up to, usually after a deal of ale or rum had been drunk. The two men had grown accustomed to hearing and sharing each other's troubles on their journeys across the Atlantic, when there was little else to do but talk and drink in the cold days and nights as they searched for Hudson or the North West Passage.

Digby smiled. Button had developed a passion for the mission. The Welshman was sure the passage existed and would one day be found. Hudson believed it too. It was the reason he'd not returned to England. The explorer was still out there searching. Perhaps that was where Button had gone. Digby knew his friend was keen to return to the Americas and try again.

Digby was also determined. Despite the veiled threats made by Northumberland, he was going to return to North America. There was little left for him in the old world but potentially much in the new. They could publish and be damned. Whatever it was they had on him, he was convinced it couldn't be his role in 1605. Too few people knew the truth. There was Mary and Button but he'd trust both with his life. The others were

43

dead, apart from one of Catesby's lieutenants, Thomas Wintour, but the man had lost his mind. Surely nobody would believe the ravings of a madman locked away in Bedlam? And if they did know, they'd have arrested him already.

The request to attend Suffolk's house in London reached Digby on the Friday evening, just after he'd returned from Gayhurst. A private meeting was to be held in the morning at the Secretary of State's home in Whitehall. This unofficial location was a little surprising but no doubt the earls wished to apply more pressure on him.

Digby remained adamant. Ireland was a dangerous place, full of dangerous people. If he did what they asked, he'd have enemies on both sides. The only advantage he could see was it would make it harder for the French to find him, if they'd been the ones behind the knife attack in Greenwich. He hadn't forgotten about this. In London, Digby made a habit of walking in public places and watching his back.

Suffolk's house was just off King Street, the great thoroughfare which linked Whitehall and Westminster. It was a convenient location for the Secretary of State, as it connected his two main places of work, and gave easy access to the river and transport to the palace in Greenwich.

It was a fine late summer's morning and despite his misgivings, Digby was beginning to enjoy the walk to King Street from the inn on the Strand. In the distance he could see the new Parliamentary buildings. Ten years in the making, they were finally nearing completion. He was sure the construction looked bigger than the one Guy Fawkes' gunpowder had destroyed. There was talk this new Parliament House would be opening soon, potentially as early as November for the next parliamentary sitting. Digby doubted it, it appeared there was much work still to be done.

The London streets were bustling with horses, people and commerce. The smells were pungent. The tide was in. Digby could almost taste the influence of the sea around him. Gulls circled overhead. Some swooped to the ground, vying with rats and pigeons for scraps the humans left behind. Digby loved the sea. To him it meant travel and the way to North America. As he walked, his mind wandered back there.

Chasquéme was special. She was one of the Muhhekunneuw people, a collection of tribes who lived inland not too far from the eastern seaboard. Chasquéme was an intelligent and extremely strong willed woman. She stood tall. Digby liked the way she held her head high, with her chin in the air. She had confidence without arrogance and was unlike any woman he'd ever met.

The language barrier was difficult but they got by. Digby began to learn a few words and phrases of her language, discovering her name meant maize or corn. For some reason Chasquéme refused to speak in English. It didn't matter. The understanding between them was deeper than words. They made love secretly in the woods.

As always, his thoughts returned to their last night. As Digby walked in the forest, he had been on his guard. The mutineer Abacuk Pricket had escaped from his chains and disappeared. An extensive search had found no sign of him. The undergrowth was so dense in places, often a man couldn't see further than fifteen feet in front of him, but Digby knew the way. He didn't need a path to take him to where the two streams met. It was their favourite place.

When he heard the screams he began to run. As he reached the clearing, Pricket was crouching over Chasquéme, holding her down and disrobing himself. Pricket growled at her, 'I've been trussed up too long. Stay still, damn you, and be quiet.'

When Pricket slapped Chasquéme something snapped inside Digby. Pricket was too busy to hear his approach. He remained unaware of Digby's presence until the first blow struck him on the side of his head. When Pricket fell to the floor, Digby followed, kicking and punching in a frenzy of violence until the other man's face was covered in blood.

If he was unconscious, Digby didn't care. In his rage he'd have continued until the navigator was dead, but Chasquéme stopped him. Not by screaming but with a single word. It was the first and only time Digby ever heard her speak in English.

No!' she shouted.

Digby desisted and stood up from Pricket, ashamed of himself. When he released Pricket's collar and let the unconscious man drop to the ground, Chasquéme pulled up the torn deerskin tunic she'd been wearing to cover herself and ran into the woods. Digby knew he should have followed her but for some reason he didn't. He just looked at his bloody knuckles and the mess of a man beneath.

They never saw each other again. The next morning she wasn't in the village when they set off in the longboats back down the river.

Leaving the village was another mistake. He should have stayed. Why didn't he stay? When they returned months later, the village was abandoned. The tribe had moved on. In the subsequent years, Digby searched for her many times. But he only found Chasquéme in his dreams, too often accompanied by Pricket's battered face.

Eventually when Button and Digby returned to England, the Discovery's mutineers were put on trial. Hudson didn't return but his testimony was well written and accepted. The attack on the loyal crew members had been carefully planned. It has taken place early one morning. Three had been shot dead. Hudson and the other four, including his son, had been outnumbered but not out-gunned. The rebels had offered to end the stand-off by provisioning a rowing boat. To prove their good faith, Hudson had been allowed to take two of the mutineers, Greene and Wilson, as hostages. He would leave them on the beach for the Discovery to pick up when they made land.

Hudson and the others clambered down into the rowing boat, holding their weapons at the heads of Greene and Wilson. As the Discovery set sail and left them, they realised only too late their boat had been deliberately holed. Greene, Wilson and Hudson junior were set to bailing duty, whilst the others took to the oars in a desperate attempt to reach land before they sank, but the oars were broken and proved ineffective.

When the boat went under, it was every man for himself. Hudson had strapped his son to three planks of wood with a length of ship's rigging and swam alongside him. Both survived but they never saw any of the others again. Four years later Pricket and his fellow mutineers were hanged.

The gate to the front of the house in King Street was closed. Digby rang the bell. He was obviously expected, and a footman ushered him inside. He walked past a line of ornately designed railings and through a small garden of grass and geraniums. Once inside the house, a second man took his jacket. Digby was not shown into a library or drawing room but instead instructed to walk upstairs.

Once he'd risen up the first sweep of steps, Digby stood on a landing. The walls were bordered with portraits of long gone ancestors. It was hard to see their faces due to the lack of daylight. A third serving man took him along a windowless corridor. They made their way carefully by candlelight, avoiding the occasional chair or cabinet. Digby wondered what Chasquéme would have made of such a house. He pictured her, standing there beside him but she wasn't smiling. This would have been an alien environment for her. The servant knocked on the door at the far end of the corridor. Chasquéme faded.

Digby wondered if the room beyond was at the back of the building but he'd lost all sense of direction.

'Sir Everard, you may enter,' came a voice from behind the door.

It was not the voice of a man or a young woman but it was a female voice. The servant opened the thick wooden door and Digby entered. The room was even darker than the corridor. A single shard of light crept out from beneath the thickly lined curtain which covered the window opposite. The door closed from behind him and the voice spoke again.

'There is a chair in front of you, Sir Everard, please do sit down.'

Digby scanned the space immediately before him with his right hand. After a few steps he felt the back of an armchair. Feeling his way around, he navigated around it and sat down.

'Do you know who I am?' asked the voice. It came from the darkest corner of the room away to his right.

Turning to that direction, Digby observed the feet of the person talking to him positioned in a slither of light. They were small, dainty and dressed in black velvet slippers. The attached body was invisible, masked completely by gloom.

'The Countess of Suffolk, I presume?' replied Digby softly.

He'd met the Earl of Suffolk's wife several times as a young man in the courts of Elizabeth Tudor and James Stuart. The Countess had once been renowned as one of the royal household's greatest beauties. Suffolk had been the envy of many of his peers for being her husband. But there had been rumours of affairs also. It was said she'd bedded, amongst others, Robert Cecil, her husband's predecessor as Secretary of State.

'I am she,' she said. 'I recall you also, Sir Everard. You were a dashing young man in those days. Many in the court felt you were destined for greatness. I won't ask what went wrong because now of course you're a famous explorer.'

'It's very kind of you to say so, my lady,' replied Digby bowing his head. 'To be spoken of in such terms by a woman of your great beauty is an honour indeed.'

'Hmm.' The sound was an abrupt one. When she spoke, it was with a degree of regret. 'Alas, the last few years have not been so kind to me, Sir Everard. Sometimes I worry my afflictions are punishment for my mistakes of the past.' When she paused, Digby listened. 'Do you ever worry about the past, Sir Everard?'

He shook his head slightly, as if to clear it. Suffolk must have put her up to this. What did they know of the past?

'I understand what you're thinking,' said the Countess. Digby felt unsettled. 'But it wasn't my husband who asked me to speak to you. I made the decision myself.' She laughed. 'It's the first time I've been able to get an eligible man into my bed chamber for some time. You see, the Secretary State doesn't even know you're here.

'What is it you want from me?' asked Digby 'Are you not afraid the servants will tell him of my visit?'

'Of course not,' she replied. 'Every last one of them is loyal to me. The discretion of one's servants is important. I learned this from a great man I knew many years ago. For some time before his death he was quite dear to me. His name was Robert Cecil.'

Cecil's name ran down Digby's back like ice. This was the man who'd instructed Suffolk and his militia to cut down Catesby and the others, show no mercy and leave no survivors. If Digby had stayed loyal to Catesby, he'd be dead too. He was thankful he'd instructed his men to return home. It had saved their lives. In the intervening years he'd never once blamed Suffolk for the death of his friends. In his mind Robert Cecil had always been the man responsible.

'Robert was not the monster people and history have made him out to be,' continued the Countess, as if once again hearing Digby's thoughts.

'Really?' said Digby. 'He led the persecution of Catholics under Queen Elizabeth and encouraged King James to re-double his efforts. It was no bad thing for the people of these lands when he was killed in Parliament, or otherwise the tolerance laws would never have happened.'

'Some of what you say is true but most of it is ill informed,' said the Countess. 'Under Elizabeth, Robert did continue to enact the policies of his father, and under James he put down a number of treacherous plots which threatened the King. What else could he have done? But by then he also started to see things differently, quite differently. I don't think he would have warmed to the word "tolerance" but he was the man who enabled my husband and the Earl of Northumberland to implement their policies.'

'What?' Digby was incredulous. 'Have you asked me here simply to give me a lesson in false history? This is nonsense.'

'Don't get up, Sir Everard, hear me out.' The words were spoken quickly but with enough meaning by the woman sitting, shrouded in darkness.

Digby sat back down, resisting the urge to leave.

'Robert spoke at length with James and realised he would be unable to dissuade him from denouncing his hard-line policies but he watched and he learned. Every time a Catholic was imprisoned or killed, another took their place. They couldn't take much more. The next crackdown may have caused a major insurgency. It was something the country couldn't afford. Do you remember how things were a decade ago? There was no money. The country was desperate. We had to forge a deal with Spain. I should know. I was there.'

There was a pause in the conversation. Digby believed the Countess was remembering something.

'Robert had watchers everywhere. He used to talk about information and intelligence as being his two eyes. He knew everything that was going on and of course he uncovered your friend Catesby's plot to massacre everyone in Parliament.'

Digby was quiet now, almost transfixed. He wanted to hear more.

'Do you remember the letter to Lord Monteagle? Yes, of course you do. There was such a fuss at the time. It warned of a plot to destroy the Palace of Westminster. The sender implored Monteagle as a Catholic not to go there. Robert sent his men to find the author. They found one of the other traitors and tortured what they could out of him. Torture? It may be dark in here but I'm not blind. Robert was no angel but, sweet Lord, he was effective. His men then went on to intercept a second plotter, the one who'd written the letter to Monteagle. But they didn't torture this one. Threats against his family were enough. Robert uncovered the rest of what was planned in Westminster, where Fawkes was hiding and even the details of the second bomber. Eventually he knew everything.'

It was dark in the room, which was just as well. The colour had drained from Digby's face. *Everything.*

'Everything, Sir Everard. He told me all about it. Imagine.'

'What do you mean?'

'There was a second part to the plan, wasn't there? An operation to kidnap Princess Elizabeth, transform her into a Catholic and crown her Queen of England.'

'This is ridiculous,' said Digby.

'Not at all,' replied the Countess. 'Robert knew everything. In the end he knew as much as Catesby did. He was aware of the plan to abduct Princess Elizabeth. It is one of the reasons Robert ordered my husband to go so quickly to Warwickshire. Catching Catesby was his secondary task. First of all he was to protect the princess.'

The Countess paused. 'And then we come to your role. Robert was told about a young man, a favourite in the royal court, who'd been knighted by the King. The man had a wife and two sons. Even so, he was willing to do anything to support Catesby and their common religion. Anything! Including kidnapping a child, a princess, the woman who is now our queen. There is only one thing I don't understand, Sir Everard.'

'What?' His voice was a whisper.

'Why did you pull out of the operation? Why didn't go through with it until the very end?'

Digby considered before answering but what was the point of not talking? She knew so much. He was as good as in the Tower already. 'I was unaware of what was planned in Westminster,' he confessed quietly. 'I knew Catesby intended to assassinate the King but when I discovered he also planned to kill hundreds of people, including innocent Catholics, I couldn't support his plan. I disbanded my group and left Catesby and the others to it.'

Once again there was silence in the room, broken only by the rustle of a butterfly's wings. It had entered the bed chamber overnight, sleeping upside down tucked into a ball in a corner of the ceiling. Now it was trapped. The insect flew around looking for a way out. Digby knew how it felt. The butterfly put its wings together, attached itself to the ceiling and settled down once more.

'Wait,' said Digby, 'you said *two* bombers. Are you saying Robert Cecil knew there was a second bomber after they caught Fawkes and he let the ceremony carry on? Surely this cannot be true?'

'Would you die for a cause, Sir Everard?'

'If I thought it was the right thing and there was no other way.'

'Then you have more in common with Robert Cecil than you think. He had his faults but most of all he loved this country. It was he who persuaded the King to postpone the opening of Parliament for twenty-four hours and limit the attendees to hard-liners only. It was he who ordered my husband to Warwickshire so he would miss the ceremony. And it was he who encouraged me to afterwards persuade my husband and the Earl of

Northumberland to drive the policies of reconciliation rather than reprisal.'

'Afterwards? But if he knew what was going to happen, why did he attend the opening of Parliament?'

'The answer to that we will never know. He assured me he was going to make an excuse late in the day and slip out. I've two theories of why he remained. The first is he believed James would suspect something was wrong if he didn't attend.'

'And the second theory?'

'I shall take that one to my grave, because it frightens me to even think about it,' she replied.

'But I still don't understand,' said Digby. 'Why did Cecil do any of this?'

'So England could recover, rebuild and start its march to greatness. For that to happen the fanatics on both sides had to be eradicated. It was the only way. Queen Elizabeth will make this nation great, wait and see. It's ironic really. Catesby planned to kill the King and put Elizabeth on the throne, so he's achieved much of what he set out to do. Although no doubt he would have wished to turn her into a Papist zealot hell-bent on burning Protestants like Bloody Mary. You must understand, Sir Everard, Catesby was as much an extremist as the Protestant hard-liners he sought to destroy. He, and they, had to be got rid of. Robert Cecil understood this, and was the only man who could make it happen.'

Digby was stunned. A few moments ago if he'd been told this story, if anybody else had told him, he would have laughed in their faces but now he believed it, every word.

'The facts I've shared with you must remain our secret, of course. They threaten us both, although what happens to me is of little importance. I could easily expose your role in the plot, and I'll have no qualms in doing so if you refuse what my husband asks. But it's not just about you, Sir Everard. Think of your family. Would you wish your sons to be forced to watch as you're hanged, drawn and quartered? Do I make myself clear?'

Digby peered into the darkness. The woman remained invisible apart from the velvet slippers but no amount of gloom could mask her intent. He believed her. 'Yes, very clear,' he replied. 'I'll do it. I'll go to Ireland.'

Chapter VII

Stepping on the bank of the River Thames at Greenwich, Inigo Jones was a man on a mission. When he designed something, he believed it was important to become fully immersed in the context and setting. He surveyed the area, paced around in each direction and shielded his eyes from the late afternoon sun.

The river bank to one side of Greenwich Palace had been bulked up decades earlier to provide a barrier against high tides and flooding. Jones understood this. He looked across the water towards the Isle of Dogs. The river meandered and bent around the area on the opposite bank, creating an almost perfect three quarter loop hemming in the marshland.

Jones twisted his body and turned around. His main challenge lay to the south. He smiled at the house, grounds and building of the Palace of Placentia, better known by most as Greenwich Palace. This had been the Queen's main residence in recent years and where she'd had held her birthday celebration. It was also where Jones had delivered some of his favourite commissions - set designs for masques and and changes to modernise the current buildings.

The Londoner issued a happy sigh. He'd recently received a challenge on a far grander scale. It would mean extra work and responsibility but do it right he'd make his fortune. Perhaps he'd be remembered for posterity. This time he wouldn't be tinkering with the work of others. Inigo Jones was now the Queen's official architect and would be laying down his own marker from the start. The new building would be constructed to his design. The new palace would be conceived, born and grow out of Jones's vision of what the future should look like.

The work would be based upon Anne of Denmark's concept of course. She'd asked him to construct a new palace fit for a queen. But after that it would all be down to Jones. Queen Elizabeth liked the idea and he was sure she'd take an interest but in all things architectural, the Queen and her mother would trust in their architect.

Jones was to build a grand new palace on the grounds to the south of the current royal residence. It would be called the

Queen's House. Why a House and not a Palace? When he'd asked this question, Elizabeth had been adamant. Her people didn't live in palaces, she said, they lived in houses and so should she. But Jones wasn't concerned with semantics. He was going to build a palace alright, whatever anyone called it.

His mind wriggled with ideas. The new construction would be revolutionary. Most of his peers in England were stuck-in-the-mud traditionalists. Nobody could ever accuse Jones of being boring. He wasn't held back by tradition. He was going to build a palace which would look like nothing built in the country before.

What would his father have thought, he wondered, of his son rubbing shoulders with royalty and travelling around Europe as he had. Also called Inigo, the older Jones had been a cloth worker born and bred in Wales. He'd only travelled once. For economic reasons he'd migrated with his young wife to London and it was in this city his offspring were raised, including the younger Inigo.

The revolutionary building Jones had in mind would be inspired by his own time abroad. He'd travelled, studied and learned across Europe, particularly in Italy. If there was one place an architect should go, he thought, it had to be Italy. The influences were fantastic – Roman, Palladian, Renaissance, you name them. What's more, he loved the wine, so much better than what the French drank, but most of all he loved Italian architecture, the art and the culture. It was these he proposed to evolve and build into his own design for the new Queen's House.

#

Elizabeth could just about make out Jones's silhouette in the distance as she walked through the grounds but she lost sight of him when she entered the maze. Before turning the first corner to cross the threshold into the labyrinth, she gazed at the mirror. The Queen envied Anne Dudley's beauty but was comfortable with what she saw.

If you're not at ease with yourself, she thought, how can you command others? There were decisions ahead. Parliament had taken on more powers in recent years but she was still their queen and reigned over the politicians. In future, no doubt, she would authorise executions. With trouble spreading across Europe, she'd probably need to send armies to war to meet and greet death on a grand scale. Could the woman looking back at her from the looking glass live with these things?

Once she passed the first corner, there was a choice to be made. Left or right? She took the latter option but after a few yards the way led to a dead end. Elizabeth had forgotten the gardeners had found damage in the hedging following her birthday celebrations and reset the route towards the centre of the maze. Retracing her first steps, the Queen passed the entrance corridor with its mirrors and took the next corner. This was followed by a succession of short straights and bends, each with at least two and sometimes three choices. The grass under her feet was short and green and the privet hedging had a glossy sheen, despite having been patched up and replanted in places.

It wasn't often she entered the labyrinth alone. Usually she'd be accompanied by Anne Dudley and other ladies-in-waiting. They'd walk and talk and laugh but today she'd shoed them all away. Elizabeth wanted her own space. The ladies had been instructed to wait for her in another part of the garden.

Elizabeth thought of Frederick of Palatine but she knew her feelings were unimportant in the grander scale of things. It wasn't love but it hurt all the same. She knew she'd angered Frederick at the ball by feigning disinterest. In response he'd quickly left her table, the ball and, soon after, England. It was for the best. He was too close to the back of the growing queue who sought permission for her hand. Most of the others were old, fat, ugly or all three of these things. The thought of laying down with some of them in her royal bed chamber made her skin crawl. Elizabeth accepted it was most likely she'd not marry for love but was it to too much to ask, she wondered, to at least have some liking or respect for her future husband? And she'd liked Frederick much more than any of the others. Sadly he was history now, feelings for another lifetime in a different universe.

The others who'd visited Elizabeth at the table during her birthday evening had fared no better. As a courtesy, the French had sent Charles d'Albert to speak to her. After saying how much King Louis regretted not being able to make the party, he'd looked at her with his dark brown eyes and showered her with heavily accented French phrases and praise. She'd paid no attention. Forlornly Elizabeth had stared over d'Albert's shoulder in the direction of Frederick's empty seat.

Rouse yourself, she told herself, you are the queen of these isles. You don't have time to feel sorry for yourself. She turned another corner in the maze and listened. The centre was close now. After another dead end, she returned to an earlier point. This time she made the correct choice. A few moments

54

later she entered the beautiful clearing with its statues, water-pressured fountain, scented flowers and love-seat for two. Elizabeth reflected sadly. She had no lover to share the seat with. Would there ever be one?

She sat down and wondered if it had been the same for her namesake Queen Bess? So much pressure to make a match when all she wanted was to select the right one in her own time. But for Bess the years had gone by and she'd remained alone right until the end. There may have been lovers, one in particular, but they has all failed her long term suitability test. None had been fit to marry.

Elizabeth II was adamant this wouldn't happen to her but neither was she going to rush into the arms of an older man twice her age who hardly spoke any English and gave the impression, backed by the smell, he never bathed. She shuddered at the memory of that one. Thank God for her mother. Anne of Denmark had intercepted this particularly rancid prince and politely led him back to his table, explaining the Queen of England had had a long day and was growing weary. When the Queen Mother put her mind to it she could lie for England, Scotland, and probably Denmark too to protect her daughters.

But if she was to marry for strategic purposes, who should it be? A Hapsburg perhaps? People said the mountains of Austria were lovely. Higher and snowier than the ones she'd seen in North Wales or in her homeland of Scotland. Or how about a Welshman or one of the Irish? God forbid! Then again, if this were to happen at least three out of her four kingdoms would be represented by the royal couple. What an idiotic notion! She laughed at herself. And why were they called *kingdoms* and not *queendoms*? They were ruled by a queen. To be known as leader of her four queendoms, that would be something. She doubted Northumberland would be supportive, stickler for tradition that he was, but perhaps there was a precedent in English law or history? It was worth looking into.

#

Things don't happen quickly in this country, mused Digby. After confirming he'd go to Ireland, there'd been a hiatus in activity. The mission wasn't ready for him. Arrangements had to be made. Work was underway to confirm the identify of the guides who'd accompany him on his journey across Ireland.

At first the waiting appeared intolerable. Digby deplored sitting around doing nothing. When a man was at sea inaction was inevitable but not on land, where he believed there should always be something to do. After a few days he got into the habit of taking a daily walk. He started out early each morning and continued until late in the afternoon.

Over the weeks the walks grew progressively longer. Digby enjoyed scaling the heights of Hampstead Heath to take in the views. On other days he crossed London Bridge and ventured south. Before long he'd travelled all over London and beyond. His body regained its fitness. On some days he even reduced how much ale he drank.

All the time his thinking sharpened. He honed his plans. If he was to go to Ireland he'd make a good job of it or be damned trying. In the early evenings he read all he could about the place. Northumberland tried his best to help. A series of men were brought to Whitehall to brief the Earl personally on recent reports from Ireland. During these sessions Digby remained hidden. He sat listening, unseen behind plastered walls. The anonymity of his role remained important.

More often than not, he believed the briefers were bigots, playing back their opinions rather than statements of fact. Nevertheless he felt he was getting to know the lie of the land. Ireland was a complex place but had a simple problem - the two sets of people living there hated each other's guts.

A month later a fitter and better informed Digby left London behind him. His designated route wasn't easy. There'd be no coach to Bristol nor naval boat. Instead he was ordered to make his own way to North Wales. He was advised to create a plausible rationale for making the trip. Nobody should suspect he was en-route to the province of Ulster.

It was an easy decision. He'd repeat the pilgrimage he'd made a dozen years earlier with Robert Catesby and many others to visit St Winifrede's holy well near Flint. Digby found the journey and English coach travel in general frustrating and fascinating in equal measure. There were annoying delays when a wheel was damaged or a driver late for a shift but also unexpected pleasures from forced companionship with strangers.

On the first day he sat inside a coach constantly being shaken up and down on a cushioned bench. Opposite him sat a pair of churchmen. They'd accidentally fallen into each other's company. One represented Rome. The other was a Protestant from the Church of England. Before long they were warmly engaged in wide-ranging conversation. Over the passing hours it became clear the two ageing holy brothers shared a fondness for topics as diverse as the psalms, poetry and offal.

In between fits of dozing, Digby smiled. The scene playing out in front of him was encouraging. Perhaps it was an omen. If these strangers from different faiths could refrain from tearing each other's throats out, perhaps others could too. Even in Ireland. He spent the following days alternating between travelling in the daytime and sleeping overnight in smoky coaching inns.

#

Shots had been fired. Everyone in the fort was on high alert. Men with rifles scanned the fringes of the forest. The mist had risen and the morning sunshine was breaking through. A hundred yards of no-man's land had been completely cleared of scrub and bushes around the stockade. If an attack came in the daytime, hostiles could be picked off as they approached. It was different in the dark. There was the sound of horses. Of three incoming riders, one slumped forward. His reins hung down and his mount only followed the others on instinct.

It was unusual for Digby to be so far inland but he'd planned to attend an important meeting. It was a conference which the French had attempted to stop taking place. They'd got their way. Three of the main tribal leaders failed to show up. Without them the negotiations were worthless. When it was clear the whole trip was a waste of time, Digby asked for a patrol to take him back to the coast. One of Button's boats would be waiting. He hoped the incoming riders wouldn't cause a lengthy delay.

The English soldiers slid back two heavy wedges and partially opened the gates. The riders entered. The slumped man looked as if he was already dead. Orders were issued and the gates were closed. Blood ran down the horseman's tunic. Digby realised he was French. The man's companions dismounted. One was a man and the other a woman. They gave the impression of being man and wife.

The men defending the gates took the reins of their horses and pointed muskets at the visitors. The pair talked hurriedly in broken English to the officer of the watch about being attacked by natives. Most of the fort's population watched with suspicion as the wounded man was taken from his horse. With his body laid on the ground, the surgeon was summoned. The doctor examined his new patient, called for a stretcher and accompanied him to the infirmary.

The garrison leader appeared. He nodded at Digby across the way, busy saddling his borrowed mount for the journey to Button's boat. Continuing on, the military man marched to the gate. Once there he bowed to the lady, addressed her husband and led the pair to his hut. The woman turned as she walked and looked around. When she spotted Digby she stared as if she knew him.

Digby sat bolt upright. He was suddenly awake in the carriage. It was her.

His surprise startled the merchant opposite him. 'Bad dream, was it?' asked the man. 'I get them all the time. I put mine down to life on the road and perhaps too much cheese. Do you like cheese? I love it. I've eaten different types from all across the country. Cheshire is popular around here of course but too crumbly for my taste. I'm a Cheddar man. They make it in caves. I don't mean that's where they keep the cattle. No, it's where they mature the cheese. The humidity and temperature are ideal, so they say. Good God man, are you alright? You've look like you've seen a ghost.'

Digby ignored him. It was the Frenchwoman. He was sure she was the one who had ridden into the fort all those years ago. When they'd met in Greenwich he'd not knowingly recognised her but his mind must have picked up something familiar and had been searching his memory ever since. Finally it had worked out who she was and passed the information on through the dream.

Digby racked his mind to remember what had happened next. Before leaving the fort he'd discovered the French couple were called Blanchet. It was the first time he'd encountered the Frenchman close up. He'd only do so once again. At the time the woman had meant nothing to him. A patrol had been sent to scout the path and when they reported no signs of trouble, Digby's group departed for the coast.

Was it her? Could he be mistaken? No, he was certain. The Frenchwoman he'd talked to in Greenwich Palace and the woman in the fort were one and the same. She'd been Blanchet's wife. Now she was his widow. Did she seek revenge?

Chapter VIII

Digby stood waist high in the water and looked down at his body. There were signs of age and wear and tear but the recent walking had done him good. He hadn't gone completely to seed. There was one major scar to the left of his stomach. The red weal was made by a surgeon two years previously. An iron brand cauterised a wound made by an arrow shot from a bow held by a native, ordered by the French.

Above the water line Digby was naked. Beneath it he wore a simple pair of breeches. He closed his eyes and prayed to God for the first time in years. St Winifride's appeared an apt location for this. The well was famous for the holiness of its water. It was one of many ancient wonders of Wales. Over the years its importance had increased and it was now a sacred site for the Catholic Church and a popular spot for pilgrimages. The water issued from the well was believed to have healing powers.

The well was where the ancient Welsh warrior Caradog had propositioned Winefride, a chaste local maiden. When she'd rejected his advances he'd severed her head with a single slash of his sword. Due to the prayers of her uncle, Winefide returned to life. The well formed around her, holy water spurting out from the ground. Digby recalled the legend but couldn't remember what became of Caradog.

In early 1605 Digby had taken part in one of the major pilgrimages to Holywell. Many of the leading Catholic families of the faith of the day were represented. Digby was accompanied by his wife Mary. They were happy in those days and he cut a popular figure, knighted by the King and a convert to the Catholic faith. Jesuit priests and others had spotted the benefits of recruiting such a rich and influential young man. It was a heady mix for their cause. The Jesuits linked him to Robert Catesby. The rest for good and bad was history.

'Are the waters working for you?'

Digby was surprised. He'd been sure he was alone. The voice came from beyond the doorway of the stone walls built to surround the shrine. As the door opened further early morning sunshine filtered in. Digby couldn't see the face of the person before him. The speaker's head appeared in a halo.

'Do you not know who I am, my son?'

A man walked forward. The halo dissipated. Underneath a long coat, the man wore the robes of a priest. Digby recognised his voice and then the man. It had been twelve years since they'd last met. The priest had aged considerably.

'Father Newcorne?' said Digby in surprise.

'Yes, it is I,' said Newcorne. 'I heard you'd returned from the Americas but what are you doing in Holywell? Did the maiden appear before you?'

Digby stepped out of the water. He shivered slightly. Using the woollen blanket which served as towel and sleeping cover he dried his body. Out of modesty, he covered himself as he exchanged his breeches for a dry pair and pulled on a shirt.

'I'm afraid not, Father,' replied Digby. 'The only visitor I've seen this morning is you, although you did appear to arrive out of thin air.'

'God helps me to walk in mysterious ways,' commented the priest cheerfully. 'You're all alone here, I see. How are Mary and your family?'

'They are well. My sons are growing into fine boys but I see little of them these days.'

'I'm aware or your separate lives but remember in the eyes of God you will always be man and wife,' said the priest. He now approached closer and stood beside Digby at the edge of the pool. He shook Digby's hand warmly. 'I must say this is a pleasant surprise, Sir Everard. It is good to see you again after all these years.'

'And you too, Father. Are you here with others?'

'No, I'm quite alone, my son. I travel to this place several times a year for group pilgrimages and now and then for individual ones, as today.'

Digby tried to hide his relief. He didn't want to meet anybody else. His plan was to leave Holywell before noon, which was different to the cover story he'd invented, where he'd remain in the area for a number of days.

'The saintly maiden of the well gives strength to all those who visit her,' added Father Newcorne. 'I believe this comes directly from our Lord God, the Holy Father, to us sinners here on Earth. Visiting a shrine like this is the second best thing any Catholic can do.'

'The second best thing, Father. What is the first?' asked Digby innocently.

'Why confession of course, my son,' replied the priest. 'When did you last confess your sins to God?'

#

An hour later Digby, the sinner, and Father Newcorne, the representative of the Saviour, stood in the sand dunes.

'In the name of the Father, and of the Son, and of the Holy Spirit, my last confession was many months ago. Forgive me for I have sinned.'

Which sin should he cover first? There had been so many and he'd avoided visiting the confessional for so long.

'Take your time, my son,' said Father Newcorne. 'God knows it has been a long while since your last confession. He knows you have travelled in foreign lands but He's pleased you've returned to Him. I'm not in a hurry. Perhaps start with the more major sins?'

'Forgive me, for I have sinned,' said Digby quietly. 'I have killed other men.'

'How did this come about?'

'It was in the duty of my country. If I had not killed these men, they would have killed me. I killed only to defend myself and my countrymen in the heat of battle.' Digby hesitated. 'Apart from once.'

'What happened then, my son?'

'He was a Frenchman, Father. Their leader in the vicinity. With him at their helm they would have gone onto greater things. Without him they became rudderless. I killed the man in the night in cold blood with the help of another. It was an act of revenge, and to prevent the Frenchman from further threatening the plans of my country. He wasn't a good man.'

'I see,' said the priest. 'God understands you were only doing your duty, my son. I absolve you from these sins in the name of the Father, and of the Son and of the Holy Spirit. Please, do continue.'

'Forgive me, for I have sinned. I have committed adultery. I married a good woman but I've been unfaithful to her.'

'This is a sin which requires greater penance, my son. Please be silent for a few moments, whilst God helps me determine what must be done to gain His forgiveness.'

Apart from the wind, the gulls and the steady flow of incoming waves, there was silence. The dunes stood at the edge of the beach about half a mile away from the shrine. From their spot on the marram grass, Father Newcorne gazed southwards toward the county town of Flint and then north in the direction of the mouth of the estuary of the River Dee and beyond to the the lapping waves of the open sea.

The priest spoke quietly 'This is indeed a grave matter. You've been blessed by God with a wife and should count this blessing. It is imperative you repent these sins from your past. I believe you are doing that. If this is the case I absolve you, on one condition, from those sins in the name of the Father, and of the Son and of the Holy Spirit.'

'Forgive me father but what do you mean by *"one condition"?'* asked Digby.

'I am pleased you noticed those words, my son. They're extremely important,' answered Newcorne. 'You are absolved of the sins of the past but only on the condition you become a better man in future. From here on you must pray to Him and think and act in a way which befits your status as an honourable man on His earth. Only if you do these things will you be able, at the right time, to enter the gates of heaven and find eternal happiness.'

'I think I understand,' said Digby, 'but specifically what must I do?'

'You must not kill, unless it is in the line of duty. You must not commit adultery, and you must not break His other Commandments. In addition, you must do what is asked of you by the one true Church, whatever that may be. Do you agree to this condition?'

Digby became uncomfortable. He considered himself an honourable man and didn't want to offend the old priest but what about Chasquéme? Mary no longer wanted him. He hoped one day to find Chasquéme and live a new life with her. No matter how unlikely this might be, there was still a chance. Surely this was not wrong? He loved her and so couldn't agree to the condition laid down. In the future he may commit adultery again. He didn't want to lie.

'You look troubled, my son,' said the priest.

Digby hesitated for a moment before answering. 'I cannot promise to meet this condition, Father. There may be circumstances where I would almost certainly break the vow. Do you understand?'

The priest suddenly became furious with him. To Digby's surprise, Newcorne stood up. 'No, I do not understand. The Father, the Son and the Holy Spirit do not understand.' He was shouting now, almost screaming. 'You'll die in eternal damnation.'

Digby was confused. He thought only of Chasquéme. Over the past few days, he'd realised once his work was done in Ireland, he would go back to North America and attempt to find her one last time. Digby raised himself up too, to face Father Newcorne.

For a moment the priest managed to calm himself. 'I will give you one last chance, my son. Will you meet the condition of the Church and tell us what it is you plan to do in Ireland?'

Digby was astonished. At mention of the word *Ireland* he grabbed Newcorne by the cassock. He pulled the old man to him and held him by the throat.

'So at last, the truth. This has nothing to do with killing, adultery or coveting. Just like in 1605, you Jesuits simply want to use people like me for your own ends,' spat out Digby. 'Don't you realise, I lost my wife because of you. If I hadn't seen sense, I would have lost my life and many others would have been killed too. How can God's people, representatives of the Church, support and encourage wholesale murder as happened in Westminster? You're the one who needs to confess Father and have your sins absolved. Your life is a sham.'

'Release me! I command you in the name of his Holiness the Pope, release me now!' screamed Newcorne, struggling to free himself from Digby's grip. 'How dare you place your hands on a man of the cloth?'

But the younger man was too strong. Digby stood his ground and wondered what his next move should be. He observed the prisoner. The priest's face was the colour of damson. His eyes bulged and spittle was forming on his lips. He was raging like a gargoyle. Raging and grotesque, thought Digby.

'Calm down, Father,' said Digby. 'I have no wish to hurt you but you must tell me what you know of my visit to Ireland.'

Digby gently released his hold on the priest in a way which ensured he didn't fall over. Once freed, Newcorne patted himself down on his chest and stomach. It was if he was going through a process of cleansing himself from the dirt Digby had placed upon him.

'You shall go to Hell for this,' he said.

'Why do you think I've been avoiding Confession all this time?' asked Digby. 'Since 1605, I've been convinced that's where I'm headed but this encounter gives me an interesting dilemma. Is there a special word for the sin of killing a priest?'

There was fear in Father Newcorne's eyes now, as well as anger. 'What do you mean?'

'I think we've both come to the same conclusion. I'm a lost cause to the faith. Well, if I'm going to burn in Hell for all eternity, a few additional sins here on Earth won't make much difference.'

'The Lord sees everything,' stammered the father, speaking quickly. 'Even a few good deeds could reduce the temperature of the fire.' The priest was beginning to sweat.

'And I suppose bad ones can only make matters worse? Let's see how hot we can make the embers, shall we?' Digby squeezed his hands around Newcorne's neck. The wind was blowing strongly offshore now. It carried the priest's cries away from the land. Nobody could see or hear the two men. Digby lessened his grip but kept his hand in place, as if ready to squeeze again.

'Your plan has backfired, Father. Tell me what you know of my visit to Ireland and the questions you've been ordered to ask me.'

'I am a priest. Nobody gives me orders, other than the Lord Himself,' Newcorne blurted out indignantly.

'Then tell me what the Lord has ordered, or perhaps what men haven't ordered but politely requested you to do. But do it soon for I must be on my way.' Digby increased his grip slightly but noticeably. It was enough. Father Newcorne suddenly had the fear of God inside him and he wasn't ready to meet his maker yet.

'I know very little about your visit to Ireland, other than you are going to Ulster to do the Devil's work. My task was to persuade you to take holy orders and work for us instead of the heretic queen when you get there.'

'Who is *us*?' asked Digby. Again he tightened his hold a little on the priest's throat. He wasn't proud of what he was doing but in the circumstances it was a necessary evil.

'The Jesuit order in England.'

'And who else?'

'We work alone.'

Digby suddenly increased the intensity of his hold. He did it only for a second. He didn't want the priest to pass out.

'You are a fiend, Everard Digby. I'll see that you perish in the flames for all eternity.'

Digby tensed his fingers.

'Stop! I shall tell you. We have friends in the government of France. They want to see Protestant England weakened. Unlike you, they are good Catholics. They are of our Church and wish to support its restoration as the one and only true Church in England. Equally they wish to stop the spread of the planters and their heretical views in Ireland. They wish to prevent any chance of a peaceful settlement between the local population and the mainlanders. Our French friends informed us you were going to Ulster, working on behalf of the government, and I was despatched to intercept you and ask you to tell us what you know of the plans put forward by the evil earls of Suffolk and Northumberland.'

'What are the names of these friends?'

'I met only two, Bishop Richelieu and a woman. I wasn't told her name.'

'Describe her to me.'

'Dark hair, dark eyes. Some would say she was a handsome woman.'

Digby gently removed his hand from Newcorne's throat. 'You may go,' he said.

'There will be no peace for you, Digby, on earth or thereafter. You are damned, and so is all your family.'

At this Digby turned and grabbed the priest again, this time by the short grey hair on his head. He pulled the old man roughly back towards his own body. For a moment he thought he'd strike him. A single blow in the right place would be enough. He knew how to do it and was aware how foolish it would be to let Newcorne go, but he didn't have it his heart to kill him. Scare him, yes. Hurt him, if necessary. Kill him, no.

'If I hear one hair of those I love is harmed, I shall find you and kill you and every other Jesuit in this country. And this evening I shall pass the word onto my friends to do likewise should anything happen to me. They're good people and will protect my family and come looking for you if anything happens to even one of my kin. Now you can go. You and those like you are a disgrace to your calling. I may be heading to Hell but consider this, the Lord knows what you do and is watching you always. Where do you think you're going to go when you leave this Earth? I look forward to spending all eternity with you. We can spend our time together in the depths of Hell.'

With this, he let go of Newcorne's hair, twisted him around and gave him a gentle shove on the bottom with the sole of his boot, directing the priest back towards the shrine. The father didn't need a second chance. He pulled up his coat so he could run and fled for all he was worth, hoping to find safety in the company of any visiting pilgrims.

Digby picked up his pack, put it onto his back and set off to walk to the nearby fishing village of Prestatyn. A man should be waiting for him there. This would be the first of his guides. Digby knew the man would have instructions explaining how they'd cross the Irish Sea to Ulster. What might be waiting for them when they got there, he didn't know.

Chapter IX

'Mea culpa,' said Northumberland. 'I trusted the man but he's let me down badly. He's let us all down.'

'How much do you think he told them?' asked Elizabeth.

'I can't be sure,' replied Northumberland, 'but I fear too much.' He was ashen faced. 'You know my policy. I believe in tolerance. I employ Catholics and Protestants without favour for either side. The man must have hid his fanaticism when my steward employed him in my family's service. If it wasn't for Suffolk's people the wretch might have carried on hiding behind every door, listening to my conversations and passing on what he'd heard to his Puritan friends.'

The Queen turned to Suffolk, 'And your man is taking him to the Tower now.'

'Yes, Your Majesty,' replied Suffolk. 'If the prisoner doesn't talk…' The Secretary of State shrugged his shoulders.

Elizabeth knew what this meant. 'I will sign the papers if I have to,' she said, 'but only for the lesser tortures. The rack's still in the Tower but God forbid we should use it again in anger.'

'Don't worry, Your Majesty,' said Suffolk. 'If the lesser treatments won't work even the sight of the rack turns most men towards frank confession.'

'Let's hope it doesn't come to that and the man folds earlier,' said the Queen. Her responsibilities weighed heavily on her shoulders. The thought of inflicting pain, even on a traitor, wasn't a happy one. She turned to Northumberland. 'Can we get word to Digby to tell him the plan may be known and his life is at risk?'

'I fear it may be too late, Your Majesty,' replied Northumberland. 'He's due to catch the boat to Ireland from the Welsh coast this very evening. We'll send word to Ulster but it will be days before it gets there. By then,' he paused for a moment, 'it may be too late. We can only hope when in the Americas he learned to watch his back well.'

\#

Darkness fell onto the sleepy fishing village of Prestatyn. Two men walked along the beach, away from all the buildings. They were confident they weren't being followed. Every now and then they stopped and listened for signs of secret pursuit but heard only the waves and the whistle of the breeze.

Digby's experience earlier in the day had confirmed his scepticism towards religion. Could a merciful God condone the things which were carried out on the Earth in His name? God's representatives had lost all connection with Him. Chasquéme's people lived a different way. Their lives were connected to the land and the animals they shared it with.

The man with Digby was a Scot. He carried an unlit lantern. When the time was right he'd use it to signal the boat which should be waiting offshore, ready to take them away into the night. Half an hour earlier they thought they'd seen a signal from a clifftop above them but when it wasn't repeated they'd put it down to a shepherd ensuring his sheep didn't get too close to the edge.

The two men left a trail of unseen footsteps in the damp sand. Soon the Scotsman saw the flashing yellow light emitted from the sea. Bending down he shielded his own lantern from the wind, lit it and replied. Fifteen minutes later the two men sat with their feet and legs soaked, in the bow of a rowing boat. The small vessel rose and fell on the swell of the tide as four sailors pulled hard on their oars and eyed their visitors with caution. At the stern, a mariner watched for signals from his ship and steered the rudder towards them.

When they'd met earlier at the rendezvous point, the Scot had told Digby his name was Hamilton and he'd fought in the Nine Years War against the Irish. Subsequently he'd been part of a plantation settlement in North Down in the province of Ulster. When Digby asked him why he left, the Scot said he'd become disillusioned with the treatment meted out to the locals. The current troubles were not a surprise, he said. The Irish railed against their repression and they always would, unless a fairer settlement was made. Digby shrugged. Hamilton may or may not have been his name but he was on message with the Queen's thinking.

It was pitch black in the boat. Digby wondered at the sense of direction of the navigator and the strength of the oarsmen. It wasn't long before they lifted the oars and steadied as they approached the ship. *The Tramonata* looked more like a large fishing boat than a naval vessel. Digby and Hamilton both wondered if it was used for occasions like this when discretion was more important than a show of strength.

Once they'd clambered on board, the captain introduced himself as James Morrison. Digby was disappointed not to see

Button's smiling face but shook the captain's hand warmly. As it turned out Morrison was another Scot and he and Hamilton took to each other immediately. When they'd sunk their second dram of whisky in the small officers' galley, Digby left them to it. He made his excuses and was shown to a hammock in the officers' quarters. After his travels across the Atlantic he was used to sleeping at sea and wasn't troubled by the constant rocking. Within minutes he fell into an exhausted asleep.

The next day was uneventful. At one he shared a post midday meal with Hamilton and the captain.

'With good wind and fair weather we'll reach Dundalk by morning,' declared Captain Morrison.

'What's Dundalk like? I've never been to Ireland,' asked Digby.

'Before the English arrived it was a small coastal fishing port. It's now grown into a garrison town.'

They ate the rest of the lamb stew in silence. When the captain left them, Digby turned to Hamilton. 'What do you know of what's to come?'

'Not much,' Hamilton admitted. 'Once we reach Ulster we'll be reliant on the second guide for instruction. My tasks are to simply share my knowledge of the planters with you, and be your bodyguard if you need one, which you will. Both the Irish and the planters are fierce f... fellows.'

'You can swear in front of me if you like, you know. What do you think will be needed to persuade the Protestant settlers to consider a compromise?'

Hamilton shrugged. 'It won't be easy, that's for sure. On the positive side, there's hope. There has to be. The planters live in fear for their lives. In some places they can't leave their strongholds unless they go out in force. It's not a good way to live. If their security can be guaranteed, perhaps they'd trade some of their resources and land with the Irish.'

Digby knew a key part of his mission was to create a personal relationship with one of the leaders of the Irish cause. This assumed there was any left and, if there was, whether they could find them. He expected the task of getting the Irish on side would be even harder than with the planters. How could they be persuaded to believe an unknown Englishman, when they'd been misled so many times in the past?

After an afternoon of thinking, dozing and staring out to sea, when the early evening came Digby once again dined with Captain Morrison and Hamilton in the officers' galley. This time they were joined by the ship's master Mister Merriweather. The conversation was somewhat subdued.

Afterwards Digby passed the remainder of the evening thinking of the Americas. The tribal leaders had taken risks by agreeing to meet him. The'd been suspicious from the start and he couldn't blame them. The Europeans, particularly the English, had lied before.

Some argued the French were better. They were hungry for land but if they could make peace, the natives would be offered the option of becoming French citizens. Those who accepted would be protected by the same laws as men born in France.

Digby believed there had to be a better way. Instead of pushing the natives off their land and into the margins, the British could, and should, trade and negotiate with them. America was a huge continent and sparsely populated. There was room for the local population and the incoming settlers. The natives could teach the incomers how to survive and prosper in their hostile territories. The Europeans could share the benefits of their technology. The two could co-exist for mutual benefit.

That was the theory anyway, and some of the tribal leaders agreed. The harder part was getting the British on side. How could Digby get the army, navy, churchmen and others with commercial interests to behave in a more honourable way and not exploit the natives? It was a precarious balance but he'd made a start. In some places peace rather than hostility had broken out. A number of the natives had even visited England.

When he'd completed the job in Ireland, he'd speak to Queen Elizabeth and ask for her support to expand the new ways of thinking. He'd return to the Americas and if Chasquéme was alive he'd find her. After that he'd make things work for her people. Another wry smile. This was all for the future. First he had to stay alive long enough to fulfil his mission in Ireland. Gently swaying in the hammock, he fell asleep.

#

'Fire!' shouted the man, calling directly into the officers' quarters.

It was dark. Digby couldn't see anything from his bunk. As he pushed open the cabin door, a splinter cut into his hand for his troubles. He joined the melee outside. On deck all was chaos. Orange flames spewed out from an open hatch in the hold up into the open air. Men ran around looking for buckets to fill. The plan wasn't complex. Water was needed to douse the blaze.

70

Captain Morrison was livid. 'What do you mean there are no buckets? There are always buckets. We have loads of buckets.'

The seamen in front of him had no explanation. Buckets couldn't be found. The fire was getting worse. Flames fanned out. With no way of dampening the fire, the captain ordered all cargo doors be closed and port holes sealed in an attempt to choke off the blaze. Nobody knew the extent of the damage in the hold itself. If the fire had reached the outer hull, there'd be a breach. After that things would get serious very quickly.

The crew spent the next few hours nervously monitoring the situation. All hands were ordered to remain on deck. In the swinging lamplight, the men's faces looked grey or wild-eyed. Digby wondered whether their luck would hold.

As first light dawned from the east, Captain Morrison spoke to the men. 'There's hope,' he said. Starved of air, the fire's begun to die down. That's good news. The bad news is we don't know how much damage the old girl's taken. When it's light enough, I'm going in to take a look. In the meantime, everyone can have a swig of rum and a ship's biscuit.'

The captain turned to Merriweather. 'Stay here at the wheel on the quarterdeck, and keep an eye on the men. I want to check out the charts. We can't be far off the Irish coast now.'

Digby and Hamilton followed the captain to his cabin. Using a small iron key, he unlocked the small desk. Finding the chart he was after, he laid it neatly onto the trestle table. With Hamilton holding a lamp, Captain Morrison pointed at a tiny blob on the coast and said "Dundalk", before indicating an area a few inches from the coast.

'That's my best guess of where we must be now. With the cloud cover, I can't be sure. My worry is these rocks. We've come a bit further south that I would have liked.'

The captain pointed to a jagged row of black lines on the chart. As he did so, a call came from the rigging. Land was in sight. The three men returned to the deck. Mariners were ordered to check and ready the two rowing boats, just in case. Both were in good order. Morrison raised his thumb to Merriweather.

Digby looked at Hamilton. 'There's a good chance we'll make it,' he said.

There was a loud creak. Hamilton shook his head. The ship lurched to the left.

'She's taking in water,' declared the master.

71

'It appears so, Mister Merriweather,' confirmed the captain ruefully. 'Prepare to abandon ship. We'll leave it to the last momont and get as close as we can to the coast before we get off. You never know, we may save her yet. If we have to go over the side be careful, the channels around here are treacherous and we'll have limited control in the rowing boats. When the tide ebbs there'll be a lot of rocks. Ensure our guests get preferential treatment. I want them both on the first boat if we do have to scarper.'

'Aye, sir,' said Merriweather. 'Come with me, sirs.'

One of the crew took the wheel. Digby and Hamilton followed Merriweather from the quarterdeck to the stern. The boat was listing badly now. It wouldn't be long before they'd have to get off. At least the daylight was increasing. Merriweather assembled most of the men and explained the situation. The captain returned to his cabin, to study and re-study the charts. There were more creaks from below.

A quick roll-call was taken of all those on board. Only one man was missing, a young deck-hand. He'd last been seen in the sleeping quarters. Two sailors were dispatched to find him and bring him above deck. They returned, dragging the body of an unconscious sailor.

'What on earth happened to him?' asked Merriweather.

'I hit him,' replied one of the sailors. 'He was trying to set light to one of our bunks.'

'My God! A wrecker,' exclaimed the master

Digby pushed past the sailors. He looked at the man and recognised him instantly as the youthful zealot who'd attacked him in the maze in Greenwich.

'Ship ahoy.' The cry came from a man stationed above them on lookout duty. 'She's coming in fast from the port side.'

Emerging back onto the deck, Captain Morrison asked. 'What flag is she flying?'

'She's one of ours,' replied the man.

There was a small cheer of relief from the men.

'Thank God for that.' said Morrison quietly to Digby, 'But she'd better get to us soon or we'll run aground, and so might she'

Digby looked ahead. They were entering a narrow channel with jagged rocks on both sides. They'd done well to get so near to the coast but there was danger ahead. The swell was increasing. It appeared the ship was no longer fully under the crew's control. If they struck the rocks on either side *The*

Tramonata and its rowing boats would be at serious risk of breaking up.

As Digby considered this, there was an awful noise of wood cracking. The boat lurched until it was almost on its side. Men staggered across the deck. A few fell overboard. Everyone else desperately grabbed onto something, anything they could hold onto. The list was too big. The rigging and sails were dragging the boat onto its side. If the hole from the fire didn't sink her, the sails would definitely pull the vessel under. They'd done as much as they could. It was time to go.

'Abandon ship,' shouted the captain.

Merriweather ensured Hamilton and Digby were pushed onto the first boat. The captain ordered the master to accompany them and take command of it. Digby had wanted to take the ship-wrecker on with him but in the mayhem the prisoner was the last of anyone's concerns. There was barely enough room for half the crew on the small vessel. Some men sat, whilst others stood pressed into one another to get everyone on. Any additional loading would cause the little craft to capsize.

Digby watched in admiration as the men did their jobs. They were saving themselves but rescuing their crew mates too. The second boat pushed off. Captain Morrison was the last man to clamber onto her. Moments later *The Tramonata* keeled over. Across the waves Morrison swore loudly. Digby was aware this was the first ship he'd lost. The main sail snagged. It was already half underwater. The upturned hull shook repeatedly as it smashed against the nearest rocks. Cracked wood and ship's paraphernalia broke loose and floated all around them.

The men on the oars desperately rowed to maintain their central place in the channel. A large wave swept over them, soaking Digby and all the others. The boat shook wildly from side to side. Hamilton and Digby's bodies were pressed back against the planking lining the vessel. Digby was just about to speak when he was grabbed by the shoulders and his body violently pulled backwards.

Before he could react he was in the water. The shock of the cold hit him, the effects were disorienting. For a moment he had no idea where he was. Submerged beneath the waves, his body spun around. Shaking his head, he opened his eyes and felt the sting of salt. He didn't know which way was up. Everything was moving. He began to take a breath but sensing the water he stopped himself. Realising what had happened he tried not to panic.

More than anything he needed air. He knew he had to go up but something held onto his legs. He couldn't kick. Despite fighting the impulse, he swallowed water. For a second he thought this was the end. Another wave swept above him. The force of this and his own angle twisted his body around. Digby's head and shoulders were thrust above the surface. He coughed out water, took in a deep breath and was pulled back under.

Whatever had him seemed to possess superhuman strength. Digby attempted to kick his legs but they were held fast. He kept on trying. Due to the darkness he feared he was getting deeper. There was little time left. His lungs were bursting but still he refused to give up.

The third wave made the difference. Whatever had him was weakening. His torso flipped backwards. As he struck out this time he felt the grip loosen. He kicked and kicked with his feet and ankles and knees until the thing released him.

Digby's body was free but he needed to breathe. The air leaving his lungs buoyed him upwards. His head pierced the surface and he took another breath. Something touched his feet. Fear came over him he'd be pulled back downwards. With waves crashing all around he couldn't see the boats. His foot was touched again. He kicked madly in the opposite direction. A hook latched onto his sodden shirt. Two of Merrieweather's mariners hauled him out and lifted him back into the boat.

As Digby was unceremoniously dumped next to him, Hamilton looked concerned. 'You need to be more careful,' said the Scotsman. A pool of water formed beneath their bodies.

'No, I was…' but before Digby could finish his sentence another wave crashed over them.

The men on the port side of the boat turned and groaned as one. It was a depressing sound. Digby rubbed the salt from his eyes and looked across. Morrison's boat had capsized in the swell. Men were flailing and swimming about in the water, attempting to gain hold of the side of their upturned boat, a rope or any loose plank.

At this point the incoming ship reached Merrieweather's long boat. Ropes were placed over the side. Digby, Hamilton and some of the crew members scrambled on board but the larger vessel couldn't go any further without risking being holed or grounded. It would have to back off if it was to remain unscathed.

Merrieweather remained in the rowing boat and commanded a small number of the men to stay with him. Under their master's direction, they took to the oars and made their way back towards the upturned hull of their stricken sister vessel. Behind them the recently arrived warship did its best to maintain a position just outside the channel. The waves pushed the small boat between the hazardous lines of rock on either side. In the end it gained so much speed it almost rammed the capsized craft but the skeleton crew managed to steady themselves by braking their oars in the water.

Drenched sailors scrambled over the side and pulled themselves on board. Despite the need for haste, each was careful not to pull the boat over in their panic. They'd been in the water once and didn't want to go in again. Merriweather scanned the sea until there were no more men left alive to rescue. Two bodies were clearly visible bobbing in the water beyond the nearest rocks. A third floated out from under the capsized craft next to them. Others, including the captain, couldn't be accounted for. They hauled the one corpse they could reach on board and rowed back slowly to the main ship.

The survivors were lifted aboard the rescue vessel and the rowing boat made secure alongside her. Once this was done the naval frigate made for the safety of the open water. Blankets and hot toddies of rum were given to all the men shivering on deck. Some of *The Tramonata*'s mariners stared at Digby and Hamilton with something akin to hatred in their eyes. Their reasoning was simple. Whatever had happened, it was these two men who'd brought the bad luck. Seamen were notoriously superstitious.

Without warning, the newly promoted Admiral Button appeared on deck. He gave a rallying speech to the men of both vessels. The admiral said it had been a terrible morning but they all were heroes and should be proud of what they'd achieved. The Queen, their country and the Navy Board would thank them for what they'd done. Once he'd finished, the men gave Button a cheer and he beckoned Digby, Hamilton and Merriweather to follow him to his cabin for a debriefing.

#

The Queen was frustrated. France had made an official complaint about the behaviour of Sir Everard Digby in the Americas, demanding his immediate arrest. The letter had been addressed to the Secretary of State personally rather than the Navy Board, as Digby didn't hold a formal commission. It appeared the French wanted to make a point. The Queen's secret envoy to Ireland was being accused of cold blooded murder.

In a report to his superiors a French army officer recently returned from the Americas claimed Digby had slipped into a French stronghold in the dead of night, evaded the guards and killed the leader of the French mission as he slept in his bed. Details of the complaint had been passed onto Elizabeth by the Earl of Suffolk. The Earl believed this was a ruse aimed at undermining Digby's mission to Ireland. If this was the case, it added weight to the concern of an alliance between the Jesuits, Puritans and French. How else could the French know of Digby's involvement in Ireland if they hadn't discovered the news from the Puritan who'd been spying on Northumberland's household?

After a brief meeting Suffolk took a boat upriver. The tide was on his side and he returned swiftly to his office in Whitehall. Elizabeth was left to ponder whether or not to reply to the French. For now she favoured another option. She'd ignore the complaint and wait to see what might happen. There was no great rush. Digby may already be dead. The Queen's line of thought was interrupted by her mother as she entered Elizabeth's private rooms.

'Good morning, my dear,' said Anne cheerfully. 'I hope I've not caught you at a bad time but we do need to talk about the November masque. Master Jonson will once again be involved. I would like to know if you'll be happy to play some part in the proceedings?'

Elizabeth looked at the older woman. Masques and arts and dancing. Diversions which maintained her mother's enthusiasm for life. She knew it had been the same when her father James had been alive. They'd taken her mind off the King's other interests.

'How is Mary?' asked Elizabeth. 'It feels like I haven't seen her for ages.'

'You haven't,' replied Anne. 'She's well but missing her sister. It's not easy being twelve years old but at least she has her mother to comfort her.'

It has become customary for children of the monarchy to be removed from the homes of their parents and instead set up in their own royal households. This was the reason why Elizabeth had been living at Coombe Abbey at the time of the Gunpowder Plot. Anne had always railed against this. She thought children should reside with their mother. Since James's death, she'd had her own way on the matter and ensured Elizabeth when she was younger and now Princess Mary lived with her in their castle in Windsor.

'Is Northy making sure she's educated well?' asked Elizabeth smiling.

'The Earl of Northumberland insists that Mary has the best tutors in the land, as he did with you. If anything, I'd say she is brighter than you.'

'Be careful what you say,' warned Elizabeth. 'In previous times such a statement may have been taken as treason.'

'Then it is just as well we live in more enlightened times,' replied Anne. They both laughed. 'Now, what about this masque? Go on. You know it would make me happy for you to take part.'

Anne enjoyed all types of theatre but she loved masques in particular. Elizabeth believed there was only one thing her mother liked better than planning and watching a masque and that was playing a role herself. Sometimes Anne would play a central character in the performance. In this aspect Anne was a revolutionary. She insisted writers not only included major roles for women but they were played by women too, when previously only men had been considered able enough for acting on stage.

'Does Jonson have anything specific in mind?' asked Elizabeth.

'Yes, of course. He knows you won't be able to make time for rehearsals. In response he's created a special role for you. Did you know he describes you as the centre of his universe, as well as the jewel of Europe?'

Elizabeth shook her head. 'Putting such flattery aside for a moment, Mother, what is this role?'

'That is it. The centre of the universe. You'll play the Queen of the Stars. All you'll need to do is sit on a special throne during the final act. You'll be surrounded by a set depicting the moon, the stars and the clouds. All the other characters will be dancing and singing around you. There are no lines to learn. You'll simply have to hold a mask and wave regally. What do you think?'

'Apart from being borderline blasphemous, it sounds perfect,' replied Elizabeth. 'I'm sure I can do that.'

'That's what I thought. I'll tell Master Jonson later. And don't worry, he doesn't want the Puritans to declare holy war on him. The Good Lord is clearly depicted as giving his blessings to the whole proceeding. By the way, Beatrix and I have arranged some time this morning to meet with my special advisers. There'll be composers, writers and architects. It'll be lots of fun. I took Mary last time but she didn't like it. For a girl of her age she's easily bored. You should come along. You never know, you may even enjoy yourself.'

'I'm sure I would,' said Elizabeth lying, 'but there is so much to do.' She looked at the papers on her desk.

'I understand,' said Anne. 'Matters of state. You're politely telling your mother to go away. Don't worry, I've got what I wanted, so I shall.'

Both women smiled at each other. Elizabeth stood up, embraced her mother warmly and wondered once again what to do about the problem of Digby. She agreed with her earlier thought on the topic. Wait and see.

Chapter X

Three decades has passed since the Spanish Armada's attempt to invade England. Many veterans on both sides would never forget the experience; burning boats, cannon fire and slaughter. The Secretary of State was amongst them. Suffolk played his part in 1588, and although Spain was currently an ally he knew things could change quickly. He'd not trusted the Spanish then and he didn't trust them now.

England, or the New Britain as James and Elizabeth sometimes called it, needed to be strong. It was better to prevent a war than fight one but you could do this only if you had a deterrent. Suffolk believed this strongly. The royal marriage between the Spanish and French had exacerbated his concerns. War was starting in Europe and would soon spread across these islands if Her Majesty and the government didn't act. Some considered Elizabeth a silly young girl but Suffolk thought differently. She listened and, when she believed in something, she acted.

It was the Queen, not Parliament, who'd diverted elements of the peace dividend created by the treaty with Spain into the new Navy Board and the ship-building programme. How ironic, thought Suffolk, that the people responsible for the treaty had been his predecessor Robert Cecil and his own wife Katherine. He'd known about their affair, even tolerated it at first. He felt he had to, for the good of England, but only until the peace deal was signed. After that he'd taken matters and Cecil into his own hands.

In a darkened corridor in Whitehall he'd pushed Cecil against a wall and demanded his superior leave his wife alone. Cecil's response was extraordinary. He'd recommended Suffolk ask Katherine for her views on which of them she'd rather be with. At the time Suffolk had shaken his head, as if a woman's opinions had any bearing on the matter. Over the years his views had mellowed.

But Cecil was dead. And Katherine? She remained alone in her bed chamber. No-one was allowed to see her because her once famed beauty had been ravaged by smallpox. She'd survived the disease but retreated from the world. Before the pox had struck her, the couple had reconciled. Indeed they still talked most nights. Suffolk would visit his wife's chamber in the dark and they'd discuss the day's events. Katherine provided opinions and thoughtful advice.

Again the irony, thought Suffolk. Nobody realised the influence Katherine and by extension Robert Cecil had had on the past, current and future of their country. He opened the next ledger. The projected cost of the new warships was significant but not unaffordable. They had to prepare. They had to be ready.

#

Following a series of conferences and debriefings, Button and Digby were left alone in the captain's cabin on *The Sixth of November.* In total six crewmen from *The Tramonata* had been lost. Two additional bodies were recovered. Those unaccounted for included the escaped prisoner and Captain Morrison. Unfortunately, the Captain hadn't been seen since the second rowing boat had capsized and turned over.

After a short search Button had ordered his crew to steer *The Sixth of November* out to sea, whilst he and Digby retired to his cabin to agree a plan of action. They were ten nautical miles south east of Dundalk and it wouldn't take long to get there. The two friends knew they'd be separated again soon and shared a tot of rum as they talked.

'I told you I couldn't leave you alone for more than a few moments before you'd get yourself into trouble,' said Button, as he handed a small wooden drinking vessel to Digby.

'Believe me, I'm grateful,' replied Digby, throwing his head back and downing the fiery liquid in one. A warm sensation hit his stomach. It felt good. He savoured the after-burn for a moment before speaking again. 'Once again you've come to my rescue. You're my knight in admiral's armour.'

Button finished his own drink and shook his head ruefully. The two men looked out towards the aft deck through a pair of adjacent portholes. The glass was clear due to the novelty of the vessel. Sea-spray and salt hadn't yet had the chance to scratch the glass. Inevitably it would, whether the ship stayed afloat or sank to the bottom.

The officer and the gentleman watched as the ship's crew moved quickly about the deck. They did whatever the more senior mariners asked of them. Other sailors climbed the rigging and prepared the sails in preparation for Button's orders. They'd follow these, almost no matter what. Mutiny was rare and even rarer when men witnessed what became of sailors such as Abacuk Pricket.

'She's a lovely ship you have here,' said Digby.

'Aye, she is,' replied Button. 'She's new and one of the best. I'm lucky to 'ave her. Even more reason for me not to 'ave to follow you onto some bloody rocks. I've got a two-year mission to fulfil. Don't turn it into a one week one.'

'Two years. What do they want you to do?'

Button considered for a moment how much he should tell his friend and then thought bugger it, they'd never kept secrets from each other before, and Digby was now a government agent after all.

'Suffolk and Northumberland are worried about Ireland becoming a back-door for foreign invasion, just as Elizabeth Tudor and her government were concerned the French would be invited in from the north by Mary Queen of Scots. I'm in command of a flotilla of four vessels. Our task is to patrol the Irish coast to look for anything out of place. If the French or the Spanish, the Dutch or anyone else 'ave plans to bring in troops from across the water my job is to keep 'em out.'

'With four boats?' asked Digby.

'Aye, four,' replied Button. 'You've spotted the flaw in the Navy Board's plan? It's quite a big coastline for four ships to patrol and at least one will usually be in dock for repair or refit. It's better than nothing though, and I'm told we're building more. Of course if one of us does encounter an invading armada we'll have to engage them on our own. We couldn't get a message to the others in time.'

'What happens after your two-year stretch?'

'That's the good news. The Navy Board has promised me faithfully I can return to the Americas and command of a voyage of discovery to search of the North West Passage. That's if Hudson or somebody else hasn't found it by then.' Button looked at Digby. 'What about you? Will you return there with me?'

'I have a similar promise from Northumberland. If I can prove my worth in Ireland, I'll be free to go back to the northern lands,' said Digby.

'Will you look for her?' asked Button.

'Yes, for a while.'

'But for now you must go to Ulster?'

'Exactly,' said Digby. He smiled at his friend. 'So how are you going to get me into Dundalk?'

'Well, my immediate mission was simply to shadow *The Tramonata* to ensure you got there alright,' said Button. 'But once we saw the smoke I realised something was up and ordered an intercept course. Lucky I did, too.'

Button gave them both a refill from the bottle of rum. 'It's going to be a slightly more conspicuous arrival into port than we'd planned,' he continued. 'We won't be able to make a subtle entrance and pretend we're ferrying cargo like *The Tramonata*. There'll be people watching for naval vessels like ours and no doubt you'll be seen getting off. It will be down to 'amilton and yourself to lose any wrong-uns who try to follow you. We could drop you off along the coast of course but we'd probably still be seen and it would make it harder for you to contact your second guide.'

'I agree,' said Digby. 'Whoever he is, this man will be important. He appears to be the only one who knows the full plan. Without him, I may as well continue to sail up and down the Irish Sea and enjoy getting drunk with you.' Digby finished his rum and placed his cup upside down on the table to indicate I he wanted no more. 'Is there any chance Morrison or the young lad have survived?'

'There's always a chance but I doubt it,' replied Button. 'Morrison will be missed. He was a good man and well liked by his crew but we all know the risks. As for the other one, it's a shame you didn't finish off the treacherous little bastard when you 'ad the chance in Greenwich.'

'Yes, I wish I had,' agreed Digby, 'but I didn't really get the opportunity, if you remember? I was attacked by two assailants and they both had blades pointed in my direction until your intervention.'

'True enough.' Button nodded. 'I should 'ave removed 'is 'ead with that spade. Who do you think 'e is anyway?'

'I've no idea,' replied Digby. 'But he has the strength of a shark-fish and the madness in his eyes to match.'

'Well, at least 'e's another who won't be able to worry you now,' said Button. 'I dare say he's joined Pricket and the others down below.'

'It's becoming quite a list,' said Digby. 'They can't harm me whilst I'm awake but they gang together in my dreams.'

'Still 'aving the nightmares then?' asked Button. 'Do you ever see Catesby, or anyone else from that time in your sleep? You know I'm not blaming you. Their deaths were on their own hands.'

'No,' said Digby firmly. 'I only dream of people whose lives I've ruined since my time in the Americas. Not the ones before.'

Button finished his second tot. 'Anyway,' he continued, changing the subject. 'Put a dry shirt on, as it's time to take you into town. The tides should be about right to get us in and out of Dundalk 'arbour if we do it quickly enough. I'll chivvy the men along. Once we get there, you'll need to get off quick. We won't be 'anging around.'

Both men stood up, their heavy chairs scraping against the wooden floor.

'I wish you luck, Digby.' Button said, shaking his hand. Neither ever used the other man's first name. 'Be careful. Stay alive or I'll 'ave no one to share a tot with when I cross the Atlantic when all this is over. Ireland may be important now but it's the Americas where we both belong.'

Digby nodded his agreement. But any return to the new world appeared a long way off. His focus had to be on Ireland. He'd need to keep his wits about him. They hadn't even landed but an attempt had already been made on his life and men were dead because of it. As a wise man once him, when there are vested interests all around, the man in the middle had better watch out.

Part Two

Extract from Traditional English Rhyme - Early 17th Century
'The Welsh don't trust the English
The English don't trust the Scots
Nobody trusts the Irish
Best they be forgot'

Chapter XI

As Button had predicted, the arrival of the *Sixth of November* off Dundalk harbour created a flurry of interest from the local population. Digby and Hamilton were taken ashore in a rowing boat under the watchful eye of many of the townsfolk. Of these, a Catholic fisherman and a Puritan carpenter took a special interest. Working independently and without any knowledge of each other they made mental descriptions of the two men who landed and their vessel, including its size, shape, crew number and guns on board.

Button and the ship made a swift departure. Despite Hamilton's presence, with his friend gone, Digby felt alone. Dundalk was a tough looking place. It was a frontier town where only the walls offered protection to those inside. These were patched in places where un-matched brick and stone had been hurriedly stuffed into holes caused by previous assaults and bombardments. The corner towers above provided excellent vantage points for spying on and shooting would-be intruders.

Despite there no longer being an official conflict in Ireland, as they scurried about their business the residents gave the impression of a life under siege. Digby imagined they felt safe inside the town but not outside it unless they ventured afar in force. In a world where few enjoyed home comforts, things appeared worse here even than in England.

At the quayside Digby and Hamilton were met by representatives of the area's two main landowners, Sir John Bellew and Sir John Draycott. Both men made a handsome living from rent and by selling goods and licences to their tenants and workers. Life was little different for them than living in a manor house on the mainland, apart from needing the support of heavily armed guards at all times.

Hamilton viewed the men's stewards with disdain. 'You can be sure they demand higher prices and give less in return to the Irish Catholics and probably treat the Protestant Scots and Northern English much the same,' he whispered under his breath to Digby.

Digby nodded. Both men knew Ireland was complicated. Shades of grey existed and not just between the Catholics and Protestants. Ancient rivalries and family feuds continued. Some

Irish families despised others from their country as much as they hated the English. There were the old Irish and the new Irish. Both supported the Catholic Church but they came from different stock, anywhere from Ancient Celts to Normans and Anglo Saxons. Suspicions abounded. Protestant Scots planters didn't trust their English and Welsh comrades and the feeling was mutual.

The town clerk introduced himself as a Master John Brandon. He was irate at not being informed Dundalk was to receive official visitors. Digby calmed him by saying the two men were attending to private matters well away from Dundalk. They'd been brought over from Wales as a favour by Button as an old friend. He gave his name as Ambrose Keyes.

Once Brandon was certain they'd not arrived to check his masters's income and tax records he relaxed. When Digby asked the best way to leave town unnoticed he laughed and asked Digby to look around him. Unless they could make themselves invisible there was little chance of not being watched. Irish eyes were everywhere and none were smiling. Digby heeded the warning and asked if there was at least a good place to eat. Food and drink in a quayside tavern appeared the best option in the short term. Digby hoped the second guide would show himself soon so they could move on.

#

The young man was cold and his body was shaking but he'd made it. He may not have drowned Digby but he'd sunk his ship and made a hole in his plans. The man was a Puritan, and believed he'd achieved all he had through hard work and God's support. The Lord never left those who struggled on behalf of the righteous.

When the first rowing boat had pushed off, he'd struck one of the sailors hard in the face, taken a deep breath and dived into the water. He'd not swum under seawater before and his eyes stung when he opened them but he'd retained his belief in God and God had helped him. At first he'd remained beneath the waves until his lungs were almost fit to burst.

When eventually he surfaced nobody saw him. He approached Digby's long boat, took a huge breath and pulled his enemy into the water. He would have drowned him too, if he could have held out for just a little longer. God must have wanted him to kill Digby another time.

After that he'd been fortunate. When the second boat turned over, all eyes were upon it. Despite his weariness, the strength of the waves carried him away from the scene. In the mayhem nobody'd even noticed his escape.

Eventually, with the help of the tide he neared land but his troubles weren't over. The shore was protected by ridges of half exposed rock. He was thrown against one of these and hung onto it until another wave rolled his body further backwards. He emerged from the water onto a small ledge at the foot of the cliffs which loomed over him.

For a few minutes he remained there, getting his breath back. In the distance he observed the sails of the rescue ship. Refreshed he gave himself up to the gentler current of the incoming tide and placed his safety in the hands of the Lord. Eventually his body was guided around the rocks and into a sandy cove. He felt smoother stones and finally sand beneath his feet. As he stepped out of the surf onto the beach the Puritan assassin had gritted his teeth and smiled. Clenching his fists in front of him, he shouted, 'God be praised!'

Saved from certain death in the waves, he no longer harboured any doubt. What he'd been told was true. He'd been chosen to do God's work here on Earth. When the Puritan leaders at Sidney College in Cambridge had taken him aside and spoken to him, they'd not lied. God had selected him to take part in this holy mission to rid the Earth of His enemies. How else could he have survived what he'd just been through?

Belief coursed through his veins. He was in a heathen land but didn't fear discovery by the Irish. If any Papist scum dared approach him he'd smite them down. He knew he couldn't fail. The town he wanted was to the north. It was on the coast road. There were good people there. He'd memorised their location and would go to them. They'd know if he should continue his mission in Ireland or return to England and they'd have food, money and clothing.

Striding along, he didn't feel alone - God walked alongside him and spoke to him in the wind. What would his peers say in Huntingdon and Cambridge when he told them of his adventures? What would his seven unmarried sisters and his mother think if they could see him now? He was the chosen one. God be praised!

#

Anne Dudley could barely control her excitement. Frederick of Palatine had written back to her. Her hand shook as she opened the letter. Yes, he remembered her well and had always enjoyed seeing her when he walked and talked with Queen Elizabeth. He'd be delighted to spend some time with her when he was next in England. This would be at the beginning of November. The letter was brief but for Anne it was enough. Her hope lived on.

#

Digby sat with Hamilton at a corner table in the inn nearest the harbour wall in Dundalk. The Scot shared a little more of his background and his thoughts on what he described as the *Irish problem*.

'I hail from Stirling. Jesus, I was born within sight of the castle walls. My family was the same as the rest of our neighbours, ordinary, hard-working Protestant folk. When the call came for more troops to go to Ireland, I signed up. The next eighteen months of my life consisted of periods of boredom interspersed with intense brutality. By the end of that time, the culmination of the Nine Years War, I'd seen enough atrocities to last me a life time, dished out by both sides.'

'Who did you serve under?'

'Our group was led by Arthur Chichester, a mean old English bastard of a man. He was the sort of military leader who favours siege, starvation and scorching the earth over combat. Chichester's concept of war is to fight the whole population, not just the fighting men.'

Digby grimaced. During his detailed briefings from Northumberland, he'd seen letters Chichester had written in the early part of the century to Robert Cecil, the then very much alive Secretary of State. One line had refused to leave Digby's mind - *'A million swords won't do them as much harm as a winter of famine'.*

Chichester and his friends had been pleased when the Scots King James Stuart came to the throne. They saw him as a supporter of their cause, which he was, but the state of the government's coffers had forced him to be pragmatic in the short term. The war had been won by England but at great cost. Ireland was a wound haemorrhaging blood and money and so James had made peace and offered generous terms for the defeated.

The English and Scots armies were victorious. The Irish suspected they'd also won, but they soon learned their lesson. The peace worked out no better for them than the war. Their freedom and lands were eroded and removed. James's allies became rich. Plans for plantation, the Protestant re-population of Ireland, accelerated. Eventually the main Irish Earls of Ulster and their advisors abandoned all hope. They fled to the continent but unable to gain support for another war they died lonely deaths of exiles in Rome.

Hamilton's account was largely consistent with what Digby had been told in London, if a lot more graphic. After the war Chichester became the Lord Deputy of Ireland, the crown's leading representative on the island. He'd served in the post until very recently when he'd been replaced by his chosen successor Oliver St John. Both men had consistently ignored Elizabeth's government's policies of tolerance. Instead, repression of Irish Catholics was openly encouraged.

'Those two are a large part of the problem,' whispered Hamilton. 'It's not about religious intolerance for them. They hate the Irish, the language, the customs, the people and they're hated back.'

'Is Chichester influenced by what happened to his brother?' asked Digby.

'I don't know but I doubt it will have helped much,' replied Hamilton. 'Hearing your brother was captured, killed and his head kicked around like a ball in a field by his killers wouldn't endear you, would it? It's not just that though. I understand he's always held extremist views.'

'One thing I can't understand,' said Digby, 'is why Suffolk and Northumberland haven't brought Ireland under control themselves? Why have they let Chichester and the rest run amok?'

'Didn't you ask that question of your lords in Whitehall and Westminster?'

'Aye, I did.'

'And what did they say?'

'They didn't seem to be have an answer.'

Hamilton laughed quietly. 'Bloody typical.' He sounded even more Scots. 'They've no idea of what it's like over here. Kill or be killed. It's like living in the Highlands but worse. You can't end decades of hatred with a few nice laws.'

Digby listened intently. It was depressing stuff but he knew it was true.

'One set of people have the power and wealth and the others don't,' continued Hamilton. 'The ones who have it want to keep it. The ones who don't, want it back and they'd each love to slash each other's throats. The idea of the two sides living in harmony is laughable. You might have pow-wowed with the Americans but you can't do it with the Irish. They'll skin you alive.'

'Others have tried. So far, they've failed,' said Digby.

89

'Well, in that case we've got nothing to worry about,' said Hamilton dryly. 'But it won't come to that because when the planters find out what we're up to, they'll kill us first anyway.'

Hamilton laughed bitterly. Any optimism he'd shown on the boat had deserted him now he was back in Ireland. He took a deep drink of ale and poured more from the large jug into his tankard.

'So why come on this mission if you don't believe in it?' asked Digby.

Hamilton took another drink. He didn't answer.

'Surely there must be a reason?' Digby pressed. 'You believe we're doomed to fail and our lives are at risk. They must be paying you well?'

Hamilton snorted in disgust. 'The money's fine but I doubt I'll live to spend it. If you must know, the reason is love. Love and a promise.'

The words didn't sound like those of a dour Scotsman, thought Digby.

'Go on,' he said quietly, the mocking tone gone from his voice.

'I fell in love with an Irish girl, if you must know. She changed my life but we were soon discovered and her family murdered her. They said it was a matter of honour. Where's the honour in that? The plantation leaders then found out too, and I was lucky to escape before they caught me. My real name's not Hamilton, you ken?'

'I'm sorry,' said Digby genuinely. 'What was your promise?'

'I promised her memory. There wasn't a body or grave to mourn. I said I'd try to make things better or die in the attempt, more likely the latter. Then I was asked to do this job, and here I am.'

Digby said nothing more but thought of Chasquéme. Was she buried in the Americas in an unmarked grave? Killed by an Englishman like Pricket, or her own people, or had she simply died from smallpox or one of the other diseases introduced by the Europeans?

'So now you know everything about me, what about you?' asked the man Digby knew as Hamilton. 'I've heard about the painting of yourself and Hudson. What else is there to know and how did the lords in London persuade *you* to support this wee suicide mission? Money, promises for the future, blackmail?'

'A bit of all three,' replied Digby.

At that moment the man they'd both observed entering the inn a few minutes earlier walked towards their table.

'I'm Conn,' said the man. His voice had a heavy Irish accent but Digby felt there was something else there too, an influence of another nationality or language. 'They say the weather in London is lovely this time of year,' he added.

Conn was outwardly dressed like most of the non-military men they'd seen in Dundalk. The inhabitants, thought Digby, would fit nicely into virtually any town in England. On hearing the faintly ridiculous code phrase, Digby gestured for the man to sit down. As he did so, a coarse brown woollen shirt became visible beneath his cloak. This wasn't like anything the English would wear. The man's hair and beard were brown also, as were the eyes which scanned the room. He had the look of a man who'd be happier somewhere else.

Once introductions were complete, Conn began talking, 'I've been sent here to link you fellas to your second guide. But we'll need to go tonight. Neither you nor I can risk hanging around here until the morning, not if we don't want our throats cut.'

'Where can we go at this time of day?' asked Hamilton, his eyes narrowing.

'You, not we,' replied Conn. 'We'll travel separately. It'll be safer for all of us.'

After this he imparted a set of directions to a meeting point three miles inland from the town and left them. Once outside the door of the inn, he took a look up and down the street and slipped away.

From a brief follow-on discussion, it was clear neither of the two men had been impressed by this Conn character. His main concern appeared to his own safety. He'd watched the door nervously through the entirety of their hurried conversation. He didn't appear to be a man they should trust but they had little choice. Nobody else had made contact with them, or looked like they would.

About half an hour later, they left through the inn's side door. After this, they walked up and down the smaller streets at the edge of the town to verify they weren't being followed. They saw nobody but it didn't really matter. There appeared no choice but to exit the town through one of the main gates which penetrated the protecting walls. If anybody was stationed to watch for them, this would be the place to do it. The town clerk had been right. There was no way they could really leave the town unnoticed.

The grey stone tower which dominated the area above the western entrance was an imposing one. The gates below it were locked and well guarded at night but pedestrians were allowed access on request, including any foolhardy enough to leave on their own. Hamilton struck the knocker on the metal plate at the centre of door. Following a short conversation with the guards through a side hatch they were permitted to pass.

Once on the far side of the walls, Digby felt his back pierced by inquiring eyes. The slits in the walls were an ideal place from which to pour oil, arrows or musket shot to maim, incapacitate or kill but the soldiers simply watched the two men depart and shook their heads. Hamilton felt he could read their minds. They were thinking Digby and he would be lucky to last the night but it was no skin off their noses if they were murdered. They'd been warned.

It wasn't a large town and the two men soon found themselves walking inland along a lane through open countryside. It was eerily dark and quiet. The only significant sounds came from the river. Hamilton had told Digby it was called the Creggan. It ran down from the low hills to the sea. Conn had instructed they should follow the well worn track and despite the gloom it was easy enough to follow the route. There were no houses and no people but lots of sheep.

The sheep trotted across the grass when the two men passed close by them. The lane was neither hedged nor walled and led through open fields clearly used for grazing. The odd sheep bleated in surprise when one of the men disturbed them. At times it was difficult not to walk into or even trip over the animals in the darker spots as they stood around eating grass. Digby wondered if sheep slept. It wasn't something he'd considered before.

The pair continued to travel in a north-westerly direction. If the path hadn't been so wide, it would have been easy to become lost and disorientated as it was such a cloudy night. They were now on slightly higher ground and felt the wind as it whisked past them on the way to the sea. Everything appeared to be moving in that direction, apart from themselves.

Digby remembered the maps Suffolk and Northumberland had shown him. Dundalk was on the east coast of Ireland. The prevailing breeze blew in from the west. The winds came from the Atlantic and beyond that from the Americas. Over the ocean moisture was picked up and deposited onto all four corners of Ireland, so Digby wasn't surprised when he felt the first spots of rain touch his leather coat and hat. Hamilton swore softly and pulled up his collar.

The rain worsened quickly until both men were soaked right through. The sound of the rain on the grass was interrupted for a moment by the hoot of an owl. It was the signal Conn had promised to make earlier but they couldn't see anything. Everything was as black as tar and the rain, if anything, fell even heavier. When the owl sounded again, they both thought it came from their left. Digby tapped Hamilton's shoulder and they walked that way leaving the path. It was impossible to see where they were going. They took small steps, not to slip in the mud, and held onto each other's coat sleeves. For a moment Digby wondered how far they were from the cliff tops. It would be easy to take a step too far and enter oblivion.

Putting each foot forward carefully into the murky darkness they continued, until Hamilton stopped. There was a metallic sound to their right. They strained their ears and heard rustling and shuffling noises ahead and behind them. The owl was gone. Clearly they were surrounded by multiple men who were closing in on them.

Digby's heartbeat accelerated. There was another sound, it came from behind them. Hamilton gently released his hold on Digby's coat. Both men extracted their knives from their sheaves and gripped them firmly in their right hands. They were ready to fight. Hopefully the men out there were friends but Digby and Hamilton doubted this. Friends spoke out. They didn't circle menacingly around in silence. If their suspicions were correct, Conn had lured them into a trap.

But they couldn't see anything. Who was out there? Digby crouched low. Hamilton did the same. There was the sound of a footstep close behind them. Digby raised himself up. A whoosh missed his head. He moved swiftly to the left and swung his knife. No contact was made. The noise came again. Something struck him. He felt his temple crack and a sharp flash of light and pain. He tried to move but blacked out. His body crumpled and fell onto the wet muddy ground.

Chapter XII

Elizabeth was in a foul mood. She'd finally received a reply from the Inquisition in Rome. The response to her correspondence made no attempt to address the points she'd made. There was no mention of science, or the folly of persecuting scientists. Instead there was a dressing down in the form of a lengthy lecture on the dual topics of her heresy and hypocrisy.

In truth, Elizabeth didn't mind if Rome called her a heretic in private, as long as the message didn't go out in public. If the Pope did this he would be inviting Catholics to kill her for her sins. Most of the content of the missive wasn't unexpected. She was the head of the Churches of Scotland and England and even if she allowed others to pray in the Church of Rome, she knew this wouldn't be enough for the Vatican. Her subjects had the right to worship in Catholic or Protestant Churches but this wasn't a choice the Pope and his cardinals considered to be acceptable.

It was so typical, she thought, of their earthly corruption of God's word. Even though she defended her people's right to pray in the Catholic Church, the Queen considered it a centre of self-interest rather than what it should have been, a route for spreading the word of the Lord to His people.

If she'd been Henry VIII, she'd have managed the reformation differently, but she knew she'd have enjoyed taking Rome down a peg or two. Elizabeth believed the Bible should be translated and written into as many languages as possible so all people could understand it, rather than made the secret word of a few ordained priests and communicated in Latin, a language most people couldn't understand. She'd never support the Puritans either. They went too far the other way with their strictness and austerity, but did the Papists really need all their finery to put over the word of the Lord? She didn't think so.

So describing Elizabeth as a heretic in private was fine but how dare they call her a hypocrite? This part of the letter focused on the situation in Ireland. Where was the religious tolerance in her other kingdom, the authors of the Inquisition asked? The people of the Catholic Church who lived on the island of Ireland were threatened and punished by the Protestant representatives of Elizabeth's own government. What hurt her most about these criticisms was that they rang true. She couldn't contradict them. Damn the Pope and his Inquisition, but on this point she knew he was right.

Ireland was a mess and those who ruled there in her name had made things even worse. They continued with their narrow bigotries to the detriment of the Irish who were her citizens too, even if the majority didn't wish to be.

She wondered where Digby was at that moment. His involvement in her plans for Ireland was her idea. She loved Hilliard's painting of the meeting with Hudson, in particular the positioning of Englishmen and natives alongside each other in harmony. It was inspirational, and an aspiration. Men and women could hail from diverse backgrounds but each could be a citizen of her realm, subject to and protected by her country's laws.

Elizabeth couldn't care less if Digby shouldn't have really been in the picture. The painting was symbolic, a vision of how tolerance could be extended beyond religion to all the citizens of a new British empire. This would be bigger and better than anything Alexander or the Romans had created. Her father had dreamt a little about this but Elizabeth was determined to make it happen.

She wished Digby every success in his task. Despite Suffolk's initial protestations and Northumberland's hushed suggestions that Elizabeth was sending the man on a suicide mission, she believed Digby could make a breakthrough. Even if he couldn't, at least he'd die a glorious death trying. If that was the case, so be it. She'd send somebody else in Digby's place and try again and if necessary again after that. One day, the Irish would be citizens of her empire and be happy about it, as would the natives of the Americas and many people beyond.

Elizabeth was reassured to some degree that her plans weren't wholly dependent on Digby's mission. Suffolk was planning to recall Chichester and his replacement St John to urgent meetings in London. The Lord Deputies of Ireland would learn to sing to the Queen's tune or not at all. If she couldn't make them bow to her will, they'd be sent to the Tower of London and replaced. Elizabeth understood why Suffolk had urged caution and no, it wasn't necessarily wise to create too many enemies but she was impatient to make things happen sooner rather than later. There was an empire to build.

If she had one criticism of Suffolk's and Northumberland's leadership during her formative years, it was that they hadn't focused properly on Ireland. It was time to correct the error. Elizabeth looked forward to the day when she'd be able to tell the Inquisition where they could place their claims of hypocrisy. To do that she needed a leader in Ireland she could negotiate with. Ideally Digby would succeed. If not, somebody else would.

#

When Digby woke he had a splitting headache all over again. He appeared to be trapped in a low-ceilinged room with voices around him. Lying on the floor with his face in the dirt, his nostrils twitched at the smells of peat and sheep shit. His feet were bound tightly and his arms tied behind his back.

He attempted to observe what was going on through one half-opened eye. There was a small fire in the centre of the room. Peaty smoke drifted upwards to a hole in the roof. The place was either an animal shelter or the home of an Irish family, or probably both. He could almost taste the smell of well-trodden animal dung on the dried earth beneath him.

There were at least four Irishmen in there with him. Each wore a long woollen cloak over a brown woollen shirt, similar to the one worn by Conn in Dundalk but shabbier. Their hair was long. One had a dark mane, two were redheads and the other was blond. Digby wondered if the man's ancestors were Viking. They talked in the language the Irish used so he couldn't understand.

The men appeared to be happily sharing the contents of Hamilton's purse. The wooden door behind them was pushed open and Conn came in. The others appeared pleased to see him and passed over a share of what they'd stolen from Hamilton. As the men talked more, Digby heard the others say 'O'Neill' a number of times. He fully closed his eye when he realised the men were turning in his direction.

Digby felt himself being raised up. There was a cheer. Should he struggle? There appeared little point. He was trussed up like a herring in Yarmouth. His best option appeared to pretend he'd not come round and wait and see what would happen next. But Digby wasn't fooling himself. There was a distinct possibility he was being carried to his death.

'Englishman, can you hear me?' whispered a voice in a heavy Irish accent once they were outside. The words had the same strange inflection as Conn's had earlier.

'Aye,' Digby whispered.

'Good. Now keep your eyes closed. I'm going to pretend to kill you and throw you down the well. I hope you won't break anything but you should be alright. I'll come back for you later.

96

When I set you down I'll free your hands. Don't resist and don't say a word.'

A few moments later Digby was unceremoniously dumped onto the wet ground. It was still raining and he felt the raindrops splatter onto his face. He couldn't hear the others' voices but kept his eyes closed. There was a small cheer in the distance suggesting the other men were still in the building. A force pressed down on his hands and then relaxed. The rope which held him remained around his wrists but was now limp. He risked a peep but couldn't see anything in the darkness. An instant later he was picked up again. His body tensed. He was dropped.

This must be the well, thought Digby, as he crashed around. In the total darkness he dropped like a stone. Thrusting his arms out to protect himself made little difference; the descent couldn't be controlled. Stone scraped at his skin and elbows. And then, almost as soon as the fall started it ended.

Digby landed in shallow water. He shook his head. Hunched onto one side of the shaft, he felt around with his hands. He appeared to be positioned on an iron grating, perhaps fifteen feet down the waterhole. He wasn't dead but his body was badly shaken. He remembered Conn's advice to keep his eyes closed and stilled himself as if dead to the world.

Moments later there were men's voices above. They appeared to be laughing and cursing. One of them coughed. Digby felt what he thought might be spittle and phlegm on his face but didn't react. For all Digby knew they were holding candles or a lantern to view his body. He remained as still as he could, hands tucked behind his back hiding the severed rope. His body lay sideways in the freezing water.

It wasn't long before all was quiet but he remained in his position for a period of time, patiently counting heartbeats, and when he reached two dozen starting again. When he began to lose count of how many he'd added, Digby stopped. He had to move to avoid losing all feeling in his fingers and toes. Looking around was impossible, the world was pitch black.

Digby used his hands to explore his surroundings. There was something else in there with him. It lay partly alongside him and partially beneath his left leg. Whatever it was it was wet and covered in rags. His fingers touched fingers which weren't his own. Digby ran his hand along an arm and over a shoulder. He felt the shape of a neck and a prominent Adam's apple. The chin was covered by a short beard. He touched the contours of the face for something recognisable. With a shock he realised an ear was missing. His fingers felt sticky. He jerked his hand back. Could it be Hamilton? The prognosis wasn't good. The body was still. The man was dead.

Chapter XIII

Will Carr had always been a government man. Often he worked in the shadows. Some would call him a spy. In the month of November in 1605 Carr's life had changed forever. A week earlier, working for the Secretary of State Robert Cecil he'd uncovered the Powder Treason, a plot led by Catholic dissident Robert Catesby. Their plan was to assassinate King James by blowing up Parliament.

Using fair means and foul, Carr infiltrated Catesby's group and discovered they'd secreted gunpowder beneath the House of Lords. From that point on Robert Cecil took control of the investigation. He arrested the terrorist Guy Fawkes just hours before Parliament was due to open. Cecil informed Carr there was a second bomber, who he planned to apprehend moments before the opening ceremony started. For some reason this didn't happen.

Carr remembered looking on in disbelief as Parliament exploded. All inside were killed, including the second bomber, the King, Princes Henry and Charles, and Cecil himself. Carr suffered minor injuries, struck by masonry thrown from the blast. Whereas most of the dead in Westminster were Protestants, in the Midlands it was a different story. The Earl of Suffolk was despatched and ruthlessly engaged the remainder of the Catholic plotters, led by Catesby. No quarter was given. Catesby and his followers were cornered and virtually all were killed.

The new heir to the throne Princess Elizabeth was only nine years old. Suffolk and the Earl of Northumberland took control of the country. Somehow they managed to prevent civil war from breaking out. Suffolk was appointed Secretary of State. In this role he replaced Robert Cecil and inherited Will Carr. Since then Carr had kept his nose clean. He'd told nobody of his prior knowledge of the second bomber beneath Parliament. The information was more than his life was worth. Why hadn't he raised a warning? His master's orders would be no defence.

Twelve years on Carr was having a busy morning. He'd walked to the Tower of London where he was due to see a prisoner. As he strolled up the steps and greeted the sergeants at the desk, he wondered what to do with the Puritan spy from Northumberland's household. Well known to the men in the

Tower, Carr was ushered through to the back rooms beyond. Once there he was offered and accepted a jug of weak ale which he shared with the two Tower staff assigned to interrogate the prisoner.

'We strung him up on the wall and laid our tools out in front of him,' said the torturer's apprentice with obvious enthusiasm, and a West Country accent. 'Then we let him watch whilst we got everything ready, just like you said, sir.'

The boy's master laughed. 'Aye, we did that, didn't we? You should have seen him, sir,' he said, before being struck with a coughing fit which continued until his eyes watered.

'Are you alright?' Carr asked. In the small room the sound was almost deafening.

'Aye, sir. Nothing to worry about,' said the torturer, once he'd stopped. 'I think it's the effects of smoking too much tobacco or something. Do you like the smell of it, sir? It's a wonderful thing, isn't it? Just makes me cough my guts up now and then. Can't be helped though, can it?'

'You were talking about the prisoner,' Carr reminded him.

'Aye, sir, I was, wasn't I?'

The man smiled, revealing two rows of uneven yellowing teeth. Both of the Tower men and the room reeked of their pipe smoke. Carr didn't like it. He knew King James had felt the same. Cecil had once shown Carr a pamphlet James had written about what the King described as *the evil weed of the Americas*.

'Anyway, sir, this Puritan lad didn't like the look of what we were putting in front of him. He's only a young man and you could tell from his eyes he was terrified. After a bit of blade sharpening he started singing like a nightingale. There was no need to use the manacles or anything. Told us everything, he did.'

The apprentice looked disappointed. Carr nodded. He showed no signs of sympathy but if the truth be told he felt a pang of regret for the prisoner's plight. Another man in the wrong place at the wrong time. Will Carr didn't much like the use of torture but he understood it sometimes had its place. It could lead to wrongful confession, anything to stop the pain, but not always. Thankfully the Puritan had talked before anything else had become necessary.

During the Gunpowder Plot, Carr had apprehended Robert Catesby's cousin Francis Tresham. Inwardly he winced at the memory of watching Tresham being beaten and burned with hot irons. They needed information from him and quickly. There wasn't time for the usual protocols. Men with explosives and evil deeds on their minds were active on the streets of London. Extreme measures had to be taken.

To be fair to the torturers' methods, Carr believed Tresham had told them everything he knew. The last time he'd seen the prisoner, he was locked in a small cell in an unofficial prison. Tresham was a broken man, eating food off the floor. He'd lost the use of his hands and fingers. Carr had left the place to update Robert Cecil. By the time he returned the building was empty. Neither prisoner nor gaoler remained. Tresham wasn't seen again by Carr, his family, or anybody else, just another man in an unmarked grave.

Things were different nowadays. The Tower was an official gaol. Prisoners were treated within the laws of the land. They were only tortured when proper sanction was received. Due to the tolerance laws there hadn't even been much of that of late. The rack on which Guy Fawkes had died remained in the Room of Blood. It was regularly serviced but hadn't been used for a dozen years. Not a single prisoner had been squeezed into the cell called Little Ease.

The master and his apprentice finished their report. Carr was satisfied. The prisoner had been brought up a strict Puritan and severely disciplined by his father for the slightest misdemeanour. Poor fellow, what a life, thought Carr. The lad had been pleased to escape the hardship at home when one of his father's friends found him a place serving in Northumberland's household. Under strict instructions, and in fear for his life, he'd been ordered to spy on Northumberland and his visitors whenever possible, listening in to their private conversations.

The Puritan had been instructed to pass the information he gathered onto two men on a weekly basis. The boy didn't know their names or where they came from. They wanted to know everything about Northumberland's meetings with people like Suffolk and Digby, and showed particular interest in the planned mission to Ireland.

Only one of the two men ever spoke at these meetings. He was a Puritan. The other was 'strange looking and smelled of something'. He constantly chewed tobacco and only ever spoke one word which sounded like 'mared', although it made no sense as they had never talked about horses. Every time he became agitated or annoyed he'd bark out the word and spit tobacco onto the floor.

It was the one piece of light relief Carr had had all morning. It added up. The Puritan and the Frenchman who liked to say *'merde'*, the French word for *'shit'*. He gave orders for the prisoner's father and friend to be found, arrested and questioned and everything done to identity the men the lad had shared his intelligence with. The descriptions given by the boy were detailed but Carr didn't hold out much hope. If they had any sense, they'd be long gone by now.

The boy was to be held for the time being. He wasn't to be ill treated but should be questioned every day to verify if he had anything else to say. If he did, the Tower guards were to send for Carr immediately. He doubted the lad was holding anything back but it was worth a try.

#

Digby spent a wet and uncomfortable night at the bottom of the well. After untying his feet he made several attempts to scale the side of the shaft but escape appeared impossible. The stone was wet and slimy and he struggled to gain traction for any length of time. Thankfully a few pieces of rock jutted out near the bottom. With a little ingenuity he managed to find a position to sit and wait. Even if he was spreadeagled across the well at least he'd lifted himself out of the water and wasn't touching the body beneath.

When it was light enough, Digby looked down and confirmed the body was Hamilton's. The Scot's head had been bashed around. In addition to the severed ear there were stab marks in his back. Blood was spread across his face, shirt and tunic. His leather coat was gone. Digby felt sympathy for his erstwhile companion but there was nothing he could do for him now. He had to sit and wait for Conn to return or for someone else to happen along and find him.

Not for the first time Digby began to drift off to sleep, fearful of what he might encounter, but he was saved from his haunting dreams by a slap in the face from a ship's rope thrown from above. He peered up the shaft towards the light. It was impossible to make out who was up there but he pulled on the rope until it became taut.

His strength hadn't deserted him. Using a combination of the cord, his boots and his back, he clambered upwards. It was slow progress but he didn't have far to go. In a little while he reached the top. When he lifted himself over the edge, he screwed his eyes and saw daylight. Conn was standing a few yards away at the other end of the rope.

Shielding his eyes with his right hand, Digby gazed around. The well was a short distance from a crofter's cottage surrounded by scrubland and sheep. There were no sizeable trees and nothing to secure the rope to. There was no one else there. Conn had taken the strain himself.

'You bastard,' spat Digby.

Discarding the rope, he rushed towards the Irishman and smashed himself into Conn's body. The other man faded to the left but was caught by Digby's shoulder. Conn was knocked to the ground. Digby tumbled down after him.

The Irishman quickly rolled onto one side and jumped to his feet, but he couldn't stay up for long. Digby grabbed at his ankles and toppled him over onto his back. As Conn fell, Digby punched him squarely on the chin. When the blow struck home, it was all Conn could do to maintain consciousness.

If Digby thought he had him then, he was wrong. Just as he was about to kick the prone man, Conn grabbed at his swinging boot. Twisting it around, he jerked Digby's knee forward. The Englishman winced with pain and slumped to the ground. Landing awkwardly, he struck his head. He was now clearly dazed. Conn rolled over and sprang back to his feet. It would have been easy for Conn to finish Digby off, but instead he stepped a few paces away from the man on the ground.

'Stop it, you idiot,' shouted Conn. 'I saved your life last night. If you keep this up, I'll have to beat your brains out or you'll do the same to me. It won't do either of us any good. We need to work together.'

'You must think I'm mad,' spat Digby. He stood tall and clenched his fists. 'Why did you kill Hamilton?' The two men glowered at each other.

'It was an accident,' said Conn. 'It wasn't supposed to happen. When I hit you, you went down nice and easy like, just as I'd planned, but your friend didn't.' Conn pointed to the well. 'The other fellow didn't stop. He came back at us with his blade flying. I told the others if there was any killing to be done I'd be the one doing it, but when it's life and death, pitch black and raining things aren't as simple as that, are they?'

'So what happened?' asked Digby.

'Your mate jumped one of my lads,' said Conn. 'I think he'd have killed him too but the boy's brother knifed your friend in the back before he could do too much damage. After that they were all over him. It was too late to stop them by then. Not that it would have been a good idea for me to be seen saving a planter. The boys took his money and dumped his corpse down the well. I told them I'd finish you off and dump your body the same way. To show good faith, here's your purse.'

Conn passed Digby's wallet over to him. He looked inside. The contents were all still there.

The Irishman looked at Digby. He licked the blood on his lip. 'That was a good shot you threw at me, just now. Have you been trained in the fist fighting? It's an ancient art, you know. Started by the Greeks and practiced by the Romans themselves they say.'

Digby ignored this. 'Why didn't you tell us what you were planning when we met last night? We'd have known not to struggle.'

'Aw, come on,' replied Conn. 'You'd never have come out of Dundalk, would you? The plan would have sounded great. We'll bring you out here into a nice dark area, ambush you, tie you up and pretend to kill you, and all the time you'll play along like little lambs to the slaughter. I don't think so.'

Digby relaxed slightly. 'Well, the plan didn't work that well, did it?' he said.

'For your friend down there, no,' replied Conn. 'I'm genuinely sorry about that but he had the smell of a planter about him anyway. He wouldn't have lasted any length of time out here.' Conn gestured at the scrubland around them.

'But for you, I don't know.' He shook his head. 'Things may have gone spectacularly well. Don't you see?'

'What do you mean?'

'Well, you're dead now, aren't you? From what I hear of your visit to Ireland; it hasn't been the best kept secret, but no-one's likely to be looking for a dead man now, are they?'

'But nobody knows I'm dead, you fool.' Digby wiped away some of the mud smeared across his face with the back of his hand and glared once more at the Irishman.

'Of course, they do,' said Conn. 'Or at least they will soon enough. Do you think us Irish would bother to go to the trouble of topping a couple of planters without telling the whole world about it? I'll wager not a single Protestant will dare step outside the walls of Dundalk for a week without an armed patrol once the boys start boasting of how we ambushed and knifed the two of you. What's more, the lads all believe you're dead too. They'll be telling the tale proper happy like.'

Digby couldn't argue with that. It made sense. Hamilton was a dead man and so was he.

Chapter XIV

The meal was lukewarm at best. The mutton stew was thin and served with coarse lumps of bread but both men greedily gulped it down. It wasn't the most delicious dish Digby had tasted but after a night down a well left for dead it was wholesome and warming. As the food kicked in and the heat from the fire warmed his body and dried his clothes, Digby felt a little more his usual self. When they finished eating, Conn extinguished the peat fire in the crofter's cottage ensuring he didn't create too much smoke.

A few moments later he gave Digby a surprise by saying, 'Take off your clothes.'

'What?'

Conn shook his head. 'You'll stand out like a sore thumb in your English gentleman's apparel. You need to wear these to blend into the places we're going to, if you don't want to end up the same way as your mate. On the positive side, you're already covered in shit and your hair and beard are a mess. Well done for that at any rate.'

Conn passed Digby the same sort of scruffy woollen clothing his attackers had worn the previous night. Digby shook his head but did as he was asked. Since they'd almost come to blows earlier, far too much of what Conn had said and did made some sort of sense. His life was almost totally in the other man's hands. Beggars couldn't be choosers. Pretty soon he'd look like one too.

'Where did you learn to speak English?' Digby asked Conn, as he pulled a layer of rough wool down over his face.

'Don't you worry about that, at least not for now,' replied Conn.

Digby looked at the Irishman. It was obvious his clothes were of a noticeably newer and better quality than his own. 'Why can't I have clothes like yours?' he asked. 'The stuff I've got is full of holes and smells of sheep.'

'No surprise there. That's what they're made of,' replied Conn smiling slightly. 'The reason I'm much better dressed than you is I'm your master and you're my servant. And servants don't talk all the time and ask their master so many questions.'

He laughed at Digby, as the Englishman struggled into his newly uncomfortable footwear. He was going to miss his boots.

'Didn't they have anyone available with the proper level of experience for this job?' asked Conn. 'The sort that might be able to work undercover for a week or two without complaining how they smelled? These rags are your disguise. They might just save your life. And as I said, you're my servant now, so you'd better carry my stuff. Come on! Off we go.'

Conn stood up and tossed a large hemp bag over to Digby who caught it in the chest. It was heavier than it looked but Digby didn't complain. Instead he simply slipped the strap over his shoulder and followed Conn outside.

'At least you can tell me where we're going and what the plan is,' said Digby.

'Aye, I'll do that and then you'll shut up. There'll be no more talking. I don't want anyone to hear us speaking in English. It would be bad for my reputation and worse for your neck.'

As Conn strode off in an inland direction, Digby realised he was a swift walker. Although the Irishman was only an inch or so taller than him, he appeared to have a lengthy stride and a unique loping gait. Conn's head bobbed up and down as he went. Digby was already struggling to keep up with him but he'd be damned if he was going to let his new master get the better of him.

As they passed the well, Conn shook his head and crossed himself. He threw Digby's clothes over the side without looking down. There was a small splash as they joined Hamilton's body at the bottom.

'I told the boys I'd bury you in a shallow grave,' said Conn.

A steady drizzle started up and the rain began to seep through Digby's clothing. Conn winked and lifted the cloak he was wearing around his body up so that Digby could see the layer of sealed sheepskin beneath. Both men knew the natural waterproofing would keep Conn warm and dry in the hours ahead.

'We'll have to see if we can get you one of these too. You're probably going to need it over the next week or so. How about that, eh? How good am I? I can't allow my servants to catch their death from the wet and the cold now, can I?'

'Tell me about the plan,' said Digby.

'Me and you are going on a little tour across Ulster. We'll finish up in the new town Chichester is building. It's located on the northern coast and called Belfast. We're to rendezvous there

106

with a boat. It'll take you back to England. Before that, there are a few things I have to show you and of course you've got to meet one of the Irish leaders. The fellow has royal green blood in his veins, alright. Perhaps he'll be foolish enough to support what you're after. If you talk nicely enough and he's daft enough, there may be a chance he'll act and speak on behalf of the real Irish, not those planter fellows. I've heard your queen is a young slip of a girl though. Does she really believe she can make things peaceful over here?'

'Aye, she does,' nodded Digby quietly.

Conn shook his head and kept on walking. Digby made a conscious effort to increase his pace.

'Who is the Irish leader?'

'I can't tell you that. Not yet anyway, just in case we get captured.'

'Alright then,' said Digby. 'But where are we going now?'

'To a tiny little place called Crossmaglen. There's a shebeen there run by a man we can trust called Ó Lionáin. He'll let us stay out of sight in the back tonight and in the morning we'll set off towards Newry. If you're lucky you might even get a taste of the whiskey from Ó Lionáin's still. It's good stuff. Put hairs on your chest. He's famous for it. No more talking now, alright?'

'That's fine with me.'

With that they reached the brow of the first hill and made their way inland away from Dundalk. The river flowed past them in the distance to their right. Before long the cottage and the well beside it were out of sight. Despite his lack of religion, Digby said a silent prayer for Hamilton. He hoped the Scotsman would be reunited with his Irish sweetheart but doubted it. Once a man was dead these days he believed all he had to look forward to was darkness and oblivion. The bleak Irish landscape was already beginning to have an affect on him.

#

The Earl of Suffolk listened intently. He nodded in the appropriate places as he received the report. Carr respected his master. He lacked the cunning of Cecil but had always been honest and straight and wanted what was the best for the country, not just himself. When Carr finished, Suffolk stood up and looked out of the Whitehall window onto the square below.

'I can remember standing over there,' he said, pointing to the far side of the square. 'I was organising the men as we prepared for the great sweep search of Westminster ahead of the opening of Parliament in 1605. When we found Fawkes and the gunpowder we were so pleased with ourselves. None of us had the slightest inkling there was another bomber hidden down there. I spent some time afterwards investigating the contents of the undercroft. I don't know, perhaps I should have searched the place one more time. I've always regretted not doing so but of course, we probably wouldn't have found anything. Whoever he was, he was well hidden. Do you have any regrets from that time, Carr?'

Will Carr considered his words carefully. 'No, my lord, no regrets,' he replied. 'I did as I was ordered to do, to the best of my ability. The anonymous letter to Lord Monteagle was a great piece of intelligence for my master but the task he set me to find the author was never going to be an easy one. There were many suspects and too little time.'

'I remember it well,' said Suffolk. 'My money was on Monteagle having written the letter himself or some skullduggery from that blackguard Cecil. You know, I've always thought he knew about the plot and exploited it to his own ends, so he could foil it himself to gain the King's favour. Sadly for him, he must have made a mistake, as we all did, in not knowing about the second bomber and it cost him his life. You worked for the man. What do you think?'

'Whilst he may have been guilty of many things, my Lord, I believe he was innocent of this charge,' answered Carr. 'From the evidence we gathered, it appeared to be straight forward. The letter was written by one of the Catholic plotters. Each had a motive due to their financial, friendship or family relationships with Lord Monteagle. I believe that's why they risked warning him not to attend Parliament.'

'*Financial, friendship or family?* That's the sort of statement Cecil would have made. Do you miss him, Carr?'

'Your predecessor had his merits,' Carr admitted. 'But he was also a secretive man with his own agenda. At times this made him difficult to work for. I prefer the straight shield and sword you use when addressing problems of state. In my opinion the achievements of yourself and the Lord Northumberland are second to none. It is an honour to serve you both, my Lord.'

Suffolk's mind wandered. He recalled arguing with a cavalry officer down there, in the corner of the yard back in the day and seeing Cecil grinning at him from the window where he now stood. He hadn't really listened to Carr's reply. Robert Cecil, his predecessor, the Earl of Salisbury, his wife Katherine's lover, whatever anybody wanted to call him, was a bastard and that was all there was to it. He stepped back from the window and returned to his desk.

Once he'd sat down, Suffolk opened a drawer and extracted a pipe along with an intricately patterned leather pouch filled with tobacco. He suspected the dried weed caused the hacking cough he'd developed in recent years but he lit the pipe and enjoyed his first inhalation of the day. What a hero Raleigh had been to return from the New World with riches such as this, he thought. It was a shame Raleigh wasn't here now. They could have sent him to Ireland if Digby failed in his mission.

Although the Queen had released Sir Walter from the Tower, she'd despatched him to the Americas in search of the mythical golden city of El Dorado. Suffolk admired the Queen and considered her wise for her years, but at times he worried she was too much of a dreamer, which he put down as a female failing.

After a second puff on his pipe, Suffolk shook his head and put the wood down. Thinking of Cecil always put him into a foul mood. How could the blasted man still get under his skin after all these years, he wondered.

'Which of the plotters do you think wrote the letter?' he asked, almost absentmindedly. 'We can't get the truth directly from any of them now. I should know. I led the militia which killed almost every last one of them.'

Suffolk retained a level of guilt for the brutality of his part in the battle of Coughton Court. He'd been under strict orders from Cecil and the King before their deaths - no mercy should be given and no prisoners taken. Being a military man he'd followed his orders to the letter but often regretted it. His men had ruthlessly chased and killed Catesby and everyone with him during the engagement.

Carr spoke. 'Most likely it was Thomas Percy. Lord Monteagle owed him a great deal of money.'

'You're probably right,' said Suffolk. 'Money makes men do strange things. I'll leave you to get on with your work. Now you've confirmed the link between the Puritan extremists and the French, we must do all we can to find the Puritan contact and this Frenchman who says 'merde'. And you need to verify if they're also in league with the Jesuits. If that proves to be the case we'll be facing an unholy alliance and they need to be stopped. If they're all working together they could create a shit storm and scupper our plans in Ireland, perhaps even undermine the Queen's plans beyond such as in the Americas.

Which of course brings us back to Digby, poor sod. By now he's probably dead. Too bad really. I quite liked the man.'

#

'Merde,' said the Frenchman.

What else could he possibly say? The boy the Puritans had placed in Northumberland's household had disappeared, and the obvious conclusion was he'd been taken by Suffolk's men. As one of the boy's contacts, he realised they might be looking for him already. If the boy had talked under torture, the Frenchman was worried the English may already have his description. In any case, if he wasn't arrested, he'd be recalled back to France for his own safety. It was a shame. He liked London. He could get away with things there as long as he kept them quiet.

Madam Blanchet would blame him for this, he was sure of it. She disliked him and didn't shy away from showing it. To put a woman in charge of their spying activities in England? What folly. What were they thinking? It was incredible. He spat out a mouthful of tobacco and watched with disgust as it hit the ground between his feet. Perhaps he'd go on one of his walkabouts tonight, have a little fun before he returned home to France.

The Puritans were idiots, Protestant extremists. He didn't like doing business with them. Why couldn't he have been part of the other cell which was working with the Jesuits? Anything would be preferable to collaborating with these Huguenot sympathisers. He'd even been instructed to keep signs of his Catholicism hidden when working with them. Apparently it didn't pay to antagonise them. Unbelievably, he'd received this order from Bishop Richelieu, himself.

'Merde.'

There was a tap on the door. He looked through the spy hole. It was Madam Blanchet. There were two men with her. Perhaps he was being recalled already? There'd be no opportunity to go on the prowl. He was disappointed. Probably he wouldn't get another chance until he was back in Paris and it was more difficult there. The risks of being identified in the streets and alleyways of his home city were much greater than in London where he was an anonymous stranger.

He opened the door. The shorter of the two men was holding one of the new hand guns he'd heard about. Perhaps they'd been followed by the English authorities? Quickly he ushered them inside and closed the door.

'Do it,' ordered Linda Blanchet.

Before he could say 'Merde!' one last time, the Frenchman was shot at close range in the chest. He was dead.

#

Across London, the Puritans acted a little less ruthlessly. The father of the boy who'd been arrested and the man who'd got the lad the position in Northumberland's household were helped to disappear. That night they left London, never to return. They'd been added to the passenger list of a ship scheduled to leave Bristol in three days time. This would take them on a journey to a new life in the New World. There would be no coming back.

A third Puritan, the man the boy had passed information to, was staying in London. He was confident. The most Suffolk's spies could have on him was a sketchy description from the boy. They had no other connection. He was safe. He'd detested the Frenchman and was pleased to hear he'd been killed. There was something particularly unholy and evil about him, he thought, even for a Catholic.

The Puritan's job now was to continue the work of the Lord and he couldn't do that from across the Atlantic. His calling was to remain in London to see the job through to completion. His instructions were to wait and, if needed, give shelter to a young man who'd been chosen for a special mission.

#

Shapes swam in and out of focus. Digby could find no other way to describe it. Then everything became clear, apart from one or two puffs of smoke. The village had been levelled. People lay on the ground dead. The tribe had worked with the Englishmen. The French had found out. Most of the surviving men, women and children had been taken away, possibly by one of the tribes who worked with the French. Possibly by the French themselves. Nobody knew.

A few youths stood around. Along with a small group of women and infants they'd managed to slip away and hide in the forest. They stood around the charred embers with blank faces, stunned at the devastation which had once been their homes. Their world had been taken away from them, abducted or destroyed. The tribespeople who remained would be taken to the relative safety of one of their sister villages further up river but even these would not be safe now. This was a warning. Work with the English and this is what happens. Nowhere would feel safe from the French and their allies. These were trading people. Word would soon get around.

Digby decided the act could not be left unpunished but it was important the French thought the damage was done by the

English, not by the tribesmen. The French leader who had ordered the raid was called Blanchet. He was the most ruthless man Digby had ever met and he had no wish to see further retaliations to the indigenous population. Blanchet had to be taken out in a way the French would blame on an Englishman. They knew where he was. They knew exactly where he slept at night. The French stockade was well protected but there was a way in for a small party, perhaps one or two men, armed with sharp knives.

It was risky but the plan was agreed. Digby and Ahanu travelled the last eight miles by moonlight. They bedded down during the next day and hid beneath branches and leaves in the woods that surrounded the French fortification. The two men took it in turns to remain on watch. Only once did anyone come near them but they were too well hidden to be discovered.

The way into the fort was through a secret tunnel the French had created as a means of escape in case of attack. If they ever came under heavy bombardment, it was a way a small number of men could use to get out to seek reinforcements or create a second front against their attackers. Digby didn't know how Ahanu knew about the tunnel but he was glad he did. They set out four hours after nightfall.

The tunnel was horrible. It was damp, dark and cramped. In the narrower parts Digby felt it would be all too easy for his body to become stuck. Once or twice he thought he might die down there. There wasn't much air and the only sound he could hear was Ahanu's body wriggling forward ahead of him. There was no possibility of turning back.

If he didn't keep going, Digby knew he would be left alone in the hole. He remembered the stories of the people in an English city, he thought it might be York. They suffered from a new sleeping sickness. Believed to be dead, they were buried in their coffins. They woke later in the darkness later, trapped and alone. By the time their families found out what was happening and dug them out, it was all too late. Desperate scratch marks were discovered on the inside of the caskets which had become their tombs. The victims died a second time.

Digby began breathing more quickly, as a feeling of panic came over him, He had to force his mind to think of something else, anything else. Memories of his childhood, grassland and most of all sunshine. His body settled into the rhythm of crawling and pulling itself through the hole in front of him. As he forced himself forward, Digby wondered why Ahanu wasn't terrified. Perhaps he was. Only once did the other man flinch. The sound of Ahanu's body moving forward stopped. As Digby's hands touched Ahanu's bare feet, he halted himself.

'Tunnel blocked, I cannot get through,' Ahanu whispered. 'Can Digby go back?'

Digby tried, but even after a few inches he figured it was impossible. Ahanu began pulling at the dirt which blocked his way with his fingers, sliding it back along the tunnel. There was a rumble. Mud collapsed onto their heads. They couldn't see anything anyway, but Digby thought it was the end of the world. But in an instant it was over. Everything went quiet.

Wiping the soil from his face and back, Digby used a flint to light the small candle he'd brought along for emergencies. Although their eyes squinted, they were grateful for the light. He passed the candle on to Ahanu to inspect what was in front of them. A hole had opened up ahead of their path. Most of the soil which had blocked their way had collapsed into it. Some had also fallen onto their backs but neither man was harmed. Clearly this was some sort of fissure in the ground.

Knowing the hole was there, they managed to clamber over it, and continued on their way. Digby put the candle away. After this, the tunnel became wider and slightly easier going. But there was still no light and Digby was still worried they'd not be able to make an opening on the far side of the stockade once they got in there. The thought of being stuck in the cramped tunnel frightened him more than anything. He'd rather fight a dozen armed Frenchmen.

Both men were relieved when they finally came to the iron bars sunk into the rock which blocked their way. Picking locks was something Button had taught Digby how to do during their voyages across the Atlantic. There was just enough room for his body to squeeze past Ahanu's.

Once the lock was open they faced a new problem. Two growling dogs had been tasked with guarding the grating. The animals were lean and mean. Keeping the bars shut, Ahanu whispered in the most soothing voice a man could muster. The dogs remained suspicious but when he tossed out a few chunks of dried meat the hounds wolfed them down. Moments later they became subdued and lay down on the grass together. When the dogs no longer moved, the two men crawled into the open. Digby took a deep breath and his body bathed in the clean air around it.

Everything else inside the camp was dark and quiet. Crawling around, they found Blanchet's tent easily enough. Thankfully he was alone. The woman Digby had sometimes

113

seen with him in the distance, presumably his wife, wasn't there. The French officer slept quietly. He never really woke up. As Ahanu gripped the Frenchman tight and held his mouth shut, Digby sunk a blade deep into the man's jugular vein. Once inserted, he removed the knife. Blood spurted out. It would have covered everything inside the tent if Digby hadn't caught the flow with the Frenchman's blanket. Still held by Ahanu, the prone body convulsed once and then became limp.

Once they were certain he was dead, Digby carefully placed a button on the ground by the side of the bed. He hoped it would appear as if it had come loose from a garment and dropped unnoticed. Surely anyone finding it would know it was English, and suspect the assassin must be too.

What a ridiculous notion, he thought. He was framing himself, but he had no wish for the French to suspect and persecute Ahanu's tribe. Better they thought it was him, acting alone. The job done, they left quietly. Digby looked back at the ground they'd crossed in the dim light of a lamp hanging from a wagon. When he was satisfied he could see traces of the marks left by his own boots but no signs of Ahanu's un-shoed feet, he moved on.

Although he didn't relish going back through the tunnel, he knew he had no choice. By the time he passed the pair of dead dogs, Ahanu was already inside. As Digby crouched to enter the darkness he felt a hand on his shoulder. He jumped.

Conn shook him for a second time and whispered. 'Will you shut up. Do you not know you whimper in your sleep like a wolf hound? We're supposed to be hiding, or had you forgotten?'

Digby squinted at the Irishman but it was pitch back in the outhouse behind the Crossmaglen shebeen and he couldn't see the other man's face. He wondered why his head hurt so much, before remembering how Conn's friend Ó Lionáin had plied them with his home distilled whiskey. It was why most people came to the place. The drink was heady stuff. It smelled pretty badly but Digby remembered the pleasing warm sensation when it hit his stomach. The drink had ensured he got to sleep quickly but, as usual after a while, he'd begun. To dream.

'I'm sorry,' he said quietly. 'I'll try not to do it again.'

They both settled back to sleep.

Chapter XV

It was a beautiful morning. Fairer weather had moved in overnight, and the rain had cleared. Warm sunshine soothed their backs, although a low mist still hugged the ground. As the damp air rose a magical sheen formed on the grass but within a few minutes the mist evaporated and was gone, as if it had never existed.

The pasture was green but Digby felt it was more than that. There was something else, a clarity, an intensity, a message of life. The weather, atmosphere and mood all felt right. The colour of the grass was like an emerald in a jewel of a day. The two men walked past a number of loosely connected copses of trees where the foliage was dappled with shades of olive, brown and yellow. Further on the leaves turned to gold, silver and bronze.

One lane was filled with bramble bushes. The tops and sides were covered with sun-ripened blackberries. Conn and Digby shared the fruit with a host of sparrows and other winged species. All around them birds were bobbing and singing. It felt like springtime rather than autumn. Everything spoke of some sort of hope. The men didn't even mind that their fingers were red with juice and blood from the prickly thorns.

'You see it doesn't always rain in Ireland,' Conn said quietly after a while.

'Apparently not,' replied Digby smiling.

When Conn continued in lilting Gaelic, Digby took the hint. English should be kept to a minimal whisper. Avoiding further utterances he enjoyed the luxury of the morning's ramble through the countryside. He couldn't say he didn't have any cares in the world but for a while he managed to push these to one side.

Hearing a piercing cry from above Digby grinned. Birds of prey had always fascinated him, wild ones in particular. It must be paradise for them here, he thought. Earlier a buzzard had glided off away in the distance near the shebeen in Crossmaglen. Further on a sparrow hawk had surveyed the world from the bough of a lightening-struck tree.

When Digby saw two shadows moving on the grass he glanced up and observed a pair of kites. He loved the shape of their wings and forked tails. The birds swirled effortlessly around, swept along by the warming air. Eventually one and then the other circled lower and neared the ground. When they did this, Digby held his hand over his eyes and gazed at their distinctive colours and markings.

The local mice, rabbits and shrews were alert to the danger. They spent much of their day hiding, only popping out occasionally to forage and graze for food. Their white tails flipped, flopped and bobbed to warn of the potential hazard when the men walked past them. Mostly the creatures disappeared quickly into the longer grass. Even the sheep appeared to be happy here, although a few struggled with the heat. Their wool had grown back and they were ready for winter, not a day like this.

After a while the men entered a wood. It was a peaceful place. It was the sort of glen which inspires poets, thought Digby. A moment later Conn raised his hand to indicate caution. He dropped to the ground and crept along keeping low to the edge of the trees. Digby copied him. They crawled together through the last piece of undergrowth. Below them, no more than two hundred yards away, was a small Catholic church with a cluster of stone cottages dotted around it and a graveyard half full of domed grey headstones.

'The heart of Creggan,' whispered Conn. 'Underneath the church there's a secret vault. It's the last resting place of some of the more ancient members of the O'Neill family. I'd take you inside and give you a look around but it's a pretty obvious place for a planter ambush and things look a little too quiet for my liking. It's a warm day but I'd still expect to see something coming out from the fires in the cottages but I can't see any smoke. It's probably nothing but we'll give it a miss, just in case.'

The two men back-tracked through the trees and skirted around a small hill to the south of the hamlet. Digby was sweating and took off his woollen cloak. He stretched it out, tied it around his waist and did his best to ignore the rancid smell emanating from it. Conn carried his own cloak. He'd folded it neatly over his shoulder as he'd done many times before. After a couple more miles of pleasant countryside there was another farmer's cottage. Around this grew rows of neatly lined vegetables.

'I'm going to have a chat with Finnegan, the man who owns the place down there,' said Conn. 'You stay here.'

He left Digby hidden in a little dip in the ground which he shared with two sheep and a mass of rabbit droppings. The heat from the sun warmed his face and made him dozy. He struggled to keep his eyes open but Conn was soon back carrying a flask of weak ale. Digby drank this down quickly, pleased to quench his growing thirst.

'I hope you like carrots,' said Conn, and he handed a small bunch of the purple roots to Digby.

The carrots had been washed but still had their green tops on them. Conn took a healthy bite from one and crunched away at the tapered vegetable. Digby followed suit.

'He didn't have any bread,' said Conn in explanation. 'And I'm not keen on raw turnip.'

They left the tops for the sheep and walked on. Not long afterwards, they passed two small natural lakes.

'Good fishing down there, alright,' said Conn. 'But not for us today. Not enough cover. We'd be sitting ducks.' He laughed. 'Sitting ducks. By a pond. Quack, quack.' He then said a few more words in Gaelic and laughed at himself. Digby shook his head and carried on.

After a while, Conn told Digby in a low voice they'd travelled about half the way to Newry. Shortly after this the usual bounce in the Irishman's gait became more pronounced. At times he was almost jogging across the grass. Carrying the heavy bag behind him, Digby struggled to stay in the wake of his new master's footsteps. The pace and stride pattern of his companion didn't suit Digby, it was too quick for walking and too slow for running. Every twelve paces or so Digby had to canter a few steps to prevent the other man from getting too far ahead.

As they rounded a bend and emerged from a densely planted group of trees, Digby could see why Conn had been so enthusiastic. Both men stopped for a moment and stared at three magnificent standing stones in the distance. They were capped and connected across their tops by a huge flat and equally grey stone. It must have been an enormous effort to lift it up there, thought Digby. He wondered what the ancient monument must signify.

As the men came closer they could see there were two rows of smaller stones at the edge firmly imbedded into the ground. Or perhaps they were equally huge but only their tops were showing. Digby remembered the icebergs he'd seen with Button which had broken off from the pack ice in the northern waters. Most of their volume and mass lay beneath the waves. Either way it was an impressive sight.

'Ballykeel dolmen,' said Conn in explanation as soon as he was sure nobody else was around. 'The place was constructed by my ancestors. Hundreds or even thousands of years ago, I expect. It's a burial chamber, alright. Probably a bit older than the one in Creggan but it'll be full of my lot, no doubt about that. Even if they weren't called O'Neill back in the day, I'm sure we'll be closely related.'

Digby was impressed. The stone monument was splendid in itself but the setting was stunning, probably part of the point for the men and women who'd placed it there. The land all around was overlooked by a steep red heather-topped mountain situated about a mile to the south. The sudden peak dominated the green and pleasant landscape around them.

'Fantastic here, isn't it?' said Conn. 'That's Slieve Gullion, It means mountain of the steep slope. Very apt, don't you think? There's all this gently undulating farmland here and suddenly bang! Out of nowhere comes that. My uncle used to take me to the top when I was young but the truth is I've not climbed up there for ages. At the summit there's this lovely little lake. It looks grand but when you go into it for a swim you soon find the water is bloody freezing. There's also a set of burial cairns. They certainly went out in style in those days, didn't they? I doubt anybody's going carry you or me up to the top of a mountain when we go.'

Both men looked at the hilltop. Digby liked this place.

'On a grand day like today,' said Conn, 'from up there you can see half way across Ireland. The view goes on for miles and miles. There's all sorts of stories and myths and legends about the place, with kings and giants and buxom maidens. You know the sort of thing.'

Digby thought of Holywell. 'Yes, I do,' he said. 'I had no idea your country was so beautiful.'

'Too few of you from over the water ever stop for a moment to have a proper look and get a feel for the place. But when you do… It's worth fighting for now, isn't it?' said Conn.

Digby didn't answer but he couldn't help but agree.

'But it's not all like this either,' said Conn. 'Come on, we've still got seven or eight miles to go before we get to Newry.'

As they pressed on they had to divert their route to the north. The direct way ahead was blocked by the clear dark waters of Camloch. So far the only men and women they'd seen had obviously been ethnically Irish. The Englishman and Irishman spied on the local people from a distance as they worked the land with their hands or small horses, whilst others used dogs to tend to sheep or a few cattle. The farmland was good and Digby was almost lulled into a sense that things weren't as bad for the Irish as they sometimes made out.

When they reached the head of the lake, Conn indicated a place where they could rest and enjoy the view for a few moments. It was a fantastic spot. The wind made ripples in the water and it moved like swathes of corn in a breeze.

'Will I get to meet the Irish leader you spoke of when we get to Newry?' asked Digby as he put the bag down.

'Perhaps but I think it'll be a while before he'll expose himself to you,' replied Conn.

'Can you at least tell me who he is?'

'I can't do that now, can I? If we got captured and it was beaten out of you, it would do the fellow no good at all.'

After that the conversation petered out. Conn got to his feet. Digby lifted the bag and they continued on their way. The pastures became increasingly rich and fertile as they approached Newry. It was clear some of those who farmed the land here were Irish but others were not. Digby suspected this might be a dangerous place to live. It was on the front line of a peacetime war where neighbour suspected neighbour and underhand methods were used to make claims for land and expand into new territory. Those who upheld the law would favour those who were more like themselves. They always did.

For the first time they encountered an armed patrol. Although the group of men who marched down the lane weren't wearing a formal uniform, Conn and Digby did their best to avoid contact. They ducked down low between a ditch and a hedgerow, and picked out the voices of the men as they walked and talked. The language was English but the accents were a strange mixture.

'This is Bagenal country,' said Conn quietly when the men had passed on and he judged it was safe to speak.

'That'll be one of their patrols. Their old man was Henry Bagenal. He's long dead now. A peculiar fellow by all accounts. Part English, part Welsh, with plenty of Scots friends. Apparently he loved everybody but the Irish. That being so, of course he decided to come over here and take our lands away from us. The current head of the family is Arthur. I call him Arthur the Bastard but not because I think he was born out of wedlock. He runs the place and directs the local planters from the safety of a friendly little castle in Newry. You'll get to see it from a distance later on. It must be a grand place to live in.'

When they reached the outskirts of Newry, Conn pointed out Bagenals Castle. The imposing fortress was compact but strategically located in a commanding position on the far side of the river from the town. Like Dundalk, Newry was a protected settlement, ready for siege and surrounded by walls and towers. The most striking building apart from the castle was the church. It didn't look like the smaller Irish places of worship they'd seen earlier. Conn saw Digby as he looked at it.

'The cheek of those people,' said Conn. 'That's the home of the first Protestant church built in the whole of Ireland and do you know what they called the bloody place?' He didn't wait for an answer. 'St Patrick's. What do you think of that? At least you're a good Catholic like me now, aren't you?'

'I'm tied to the Catholic Church,' nodded Digby. 'But I was born a Protestant and the last Catholic priest I met probably thinks I'm somewhat lapsed, although he did hear my Confession.'

Conn looked perplexed. Digby recalled Father Newcorne's thickset legs as they ran away from him towards the shrine as fast as they would go. He wondered what the priest had done since their altercation. Whatever it was, he couldn't change things now.

'I'm sure I don't know what you're talking about,' said Conn. 'You're an eccentric fellow alright. There's no doubt in my mind you're English. Do you know that feeling when you've drunk so much whiskey you can't drink any more?'

'Aye, I do,' laughed Digby.

'Well, there you go again,' said Conn. 'I was right. You're definitely not Irish.'

#

'The news is not good,' relayed Suffolk 'There is definitely a link between the Puritans and the French. We now think the Jesuits may be involved too.'

'Should we hold a meeting of the Privy Council to discuss the matter?' asked Northumberland. He hadn't wished to raise the idea as it risked highlighting the fact his household was the source of a major leak but he felt he was left with little choice.

'I think not,' said Elizabeth. 'I want to keep this just between us. At least until we get some news about Digby.'

'I agree with you, Your Majesty,' said Suffolk. 'For now we should keep these plans between the three of us, until we have given Digby ample opportunity to progress. The Council members are all good men but one or two have major interests in Ireland. They know we're considering the matter but there is no point in giving them a chance to inadvertently put a lance in the spokes of our wagon. Not that any of them would, I'm sure.'

This was an area which concerned all three of them, thought Northumberland. Nobody could guarantee the good intentions of every member of the Privy Council. Despite the tolerance laws, things were changing slowly. Apart from one man, the members of the Privy Council were all Protestant. Most had friends who were planters or had investments in Ireland. Money talked. The only Catholic who'd made it onto the Council was Lord Monteagle, who'd heeded the letter in 1605 and not gone to the opening of Parliament. But even he hadn't openly declared himself a Catholic until 1615 when he considered it finally safe to do so.

'But when should we go public with our plans for a better future for Ireland?' asked Northumberland, although he suspected he knew the answer.

'When Parliament opens in November,' said Elizabeth. 'I will give the opening speech but both Houses have more authority now. If we are to accelerate the move towards one Parliament and one law, we must not delay. We need Parliamentary support. You should both outline your own determination to give every Irishman the same benefit and protection of English law that is enjoyed by the English, Welsh and Scots. We can judge the appetite for change and move on with our plans.'

Northumberland looked at Elizabeth. She was wearing a fine new dress, the colour of emerald green.

Chapter XVI

Linda Blanchet looked at the two middle-aged men in the room alongside her. The light was low but she could tell they avoided looking into each other's eyes as they talked. The Frenchwoman, the Puritan and the Jesuit priest. It sounded like one of her husband's bawdy jokes. She missed him. At times he could be violent but there was something about men like him which certain women, women like herself she acknowledged internally, found incredibly attractive. And in Linda's case this had nothing to do with low self-esteem.

The Catholic priest looked exhausted. He'd completed his journey from North Wales only an hour before. He'd caught and hired a variety of coaches along the way, even paying one driver to travel at night. Aching tired but elated, he was now back in London with a story to tell. He'd informed the others how he'd intercepted Digby at the shrine in Holywell as instructed. With a smug look on his face he described how he tricked Digby into taking Confession but things after that, he said, had not gone so well.

During his time in the Americas Digby had clearly become a man of the Devil, argued Newcorne. He'd refused to help their cause. Even worse, he'd attacked the priest, a man of the cloth. Newcorne said he was certain Digby had become a follower of a pagan religion influenced by the heathen Indians he'd spent too much time with. Linda raised an eyebrow but said nothing.

The Puritan grinned at the other man's discomfort during the final sentences of his report. When Newcorne finished, he gave his own feedback. His men stationed in North Wales had received the message from Newcorne in the afternoon stating Digby wouldn't help them. They'd used lanterns during the evening to relay a message to the man they'd placed on the naval ship as it neared its rendezvous off Prestatyn. The man on board was well trained. He knew his mission. His orders were clear. He was to kill Digby with a knife or, if he couldn't get near him, sink the ship and kill all on board. He had no fear for his own life, his reward for doing God's work would come in the next world.

'What chance do you think he has?' asked Linda.

'Very good,' said the Puritan. 'He is a chosen one. Like me, he does God's work here on Earth.'

'Who else knows of this?'

'Nobody on my side,' said Newcorne proudly. 'You are good people but there are some in my Church who would ask the Pope to ex-communicate me for working with heretics such as him.' Newcorne nodded at the Puritan sat next to him.

In return, the Puritan shook his head at the man Linda knew he thought of as Papist scum. 'At least our man will be successful. For all your bluster, you have not been,' he said. 'How could you be? You would never be chosen to do God's will, as you serve only the Pope in Rome.'

'Heretic!' shouted Newcorne, gripping the cross which hung around his neck. 'It was your assassin who failed to kill Digby in Greenwich,' he retorted, 'or have you forgotten? You've been here in London pretending to be God's chosen spy, whilst I've been criss-crossing the country working in His name and risking my life to ensure our mission succeeds.'

The two men faced up to each other and began pushing and shoving. The Puritan raised his fists. Linda was amused at their childish behaviour but there was much to do and little time to do it. She couldn't afford to wait and watch the pair fight, entertaining though it would have been.

'Stop this,' she commanded. 'And what of your people? What do they know?' She looked at the Puritan.

'There are a few who know we work with the agents of the devil for the good of the angels but we work in cells. Each has only a few contacts. In this way, Suffolk's men can never break us. Nobody else knows about my connections with you,' he boasted proudly.

The Puritan had no notion this was probably the worst thing to say. Linda turned towards her men as they waited in the shadows at the back of the room. They'd been expecting her orders and already locked the doors.

'Kill them both,' she said, shaking her head. She was already considering what her next move should be. 'Tie their bodies together, connect them to a rock or something and throw them into the Thames.'

Both men realised their mistake but it was too late and they knew it. Whether Puritan or Jesuit, for an Englishman there was only one thing worse than making a pact with the devil - collaborating with the French. Their throats were cut and their bodies transported. It was all done skilfully with the minimum of fuss. The blood on the floor was wiped away.

Linda didn't like people who made mistakes. She had even less sympathy for those who betrayed their own kind. Unreliable people such as those were fair game for exploitation for her own advantage, until they no longer had value. At that time they would be mercilessly dealt with. It was a lesson she'd learned from two of the best. One was her husband and the other a bishop.

#

Conn and Digby stayed overnight with one of Conn's friends in a ramshackle farm building about two miles from Newry. They wished to avoid the town with its greater likelihood of interception and capture. It was becoming clear to Digby that Conn was well known and liked by the Irish they met. Equally it appeared he was feared by the planters and their associates.

That evening more whiskey was drunk. The man's eldest son was posted on look-out duty a couple of fields away in the direction of the town but they weren't troubled overnight. The men talked of land grabs and trumped-up charges, Irish families evicted from villages they'd lived in for generations and no legal recourse. How could a man claim redress when those sitting in judgement were doing the taking? It was all translated to Digby by Conn as the conversation was in Irish. As a friend of Conn's, Digby was treated with courtesy but it was obvious every man and woman viewed him with suspicion once they'd heard him speak to Conn in English.

In the morning Conn warned Digby they were in for a hard day's walking. The pair were presented with food and ale for the journey by the farmer and his wife. They waved them off with their young children around their ankles and the older ones watching from the barn.

The distance to Portadown was around twenty miles. For most of the morning the terrain wasn't troublesome but it was featureless and boring. Once away from the town, the land was sparsely populated. As they walked they encountered areas of increasingly wet and boggy marshland. Marram grass and reeds peppered the landscape. At times they were forced to walk around or step over dark patches of peaty black water.

But the weather conditions continued to be favourable. The sky was dominated by thin cloud, interspersed with the occasional bout of sunshine. As they tramped their route through the bog a breeze came up. This was a godsend for the two walkers as it diverted the flies and midges still active in late September from their uncovered faces and arms. Both were thankful for the relief.

124

Eventually they entered a lonely area. The feeling of solitude was accentuated by the occasional plaintive cry of a bird. Digby heard these noises but never saw where they came from. Every now and then Conn slowed down to give Digby sufficient opportunity to catch up with him. The Irishman would take a moment, down a drink of ale and once Digby sat down alongside him return to his feet and stride off again. Of course Digby wished he'd halt a little longer so he could rest himself but he didn't complain. It was part of the game. And he had no wish to give Conn the impression he wasn't up to it.

As he walked Digby speculated about the man he would hopefully soon be meeting. Would he be an O'Neill or perhaps an O'Donnell? These were the two Irish noble families who'd fled to Spain in 1607 to raise an army for the next uprising, which of course it never happened.

The last of the Irish earls of Ulster had spent time in France and Flanders but never reached Spain. Finally they realised they would no longer be welcome there. Sympathies had changed - the Spanish wished to retain peace with England. Eventually both earls, O'Donnell of Tyrconnell and O'Neill of Tyrone, ended up in Rome and died there. Their titles were left vacant and were now subject to dispute.

Conn stopped again. This time he passed the flask of ale to Digby so he could take a drink.

'We should sit down and rest for a while,' said Conn.

They lowered themselves onto two flat adjacent pieces of rock. As they did so, Digby took the bag off his aching shoulders and laid it out as flat as he could on the grass next to his feet. With his burden removed, he arched and stretched his back to provide some relief. Conn smiled.

'For an Englishman you're not doing too badly,' he said. 'I'd been expecting a lot more complaints.'

Digby ignored this. 'Where are we now?' he asked.

'Not far from Poyntz Pass,' said Conn quietly. 'We'll need to be careful when we get there. There could be planters about but we have to go that way as its one of the few decent crossing points across the worst part of the mire. You see, there's this strip of land ahead of us which is going to be our problem for the day. If you think it's been bad so far, it's much more boggy and prone to flooding there. I don't want us to chance getting stuck in the mud when we try to cross it. After that though the going is pretty good and we should do well.'

'Poyntz Pass? The name doesn't sound very Irish to me,' said Digby.

'You're right,' said Conn. 'It's not. It's named after a soldier from Gloucestershire. The fellow was called Charlie Poyntz. He was here in the war. He held the crossing point for days against Hugh O'Neill, the great Earl of Tyrone, despite the fact he far fewer men than Tyrone did.'

'Doesn't sound very Gloucestershire either,' added Digby. 'Did it have an Irish name before that?'

'I don't know,' replied Conn. 'The pass in the shit hole perhaps. Would you like me to translate?'

'No, thanks,' said Digby.

'The story goes,' Conn continued, 'Poynzt got his men to dig in and even though they were vastly outnumbered they fought bravely and held out for days until they were reinforced. It was a pretty important engagement by all accounts. Of course the history of battles is always written by the winners. Anyways Poynzt got promoted to Colonel and the English powers-that-be picked out five hundred acres of the best farmland on the far side of the bog, confiscated it from the locals and gave it to him as a gift for his good deeds. So just like Bagenal, he built a castle. We'll see it in a while. When I say castle, it's more a fortified house, but if I was him I'd build my walls pretty thick too.'

'Does he still live there?' asked Digby.

'Last I heard, he did,' replied Conn. 'He's also built a village on the other side of the pass. It's made up of a series of connecting farms and houses for the workers. He shipped in families from his English county to farm the place and these days I think he just sits in his castle counting his money. Perhaps we should pay him a visit and relieve him of some of it? What do you think, Digby, are you in for a little daylight robbery?'

'I prefer to do my creeping around at night,' said Digby, remembering the night he broke into the French stockade.

'Do you now?' said Conn. 'I'd better watch myself then. Come on.'

They set off at once. As they walked, the tree line became thicker in places. At one point they climbed over a set of undulations which appeared to align with the ground. Conn indicated these weren't natural. He nodded at the soil and whispered, 'Ditches built by O'Neill's men during the battle. We're getting close.'

Digby wondered, not for the first time, what Conn's age might be. He'd estimated earlier he was in his mid-twenties but it was difficult to tell. At different times there was something older and younger about him. When they reached the pass Digby was pleased to see a row of trees masked their progress. They appeared to be alone. There was hopefully no reason for Poyntz to post guards to watch the narrow raised strip of land.

Brown water flowed strongly in a ditch beneath, crossing from one side of the pass to the other. Digby couldn't make out where it went on the other side but a line consisting mostly of broken branches and dead bracken formed a flotsam layer around the banks of the channel. He reasoned this indicated a recent level of flood water. The going on either side looked to be lined with squelchy mud and very treacherous. The two men took one last look around and scurried safely over the solid ground in the middle.

At the head of the pass they saw Poynzt's fortified retreat.

'We'll skirt that way around the building,' whispered Conn, pointing to the right hand side.

Digby followed Conn's instructions and crept forward, expecting to be challenged by armed guards at any moment. Or maybe they'd shoot first, and ask questions later. He quickened his pace. At least Conn seemed to know what he was doing. As the two men slipped past the main house and circumnavigated the newly constructed village, they heard voices but kept away from the people.

The little hamlet appeared out of place in Ireland, thought Digby. Although it was surrounded by rich Irish farmland, it felt as if it belonged in England. Gloucestershire accents echoed around his head from within the stockade surrounding the housing. There was an apple orchard. Digby suspected the fruit would be used for eating, juicing and most of all cider-making. And feeding the pigs. He couldn't see the pens but he could smell the inmates. If the walk had made Digby hungry, this stench turned his stomach and destroyed his daydreams of bacon and faggots covered in gravy.

When they were safely out of sight, Conn turned to Digby. 'We've still got about eight or ten miles left to travel if we're to reach Portadown by nightfall. We're not taking the most direct route to Belfast, as there are some things your Irish leader wants me to show you first.'

'Such as?' asked Digby.

'Portadown for one thing,' replied Conn. 'It's a prime example of what's going on in Ireland. Your man wants you to experience first hand some of the impacts the plantations are having across Ulster. He told me he thinks, despite being English, you may be a decent man. He thinks when you see

127

what's happening perhaps you'll have a word with that slip of a queen of yours.'

#

'You really must spend more time in the palace in Whitehall and allow members of the court to see you,' said Anne the Queen Mother, as she admonished her daughter. 'It is expected. It is what Queen Mary did. It's what Queen Bess did and it is what your father did. People want to see you. They want to confide in you. They want to ask you favours.'

'Why should we go to the trouble of giving power to Parliament and state that everyone, apart from myself obviously, is subject to the laws of the land if we let people flout them? Why should we grant favours, just because a man makes an effort to visit me at court? You know I hate the sycophancy of it all,' replied Elizabeth.

Anne sighed. Her daughter had much to learn about the modern world.

'There is a right way of doing things and there's a wrong way,' continued Elizabeth. 'We have set up a Parliamentary circuit which now tours the country. This is something I strongly support. I have attended a number of the petitioning sessions myself and frequently sat down with Suffolk or one of his ministers and their lawyers as they listened to the grievances of the people of Warwick or York or Edinburgh. Quite rightly they use the law to decide if an individual claim should be changed or upheld. This should be enough.'

'But it isn't, my dear,' said her mother. 'It's not enough. I know you dislike these things but you are a queen. You have great privilege but this comes with responsibilities to uphold. The people expect you to hold court, give favours to those who deserve them, dine in the great hall, ingratiate yourself with the noble families of the land and be seen to do so. It is the tradition.'

'Then tradition must change,' answered Elizabeth firmly. 'How can we transform this land into a modern country if I allow people to take advantage of my patronage or encourage them into the great hall to watch me eat and indicate which of them can have what is left of the dishes I want no more of? The whole thing is archaic. For heaven's sake, this is the year of our Lord 1617. I want to drag this country into the seventeenth century. During my reign there shall be new traditions, better ones and where necessary the old ones will vanish. These are my wishes, and as you say, mother, I am a queen.'

Anne wasn't surprised. In truth she'd expected her daughter to react in such a way but she felt she had to respond to the requests of the nobility. Elizabeth would have to learn that the world couldn't be changed overnight. People in important positions expected their queen to act in a similar manner to her predecessors. Whilst Anne had sympathy for her daughter's position and was delighted she was such a popular monarch, she knew how quickly things could change. She needed to try harder if they were to keep things the way they wanted them to be.

It just wouldn't do to continue to antagonise the wrong people. Displeasure could turn into action. They could begin whispering campaigns against the Queen. Discontent was something which easily spread. Lack of time in the royal court and patronage were two complaints, but there was a more serious issue Anne was attempting to avoid bringing up. Patience was being lost with Elizabeth's lack of progress in the betrothal, marriage and childbearing stakes.

'I know what you're going to go on about next,' said Elizabeth. '*Elizabeth the chaste, Elizabeth is chased* and so on.' The Queen spoke the verse in a mocking tone. She rolled her head back from one side to the other as she said the words.

'Oh, come now, my dear.'

'Don't come now, my dear, with me, Mother. I know my duty. I'll marry in the next few years but only when the time and man is right for me and not just for the country. I'll not be rushed into marrying a child or bedding down with a man old enough to be my grandfather.'

'The people are simply nervous,' said Anne. 'They remember your namesake not marrying and your father dying before his time. They thank the Lord for your continued safety but worry about the lack of succession. You need to give them hope. At least show an interest in one or two of your potential suitors so the people can raise their expectations and have a good old-fashioned gossip about their suitability.'

'Does Suffolk have another of his lists ready for me to review then?'

'That is more than a little unkind. The man has been a Godsend to us both, and only ever has your best interests in mind. They just happen to coincide with the needs of the nation. With your actions and letters you've forced him to cross names off the list far quicker than he can add new ones on.'

Elizabeth caressed the fine laced wrist collars of her dress with her thumbs and forefingers. It was something she did when she felt uncomfortable. 'I thought you would have more sympathy for me, Mother,' she said. 'How did you feel when my grandfather forced you to accept a match with a man you'd never met?'

'I understand your point,' said Anne, 'but remember this. It was harder for me. I was much younger than you but I did what was right for Denmark. After I married your father, I began to do what was right for Scotland and now I do what is right for England, Scotland, Wales and Ireland.'

'And what is that?' asked her daughter, with a hint of scorn in her voice.

'Don't be impertinent,' replied Anne. 'You may be my queen but you're still my daughter.' She sighed. 'Lizzie, what I do for the country is this. I encourage you to find a man, the right man, someone suitable for yourself and for this country... and I beseech you to get a move on, so we can show the court and the people there is a clear pathway to your marriage and royal children.'

Anne looked at her daughter. For once, Elizabeth didn't seem to be able to think of suitable words to argue against the points she'd raised. Given the circumstances, with the French, Puritans and Jesuits all out to cause mischief, and potentially gang up on her daughter, she hoped Elizabeth was aware her choice of husband was becoming increasingly important.

There was a knock on the door. The Queen was informed that the Earl of Northumberland had arrived at Greenwich Palace a few minutes earlier. He was waiting downstairs but had insisted to the officer of the guard that his news was important and he needed to share it with the Queen most urgently.

'I will let you go off to this conference,' said the Queen Mother patiently. 'But you must consider what we've spoken about. Your lack of succession is even putting a strain on your sister.'

'What do you mean?' asked Elizabeth, with genuine concern.

'Mary knows she's next in line to the throne,' said her mother. 'The prospect terrifies her. She's loses sleep at night about it. In the daytime she wanders around the castle at Windsor with a worried expression on her face. When I asked her what caused this she admitted she's concerned with what might become of her should anything happen to you and she's forced to take your place. You should spend more time with her, reassure her, boost her confidence. She'd love to see you.'

'And I her,' said the Queen. 'I'll try to get across to Windsor and visit her soon. Or she can come to Whitehall or Greenwich.'

Elizabeth rose, accompanied by her lady-in-waiting Anne Dudley, who'd sat sewing until this point. When both women left the chamber they walked through the palace flanked by four guards. Through the windows in the distance they could see Inigo Jones and his men marking out where he planned to place the foundations for the new Queen's House. Elizabeth wondered how many years the construction would take to complete. It was obvious to her she would be long married by the time it was finished but who would be her husband? How many children would they have? How would her new United Kingdom progress against the backdrop of the bloody wars she felt certain would soon take hold across Europe? And how could she possibly keep her queendoms out of them?

Northumberland had been waiting impatiently in the meeting room. When the Queen entered, he stopped wearing out the floor. Elizabeth thought he looked worried and relieved at the same time. What news could this be? What was so urgent?

He bowed. 'Your Majesty, I thank you for seeing me at such short notice and apologise for my haste but I bring news from Ireland.'

'Already? What is it?' A look of genuine concern etched across Elizabeth's features. She would have liked to have held Anne Dudley's hand but she needed to show she was stronger than that.

'I am sorry to report, Your Majesty, that an assassin has attempted to sink Digby's ship and I'm afraid he was successful.'

'Oh no,' said Elizabeth. 'You warned me I was sending the man to his death. I should have listened.'

'Things are not quite that bad. At least not yet,' said Northumberland. 'The ship was sunk but only the captain and a few of the crew were lost. The assassin is missing and so could not be questioned but the majority, including Digby and his guide, were saved by Admiral Button's ship. Button had been escorting them at a discreet distance to protect against any naval attack. Once he'd picked up the survivors, Button proceeded to Dundalk as planned and put Digby and the other man ashore before returning to Wales. Once there, he sent express riders on the fastest horses to bring the news directly to London.'

'The Lord be praised,' said Elizabeth. 'Thank heavens! Digby is alive.'

'Well, he was at the beginning of the week, at any rate,' said Northumberland. 'But Button's message contained a little extra helping of bad news. Digby believed the man who sank the boat was a Puritan. I'm sorry, Your Majesty. This action is obviously due to the interception of conversations in my own household.' He looked at the floor.

'That can't be helped,' said Elizabeth. 'I need you to take control of this situation and not feel sorry for what may have happened in the past.'

Men! In Elizabeth's experience they were all like this. They made a mistake and then needed a woman to praise them and massage their egos back into shape. She hoped her husband would be different.

'Of course, Your Majesty,' he said. 'Unfortunately there is more. Digby informed Button that a Jesuit priest intercepted him in North Wales ahead of the sinking and asked him to work against us. Digby acted swiftly to repulse this advance but it confirms our worst fears that Jesuits are involved in the conspiracy.'

'Should we summon the leaders of the Churches and place the fear of God in them to get their houses into order?' asked the Queen.

'We could, Your Majesty,' replied Northumberland, 'although I fear this would do little good. They have little control over their more extreme members, and it would show our hand to others.'

'I tend to agree,' said Elizabeth more softly. 'But we must do something. Have you arrested the priest yet?'

'Not yet, Your Majesty, but Digby passed on his name,' said Northumberland. 'The man is called Father Newcorne. By all accounts he's a member of the Jesuit old school and may even have plotted against your father. Suffolk's spies believe he will have travelled back to London to report his findings and receive additional orders from his masters. The Secretary of State has engaged his best men case to find him. They're scouring the city as we speak. If Newcorne is here, I have no doubt he'll be discovered soon.'

Chapter XVII

Will Carr leaned down and looked over the two bodies for a second time. The stink of dirty water and effluent hit him again. His men had already searched the corpses and found nothing. The pair of unlikely river bed fellows had been tied together, attached to a rock and dumped into the Thames the previous evening but the men doing it had been seen.

Two ladies of the night had been waiting for trade on one of the side streets next to the river, in an area a quarter of mile from the Tower of London. Although the women were afraid of the authorities, the lure of potential cash had been enough to tempt them. Even a small payment might mean they could stay off the streets for a day or two. They reported what they'd seen to the Tower guards and insisted they'd only point out the location if they were well rewarded.

Their testimony was viewed with suspicion but luckily one of the sergeants passed the tip inside. Eventually a few coins were handed out and a wherry boat sought. A small area near the river bank was dredged with rope and hooks. The bodies became dislodged from their weighting and floated to the surface, still connected by their bonds. Eventually they were hauled onto the deck of a barge and brought ashore accompanied by a stomach-turning stench.

One was dressed in the forbidding dark clothes of a Puritan, the other had the inner robes and trinkets of the Roman Church. Carr had the priest placed on a stretcher and brought forward. In the past he'd investigated many of the more extremist Jesuits and recognised Newcorne's face instantly.

The bodies were placed onto the back of a cart. As the horses departed up the slope to Botolph Lane, Carr turned his back on the street and looked towards the water. He spied the houses and workshops which spanned the great crossing of London Bridge in the distance and continued his gaze across the Thames to the far bank and Southwark where he lived with his family. Eventually he turned from the river and walked up the lane, deep in thought.

As he turned into Thames Street, Carr considered the location of the crime scene to be interesting. He looked towards the warren of backstreets which ran from the road with suspicion, before picking out Love Lane. There were still a few houses of dubious reputation up there but grander buildings too those days. Carr happened to know it was also the favoured lodging area for members of the French delegation when they were in London. If they had bodies to dispose of, the river end of Botolph Lane would be a convenient place to do it.

The streets in front of him were empty but someone out there had murdered people in London. Carr was aware of the intrigue in Ireland. He'd been informed of the attempt on Digby's life but what was happening here so close to home felt much more personal. It had to be stopped before it got out of hand. As he walked away from Love Lane an idea began to develop in Will Carr's mind.

#

'Now tell me, where's the justice in that?'

The two men lay flat on their fronts on the brow of a hill. After a night sleeping rough in a barn, they'd spent the day observing activities around Portadown. As they watched the activities taking place around the building site below, both had come to the same conclusion. Things had to change.

Conn quietly described the history of the area. 'In times gone by the landscape had been lightly populated. The few inhabitants worked hard to make a living. All that changed seven years ago. The small farms Irish families had lived and worked on were forcibly taken away from them. The lands were confiscated by the English administration in Ireland and granted to an Englishman.'

'What happened then?'

'The local people's lives were thrown into turmoil. The new landlord didn't even want their estates, at least not for his own use but his stewards recognised their value and sold them all on as a job lot to another English Protestant. Whilst the seller was happy with his windfall, the Irish were evicted from their homes.'

'I'm sorry,' said Digby.

'I've not finished yet,' whispered Conn. 'As well as being a property speculator, the new buyer was a religious man, the type who prays to the money lenders in the temple rather than God. This churchman's advisers recommended he sell the land piecemeal to maximise his profits. The merged farms were broken up and each plot sold to the highest Protestant bidder. Another Englishman, Michael Obins, bought many of the plots and he's now the area's largest landowner. And all this happened as the Irish watched on, powerless to prevent it.'

134

'Was there nobody who would stand up for their rights?' asked Digby.

'No.' Conn shook his head, still keeping his voice low. 'With the earls of Tyrone and Tyrconnell flown from Ireland there was nobody left who gave a shite. Nobody could be bothered to fight for the local people. In London, your Parliamentarians talk about tolerance to the Catholics but turn a blind eye to what's happening over here in Ireland, not least because there's money to be made.' Conn rubbed his thumb and forefingers together.

'This isn't really about religion though, is it?' asked Digby. 'It's about exploitation. Out of control Englishmen, Scotsmen and no doubt a few Welsh doing a land grab and being allowed to get away with it. It strikes me this has been allowed to happen not because the Irish are Catholics but because there are profits to be made. Is anybody in London aware of the full details of this?'

'Some people know alright.'

'Yes, maybe,' conceded Digby. 'But we need to ensure the right people are aware. But...'

'What?'

'We need to consider how best to address the... the Irish reputation problem. If we don't we'll risk losing support for change.'

'What do you mean?'

'A lot of people in England see the Irish as uncivilised monsters, murderers and robbers not worthy of sympathy. History is told by the winners. Those who've fought in the wars against you have no wish to paint you in a better light. I fear the same thing could happen in the Americas and elsewhere too. Take a look at what I hear the Spanish are doing. It's easy to paint the people you wish to conquer as heathen savages. It makes what you're doing acceptable, heroic even.'

'There's nothing heroic about starving babies,' said Conn. 'And you should be asking what turned some of the Irish people into monsters in the first place. The folk around here have been pushed around, forced to live life on the margins and watch others make money from what was rightfully theirs. For now they survive because the planters need tenants and workers and are forced to pay the Irish a wage but it's not enough to feed their families on. And the rents are ridiculous. The planters have squeezed about as much as they can get from the people who fought against them. It's a long and lingering punishment for the last war and all the other ones before that. We never asked you lot to come over here. It's our land and we want it back.'

For a few moments both men were left with their thoughts before Conn turned to Digby and looked him in the eye. 'There's one thing though,' he said. 'You're a man of surprises. I'd never have suspected an agent of the Queen to have some of the views you appear to possess. Do they know about these in England? You're as much of a rebel as I am.'

'Perhaps' said Digby. 'but I shouldn't have spoken out. I thought I'd learned to keep my views to myself but I what you've shown me in Ulster does anger me.'

Digby went quiet for a moment. His mind wandered back to the villages he'd visited in the Americas. How many more settlements had been destroyed like the one which led to his incursion into the French stockade? His thoughts returned to the things he'd learned from Conn over the last few days.

The plantation leaders made frequent journeys to England to recruit and return with more of their own. He was reminded of Poyntz in the castle on the pass and how he'd imported his tenants from Gloucestershire. Good Protestant stock, one and all. Digby thought he knew why Poyntz paid to uproot whole families and bring them to Ireland. He'd consider it preferable to allow his farmland to go fallow rather than be worked by the Irish. War did that to men.

Earlier on Conn had explained that the plight of the locals was deteriorating. The conditions they lived in now were getting worse. There was less food on their tables. The Irish families were being pushed onto more marginal land. In the morning they'd seen Irish labourers working for the planters. Conn said once the planters had imported sufficient English and Scots Protestants to do their work, there'd be no more for the Irish and what would happen then, he asked.

In the meantime wages in cash and kind were pitiful and falling. Digby was moved by the plight of Conn's people. Once the new farms and towns were constructed and could be maintained and protected, the planters would want the Irish gone but where could they go? In a world like this, thought Digby, who in their right minds would not rise up and rebel? He hoped he would. He shook his head. He knew he would.

From their current position they were watching a group of men working on a construction site for a fortified tower. Conn said the building was to be called Obins Castle. A brand new settlement was to be built around it to house Protestant planters. The castle would be a stronghold from which Obins and his men could patrol and control the countryside and harry the indigenous population.

The more Digby saw of plantation, the more he disliked it and the more he worried it would become a model for controlling the lands and people of the New World. If it worked in Ireland he was sure it would be repeated across the Atlantic. He was determined to do everything in his power to stop it but, realistically, what could he do?

How could anyone reconcile two groups of people who had such a long history of violence against each other? The English and Irish had fought bitterly for generations. One side was taking control of the lands of the other. The second group was responding not with traditional warfare but hit and run, murder and robbery. The Irish believed they had no choice but to terrorise their enemies but even their leaders knew this would be unlikely to succeed in the long run. The odds, finance and military might were stacked too heavily against them.

Conn and Digby could see from their clothing the men working below were Irish. They toiled under the direct watch of a small group of overseers, each armed with a stick. It appeared to be more like a prison camp than a construction site. Although the walls were twenty feet high, the scaffolding around them was rudimentary at best. From what they could see the Irishmen were tasked with transporting and lifting heavy flat stones to be positioned on top of the ramparts.

An argument broke out between the workers and their overseers. One of the Irishmen had been pushing heavy barrows of stone around the base of the tower. His body looked thin and he'd collapsed with exhaustion. He was being encouraged onto his feet by strikes to his legs and back. Three or four of his fellow workers rushed to his side and there was an exchange of words. Although the debate was inaudible, clearly tensions were high. When it looked as if things would turn into a fight, the fallen man struggled to his feet. He supported himself for a moment against the now empty barrow and wheeled it away.

'They look like slaves but surely they can't be?' exclaimed an astonished Digby.

'Oh no,' said Conn. 'They're not slaves. They're employees alright. They get paid for their labours although it will be a pitiable amount. How well fed do you think they look? And to have the strength to work, they'll have to eat most of the food which comes into their houses. You should see the women and children. I'll take you there.'

'No, it's alright,' said Digby. 'There's no need. I believe you. I've seen enough. You've proved your point. I need to meet the Irish leader as soon as possible so we can agree how best to deliver some pretty difficult messages to the Queen and her Parliament. This has to stop.'

'Stand up!'

Digby and Conn turned around. Three men were standing behind them. They were dressed like the overseers below. Each held a thick wooden stick. And they weren't alone. Alongside them stood an English gentleman. He was dressed in a fancy tunic, hose, ruff and hat. He wouldn't have looked out of place in the royal court in London, thought Digby.

'We know you,' he said pointing at Conn. 'But who is your friend here? And are there others with you? We know you don't normally go out on your raids alone. Come on now, get up! Both of you.'

Digby thought it was best not to speak. He lifted his body from the ground. When Conn attempted to do the same, the man who'd spoken nodded towards him. One of the oversees lashed out and hit Conn hard across the back of his legs. A second man struck him on the back. The third held his club steadily and looked at Digby as if taunting him to have a go.

When Conn was struck again, he felt had no choice.

'I'll not see this man murdered,' he said softly under his breath.

With a quick step forward, Digby punched and head-butted his opponent. The man fell to the ground, already unconscious. His stick tumbled onto the grass. The gentleman was taken aback. His face displayed alarm at Digby's actions and sheer surprise at his English accent. He took a pace backwards.

Digby turned. He punched the second overseer in the back. The blow found its target, a kidney. The man winced in pain. When he turned, Digby struck again. This time the man fell to his knees. He dropped his stick. Digby reached for it but the third overseer reacted quickly. The club swung at his head. Digby dodged it. It missed.

From the floor Conn grabbed at the attacker's boot, and used his momentum to flip the man over. The overseer turned slowly in the air, as if he was a large flat pancake. As he fell to earth Conn picked up the lost club and struck him hard. Ribs cracked. Conn smiled.

The gentleman leader decided to flee. He galloped down the hillside towards the tower, whistling and calling as loudly as he could. Digby was about to go after him but realised it was too late. He turned and kicked the second overseer who was attempting to get back to his feet. All three assailants now lay on the ground. When Digby picked up one of their clubs the tables were fully turned. The overseers looked terrified, as if their deaths were imminent. This was the burden the Protestants carried with them, thought Digby. If the Irish caught them alone they'd be dead. It was no way to live for either side.

'I'm an officer of the English government,' Digby said to them. 'Follow us and I'll have you arrested and transported back to London where you'll be hung, drawn and quartered as traitors. Do you understand me?'

They nodded in fear for their lives. As Digby glanced down the hill he could see their leader had stopped running. The men with sticks at the construction site had heard him and were now charging up the hill towards him. But they still had a way to go. The gentleman screamed at them to hurry. For an instant he turned and glowered.

Digby checked the numerical disadvantage against Conn and himself. Including the three men currently on the ground, they would be facing nine foes in total. Perhaps some of the workers would come to their aid but he knew this would be as good as a death warrant for themselves and their families. He wouldn't allow that. Conn obviously shared his concerns.

'Take to the trees,' he said.

Before he'd finished speaking, they began to run. It wasn't long before the two men entered the forest. The area was densely planted and used for firewood and timber. The saplings were young and supple and packed tightly together. Digby dodged and scrambled through the trees, constantly hampered by Conn's bag. He still had no idea what was inside. The bag was sewn shut. The man running ahead of him had said he shouldn't look inside and so he hadn't. It was a question of honour. Digby considered himself a gentleman.

He wondered what Conn must think of English chivalry and honour. At times Digby felt such a hypocrite. One moment his countrymen would be doing a gentlemanly deed, in the next they would be turfing children out of their homes. There was no consistency.

Conn stole a glance back at him. Digby was still there. Despite himself, Digby was beginning to like the argumentative Irishman. The two men seemed to developing an unlikely respect for each other. The bad news was it might be short lived.

139

Digby quick realised they weren't running aimlessly. He suspected Conn knew where they were going and had an idea in his mind. It appeared they were heading towards the river. Digby wondered if there was a good crossing point.

The gallop through the glade was mesmerising. It was like a game. They ran. Young trees sprang up. The path was blocked. They would need to swerve. Their bodies moved at speed. If a pursuer stumbled their lead would increase. If one or other tripped, momentum was lost. The gap would narrow. Do this too many times and the lead would be zero. Their lives would be lost and it would be the end of the game.

Digby side stepped. Conn accelerated. They reached a place where the newer plantings petered out, replaced by older deciduous forest. The undergrowth here was different and much more varied. Digby chanced a glance behind. The loud voices weren't too far away but he couldn't see the men. They still had a chance.

'Now!' whispered Conn. 'Go this way.'

They both took a sharp turn to the right. The footprints they'd left in the woods before were more obvious than in this place. The autumnal undergrowth was beginning to thin out, and much of the ground cover was dying as part of the annual cycle. It was becoming more difficult to distinguish marks they made from the natural shade of the earth.

The land to their left had a natural rise. Staggered rows of trees and bushes zigzagged upwards. Conn decided they shouldn't follow suit. Glancing at the fallen leaves gathered at the bottom of the dip, he stopped running and waded into them. He had to make sure they were deep enough.

'Down here,' he said. 'Bury yourself under. Just there at the edge of the track. You're less likely to get stepped on. Keep your knife at the ready. If they catch us it'll be a fight to the death. It's been a pleasure knowing you.'

Digby could hardly believe it but Conn took time to shake his hand. The gesture appeared genuine. Without wasting another moment both men stepped away from each other and took to their task. It wasn't difficult to find suitable places. They burrowed themselves into the leaves and secreted themselves beneath. Each hoped they'd achieved this without causing too much obvious disturbance in the patterned formations on the ground above them.

It wasn't long before they heard the overseers searching for their hiding places. The pursuers were blowing hard and they'd slowed down considerably. It appeared they were fanning out to look for the two men. There were words spoken and a clear level of disagreement. A few of the men wanted to continue to the river but others wanted to search through the undergrowth, or head up towards the top of the bank.

A footstep passed close-by to Digby' face. He gripped the knife in his hand. He was pleased of the way he'd fought earlier, but felt it was a shame he was fighting fellow Englishmen. He had no time for these men though and if he was going to die, he was determined he would go down fighting.

On the other side of the trail, Conn held the club. If things kicked off, he'd fight his way through the men and go for their leader Michael Obins. If Obins recognised Conn as an O'Neill, he'd equally recognised him for what he was. A man with choices. The others followed orders but it was those in control like Obins who made the real decisions and they should be held accountable. If Conn could take anyone out with him before he died it would be Obins.

Conn thought of his relatives. They'd lost the war but retained a level of control at the start of the peace. As that slipped away from them they had a choice. Stay or leave? For years he'd believed his family had made the wrong decision in abandoning their people and taking the boat. They should have stayed and fought. When they left, he was young and had little choice but to go with them. Now he was a man he'd made his choice. He'd returned. This was his country.

Michael Obins caught up with his men as they scoured the woodland for signs of Digby and Conn. 'You fools,' he shouted. 'You should have caught up with them by now. That man is an O'Neill. If I know the way his mind works he'll be heading for the crossing point on the river. His view will be they can hold us at bay there for a while but they're probably long gone, unless they're scouting for a larger party and leading us into a trap. We'll call off the hunt for now, just in case. Did anybody get a good look at the other man?'

'He was covered in mud and shit, so I couldn't see his face,' said one of the overseers. 'But he told us he worked for the English government.'

'What nonsense is this?' Obins was incredulous at the suggestion.

'That's what he said,' confirmed a second man. 'And he didn't sound Irish at all. He spoke like a proper gentleman.'

'A gentleman who needs a damn good thrashing,' said one of the others.

141

Obins pulled a face. 'It just doesn't make sense,' he said. 'I suspect they must be setting a trap for us. We should return to the tower.'

It was a good while before Conn slowly sat up. He tried to rustle the leaves around him as little as possible in case Obin's withdrawal has been some sort of ruse. He scanned the area, and when he saw nothing quietly requested Digby come out too. Without speaking they crept slowly together to the river crossing. Once there they remained hidden in the woods for some time before showing themselves. Conn listened and watched the trees on both banks for signs of movement. When he saw nothing he skipped across the water.

As the coast was clear he beckoned for Digby to follow. Digby shook off some of the leaves still stuck onto his woollen cloak and walked towards the western bank of the water. He jumped across the sections of rocks as Conn had done before him, landing safely each time. At one point he halted for a moment and looked into the river but the water was flowing too fast for his eyes to penetrate its depths.

'There's salmon and trout in there, alright,' said Conn when Digby reached his vantage point on the far side. 'End of the season really but if we get through this, I promise I'll cook you a big fat Irish salmon myself. But right now we're off to see what Arthur Chichester and his mob are doing in Belfast. If we don't get intercepted along the way, I reckon it'll only take us two more days to get there.'

'Good,' said Digby. 'But you must tell me now when am I to meet this Irish leader you've told me so little about.' Digby stopped and looked at Conn. 'Or do I take it I've already met him?'

'Aye, you have,' replied Conn. 'He's a grand fellow now, don't you think?'

Chapter XVIII

The French ambassador was furious. Two hours previously he'd received an unscheduled visit from the English Secretary of State himself. The Earl of Suffolk had been polite but his message was clear. In the last twenty-four hours the authorities had found three dead bodies in the Thames. All had been murdered. From his clothing at least, one was believed to be French. Was the embassy missing any of its staff? If so, the ambassador should send someone to the Tower of London to identify and claim the body.

The ambassador assured the Englishman nobody from his household or office was missing. Of course he would make enquiries across the wider French community in London. Suffolk had then left. The ambassador's thoughts were disturbed by a knock on the door of his office. The woman he'd sent for had arrived. Shaking his head he put his tobacco pipe down and ordered a servant to pull the curtains across the window to close them. He had no wish for the meeting to be overlooked from outside.

'Show her in,' he said angrily in French. 'And everybody else get out!'

Linda Blanchet walked into the room. As always the ambassador was impressed by her looks and style. She was so different to his own wife, unburdened by children and the work of running a household. He felt she was a proud mare running free in a world which was otherwise full of cart horses.

The Frenchwoman wore an embroidered linen jacket as black as jet. Her petticoat was embroidered and partially covered by a long black dress. Did she always wear black, the ambassador wondered. But he also noticed the lace and materials of her collar, cuffs, and hood, as they glinted with different shades of gold. The contrast to her dark dress, eyes and hair was stunning. He'd always found her attractive, even if there was a little something of the night about her. A thunderstorm in the evening came to mind, like the ones in the Pyrenees. Exhilarating but deadly. He wanted her.

Linda knew this. As always what she wore was simply part of her plan. When the door was closed, she sat down sensually onto the seat positioned directly across from the ambassador's desk and smiled enigmatically. Her calculations had been correct. The man lusted after her but he was in awe of her power and looks. Women weren't supposed to behave the way she did. It scared and excited little men like this one in equal measure. Why were so few of them strong enough to stand up and fight with her?

'You wished to see me, Monsieur Ambassador?'

'Yes,' he said. 'I have just had the Earl of Suffolk in here to see me. He talked of murder and dead Frenchmen on the streets of London. You must tell me what is going on, Madam Blanchet.'

'When was he here?'

'Two hours ago, but I must insist, I have questions which must be answered.'

'You fool,' she said. 'It's a trap. They have no idea of who leads our spies in London. My cover was perfect but they share a few words with you and you send for me immediately and, fool that I am, I come here running. Don't you understand? The embassy is being watched. They'll have seen me arrive in my carriage, obviously sent for by you.'

The ambassador's face reddened. He started to speak but stammered a little. The words wouldn't quite come out of his mouth the way he wished.

'Perhaps there is one way out of this,' said Linda, thinking quickly. 'It will probably not work, but it's worth the attempt. Where is your wife?'

'She is back in Paris.'

'Good. Now, go to your bedroom and take all your clothes off,' she instructed.

'What?'

'You heard me. You want my body, don't you?'

She leaned over the table and ran her long black velvet gloved fingers down the sides of his face. The ambassador was in his early fifties. From the look of him she worried for a moment he might have a heart attack or pass out. Instead, he did as he was told and went quickly and directly to his bed chamber. Linda thought she was going to enjoy this.

She gave the man a few minutes to remove his attire and demanded one of the footmen stand her carriage and driver down for the evening. They should return to their usual own stables. After this she ordered another of the embassy staff to show her to the room where the ambassador kept his bed. She made a great fuss about this. There wasn't a servant or official in the house who couldn't have doubted they were about to sleep with each other. Perhaps the English wouldn't think she was a French spy, just the ambassador's sleeping partner?

When the ambassador's man servant opened the bedroom door she shouted angrily for him to go away. They were not to be disturbed until morning. Linda went into the room and quickly closed the door. The interior was lit by a log fire, scented candles filled the air with incense. There was a line of discarded clothing on the rich carpet.

Where was the ambassador? Oh, there. Of course. Already in bed. Waiting for her. He lay on one side of the four poster structure, his white shoulders exposed above the bed linen. On the other side, Linda's side, he'd neatly folded the sheets back, where he believed she'd be sidling in next to him.

'What do you think you are doing?' she laughed. 'Get out of the bed.'

'What?'

He stepped out of the bed and awkwardly stood up. A pitiful sight, she thought. What was French society coming to that men like this could be made an ambassador for important enemies? She wasn't worried though. He would soon be replaced and she'd been told she could make her own recommendation. There weren't many candidates but she had one or two in mind. For now, however, she would have to work with what she'd got.

She laughed at him again. As a fig leaf wasn't available, he held his hands in front of himself to cover his embarrassment. Linda leaned against the side of the bed. She took off one glove and then another. As she did so she held the end of the middle finger of each glove in her mouth, biting down on it hard and pulling her head back. Once each glove was released she dropped it onto the carpet next to the ambassador's own clothes.

He stared at her, and suddenly felt the need for larger hands. Linda didn't know what the ambassador was getting quite so excited about. Without her maid it would take her an age to fully disrobe. The old man's eyes almost popped out, as she began to loosen the layers of her clothing in front of him.

'I want you to do exactly as I tell you,' she said.

'Anything. I am your servant,' said the ambassador, warming to the situation he found himself in.

'Go to the window.'

He did as he was instructed. The curtains were drawn but Linda knew from her previous visits to the house the view from this room faced the front flower garden and main street.

Although the individual panes were small, the windows were quite large. Each had a sill which stood two feet off the ground. They jutted out about the same distance into the room. These were covered with cushions and made perfect seats in the daytime. When in London, the ambassador's wife liked to sit there in the sunshine sometimes and sew.

'Now your next instruction,' said Linda. 'You are to go behind the other side of the curtains and pretend you are looking for something. Once you've looked down for a moment, you must drop to your knees and crawl along the cushions on all fours. You must stay out there until you've counted slowly to one hundred but, and listen, and this is very important, you are not to look out of the window down onto the street. Do you understand me?'

The ambassador nodded. 'But somebody may see me and what will we do then?'

'Never mind about that. I shall continue to undress. You'd like that, wouldn't you?'

'Yes.'

He looked very keen. After a moment, he climbed onto the window sill and pushed himself through the overlapping gap in the middle of the blinds. He was now invisible to Linda but very visible to the street below. She continued to undress. How could any man find this alluring, she wondered, with all these straps and catches and buttons. A short time afterwards she'd gone as far as she wanted to.

'You can come back into the room now, ambassador,' she said.

He immediately crawled back out from behind the curtains. He stared at her. She was stripped to her corsets. These were sleek, black and made of silk. He'd never seen anything quite so exciting in his whole life. Did women really dress like this? He was almost beside himself with anticipation.

'Now you must stand over there by that chair,' Linda ordered.

He walked across the room obediently and she moved to the window where he'd been.

'It's now my turn to do a little window dressing,' she said.

As she clambered through the same gap in the curtains as he had, the ambassador stared at her thighs. Linda crouched down in the window and searched on all fours for something elusive which one of them may have dropped earlier. She knew the clear white skin of her legs would be visible to the outside

146

world and felt a little thrill. She wondered who was watching. She hoped it was a strong man.

Once she felt the show had gone on for long enough she stepped back inside pretending to hold something in her hand. She ensured the curtains were fully closed and stepped across the carpet towards the bed. Every second she could feel the ambassador's eyes watching her. When she reached the bed, she picked up her clothes and folded them neatly and carefully, before placing them onto the back of a chair. She didn't want them to be creased when she left in the morning.

'What happens now?' asked the ambassador.

'I suggest we both get some sleep,' said Linda.

She sidled into the bed and pulled a blanket from the bedding. The ambassador was emboldened and strode manfully towards her. She threw the loose blanket at his chest, forcing him to expose himself in all his glory, as he caught the bedding mid-flight.

'You can sleep on the floor,' she said.

'No,' he replied. 'That is not possible. We must, you know. Look!'

They both looked.

'I suggest you think about something else then,' said Linda in a sharper voice. 'Because if you attempt to get into this bed, I'll wrench that thing right off you and throw it into the fire. Do you understand me?' She felt perhaps she was being a little too dominant and relented slightly. 'But really Monsieur Ambassador it's your choice.'

The Frenchman winced, his ardour already waning. He skulked across the carpet towards a cushioned bench near the fire and pulled the blanket up over his body. As he stared into the flames, Linda wondered what he was thinking. He probably couldn't believe what was happening. This was his embassy after all, but she enjoyed being impossible, and having powerful friends helped. For once it was the man, not the woman, in this world who was powerless.

'Merde,' he whispered and closed his eyes.

#

Across the road in a small unlit room in an empty house, Will Carr was amused. The Frenchwoman had put on quite a spectacle for him. He'd particularly enjoyed the second half and called quietly for an encore but sadly it didn't happen. Would she stay there all night? Carr doubted it very much. He didn't believe for a second she'd actually sleep with the ambassador. She was something special and frankly the ambassador wasn't up to it.

Carr found the woman attractive but there was something else he didn't like about her, even at this distance. In any case, he knew she was out of his reach and he was happy at home with Margaret. Sometimes he might look at another woman but he never touched.

For the next hour or so there was nothing else to see. Eventually there was a tap on the door of the room. Carr ordered the man with him to keep watching the front of the embassy. He slipped into the hallway and spoke to one of his other men who was waiting for him in the corridor. Once the man had caught his breath he gave his report.

When the lady's coach had departed from the embassy buildings some time ago, even though she hadn't got into it he'd followed. It had been quite a struggle without a horse but he'd run as fast as he could and most of the time he'd been able to keep up with the carriage as it passed through the streets of London. Only on two occasions had he been forced to make an educated guess and take a short cut to keep up with the vehicle. Thankfully, he'd chosen correctly each time.

Eventually the coach and horses completed their journey and arrived at a set of stables in one of the back yards off Thames Street. Leaving a stable lad to see to the mounts, the driver had left and walked a few hundred yards to a large house on Love Lane. He'd tapped on a door and been admitted inside. From all accounts the house was well guarded, with a man stationed at both front and back gates.

Carr thanked the watcher. He was confident they'd discovered the new centre of French spying operations in England. He despatched half his men to Love Lane to begin watching the house. The idea he'd taken to Suffolk had worked out well. The talk of dead Frenchmen on the streets of the English capital had concerned the ambassador sufficiently for him to immediately summon his head spy for an urgent conference. The only surprise was the spy was a woman. The next trick was to identify her.

Chapter XIX

'So, here we are,' said Conn. 'The new town of Belfast. Even more O'Neill lands in the hands of the bloody English.'

Over the past few days Digby had discovered a great deal about Conn O'Neill's background and history but the picture was still a little confused. Conn claimed his father was Hugh O'Neill, the last Earl of Tyrone, and he'd travelled with him, his mother and more than ninety other members of Irish society on the fateful boat journey to exile a decade ago.

Conn said he'd never been close to his father. There was too much competition. In his heyday, O'Neill senior had been a promiscuous man. He'd had numerous children with his four wives, as well as illegitimate offspring with many other women. Conn indicated he fell into the first category but wouldn't say which wife had been his mother. He claimed she still had relatives in Ireland and he didn't want to risk compromising them. Apparently his old man was good at fighting but struggled with many other things in life, such as the peace. Why else, said Conn, would an earl give multiple sons the same Christian name? It turned out there was more than one Conn O'Neill in the immediate family.

When his father passed away in Rome the previous year, in many ways it had been a relief for Conn. It was time to go home. Others may lay claim to be the title of Earl of Tyrone, he said, but they all lived abroad and sought solace in the Bible, the bottle or both. A few fought for the Spanish. One had even joined forces with the Portuguese, but none of the others planned to come back so how could they claim to be the true Earl of Tyrone? Only he was ready to live in Ireland and, if necessary, die there too.

From the moment the boat had left Ireland, Conn said he'd been determined to return one day when the opportunity arose. He'd learned the skills of war fighting for the Spanish in Flanders, and from his Protestant enemies. The Dutch were masters of small scale skirmishes, targeting and attacking groups of soldiers who'd become detached from the main Spanish army. This explained his slightly odd accent, thought Digby. Conn had learned to speak in the English language whilst fighting alongside English and Irish Catholics in a Spanish unit in

149

the Low Countries. He described himself as partly European but mostly Irish.

Conn returned to his own country early in the previous year, along with two others. They were comrades with similar ideas of establishing an armed resistance in Ireland, fighting the English enemy and disrupting the occupying forces from within. The others were both dead now, killed in small-scale exchanges with English planters.

Conn believed he would eventually share their fate until the day when he met Ó Lionáin, the man who ran the shebeen in Crossmaglen. One evening the two men had sat down to drink whiskey together. The session lasted long into the night. A drunken Conn gave away his identify as one of the sons of Hugh O'Neill. When Ó Lionáin said the Irish word for bastard, Conn told him to shut his mouth. Ó Lionáin laughed and said, 'No, not you son, your father.'

He went onto explain his view that the Irish earls were little better for the ordinary Irish people than the English planters. They killed and murdered each other to gain position and cared nothing for the people beneath them. We didn't matter as long as they got what they wanted, and when things got rough, what did they do? They pissed off and left us. If you want to change the world for the better, sonny, don't throw your life away by trying to make things like they used to be. Keep yourself alive and make Ireland a better place for all the people who live here.'

The drunken statement struck a chord with Conn. His experiences had led him to believe a long armed struggle would eventually be futile, and could only lead to the death of his people. Despite everything he'd been brought up to believe in and the ideas he'd developed himself on the Spanish battlefields, that night in the shebeen changed his mind. He wasn't even deterred the next morning when Ó Lionáin said he couldn't remember a word of the conversation and it must have been the whiskey talking. For Conn knew an inebriated man often speaks more truth than when he's sober.

It was a stark truth too. Ireland was at a crossroads. The way ahead looked bleak but there was no going back. A different direction had to be found. Violence would be needed at times but Conn felt he also needed to learn the art of politics. Over the next few months he'd spoke with the few Irishmen he knew who still retained some influence. A few of them told him where to stick the talk of politics. Others shook their heads but somehow connections were made, and here he was standing next to Sir Everard Digby, the secret envoy of the Queen of England. Conn smiled in disbelief. Was he a visionary or a traitor?

'Tell me more about this place,' said Digby as they looked towards the growing new town of Belfast.

'The land used to be under the jurisdiction of my family, until Elizabeth Tudor took it away from us. She granted it to an English fellow named Smith. The O'Neills were naturally not so keen on the idea and Smith struggled to keep control. There was a bit of to-ing and fro-ing but eventually the land was handed back to the English crown, so your new Queen Elizabeth owned it for a while.'

'I bet she had no idea,' said Digby. 'She is young but a good woman. If she knew what was going on here, she wouldn't allow it. Is much of the land in Ireland still in the name of the crown?'

'Some, I think, why?'

'Just an idea but it can wait for now,' replied Digby. 'What's happening here? There seems to be a lot of work going on, even more than around Portadown.'

'More recently the lands for this town, the castle and all the local estates were granted to Sir Arthur Chichester.'

'How and why?'

'I don't know for sure, but it might be something to do with the same chap having been the Deputy Lord Lieutenant of Ireland for so long, and pretty much able to do anything he wants.'

'What is he planning?'

'Plantation of course, but on a grand scale. Belfast is Chichester's personal project. He wants to create a new gateway into Ulster, a big town and port where he can ship things in and out. He's looking to create a trade monopoly so he can tax everyone else's imports and exports too. Before you know it, he'll have his own customs house down there. It is crooked bastards like him who give you English a bad name. Not that you need any help on that score, present company excepted.'

'What do we do now?' asked Digby.

'Since we lost Hamilton you've had a bit of a one-sided story. I know it sounds daft but I think you should talk to Chichester, so you can make up your own mind about the man. He's no longer the Lord Deputy. These days he's usually here in Belfast or in his castle in Carrickfergus, a dozen or so miles along the coast. Over there.' Conn pointed to a distant headland across the dark blue water.

'Carrickfergus is also where the ship will come in to take us to London,' Conn continued. 'The water down there at the mouth of the river in Belfast isn't deep enough for a big boat like Button's. Chichester's getting it dredged and the channel widened but it's not done yet. Once it is, there'll be a harbour and dockyards. Then nothing will stop the man.'

'Do you think I'll be safe?'

'You? Once you open your big English gob, God yes. If you tell Chichester you're here on government business, he'll probably want to have your babies. But there is one last thing, Digby.'

'Yes?'

'They'll probably want you to change out of your clothes and take a bath. You stink like the back end of a sheep.'

Both men laughed.

'What about you?' asked Digby.

'Belfast isn't a safe place for an O'Neill,' said Conn. 'Chichester would have me strung up from the nearest gate post before you could ask if there's time for another whiskey.'

'Where will you go?' asked Digby.

'I've got a few things to do. Speaking of which, hand over my bag, will you?' said Conn. 'It's been good of you to carry it all the way from Dundalk but I can take it from here.'

Digby handed the bag over and shook Conn's hand.

'I'll meet you by the harbour in Carrickfergus at noon on Wednesday,' said Conn. 'Just stand by the sea wall and I'll find you. Good luck in the meantime.'

'You too, Conn,' said Digby. 'Be careful.'

When the Irishman was gone, for the first time in a week Digby stood alone. Would he miss the man who'd pretended to kill him, thrown him down a well, made him smell of sheep shit and forced him to carry his bag across Ulster? Digby thought, yes he would.

Part Three

Extract from Traditional English Rhyme - Early 17th Century
'Linda was a Frenchwoman
Linda was a spy
She killed seven Englishmen
We don't know why'

Chapter XX

'The French spymaster in London is a woman.'

'Are you sure about this?' The tone of the Earl of Suffolk's voice betrayed his disbelief.

'Absolutely certain, my lord,' replied Will Carr.

Meetings between the two men were occurring more frequently than usual. Sometimes weeks, even months, would go by without Carr being summoned to see the earl but these days their conferences took place almost daily. This one he'd convened himself.

'Do you think she really slept with the ambassador?'

Carr smiled. He was pleased with himself. 'We can't be sure either way, my lord, but I'll wager she didn't. I'd wager she was angry with the old boy for falling for your trick which flushed her out into the open. Most likely she created the bedroom scene as a simulation, an attempt to throw us off the scent by asking us to believe she was merely his sleeping partner for the night.'

'What does your maid in the embassy say?'

'Unfortunately we couldn't get her onto the work rota that evening but she claims it's the main topic of conversation in the house. Apparently the ambassador has gone up in most people's estimations. The staff hope she'll return soon. It was the biggest excitement they've had for years.'

'But who is this mysterious woman?' asked Suffolk. 'I take it you wouldn't have called for a second meeting in two days unless you had something new to tell me?'

'Indeed. Perceptive as always, my lord,' replied Carr. 'Her name is Linda Blanchet. She's the widow of a French officer killed in the Americas. From what we've managed to piece together, her husband was the Frenchman we received the complaint about.'

'The man they claimed was murdered by Digby? Good Lord.'

'Yes,' confirmed Carr. 'And Captain Blanchet's widow moves in exalted circles. We believe she's a friend and confidante of both Charles d'Albert and Bishop Richelieu.'

'You're saying she's connected to both King Louis's administration and the previous one led by Louis's mother, Marie de' Medici?' A hint of disbelief returned to the Earl's voice.

'Aye, my lord. Madam Blanchet was seen speaking for some time with both men separately at the Queen's birthday celebrations at Greenwich in August. Our men thought little of it at the time, as she was merely a woman. They simply assumed they were both angling for a visit to her bedchamber.'

'Really? Don't forget you're talking about a Catholic bishop,' said Suffolk.

'Oh yes, my lord,' replied Carr. 'Often the bishops are the worst offenders. You should see the records we hold on some of them.'

Suffolk sighed. 'I have no wish to,' he said. 'I am no Robert Cecil. What do you recommend we do now with regard to Madam Blanchet?'

'We should continue to watch her closely. If she ordered the killing of the men who ended up in the Thames she is dangerous, but we need to find out what we can about her before acting.'

'Why would they choose a woman anyway?'

'Who knows? Perhaps they saw it as a perfect cover. She's fooled us up to now. The important thing is we gather proof against her. Once we have enough evidence, you can make a song and dance to the ambassador and demand her return to France.

'Why don't we do that now?' asked Suffolk.

'Why do you think, my lord?'

For the last twelve years questions such as this had been Carr's way of sharpening his master's spying and analytical capabilities. The Earl of Suffolk may have claimed he was no Robert Cecil but both men knew in some ways he had to be if he was to be effective. Dangerous enemies lurked everywhere. They needed to be thwarted.

'We should keep her out there for now because we know who she is, where she lives and we can follow her and find out what she does,' said Suffolk. 'If she leaves, they'll only send another and we'll have to sniff him, or her, out all over again.'

'My thoughts exactly, my lord,' replied Carr. We'll make a Robert Cecil out of you yet, he thought.

#

Linda Blanchet stood in the dining hall of the French safe house on Love Lane. The flames from a roaring fire burned brightly and gave off the occasional puff or swirl of black smoke as another piece of paper caught light. One by one Linda was burning her secret correspondence, the important documents she'd collected over time.

It was clear now the ruse hadn't worked. The house, her men, even she was under surveillance. The French observed the English watchers, as they watched them. One or two hadn't been professional enough as they walked up and down the street, hid in corners or nodded at colleagues as they came to relieve them. She lifted another batch of neatly written reports and orders. Of course they were in code but some amongst the English were almost as clever as the French. They couldn't afford for these papers to fall into the wrong hands.

The ambassador's head would roll for this. She'd make sure of it. Linda would work with whichever group came out on top of the power struggle in Paris. She cared little if it was Louis or if Bishop Richelieu engineered a place back for Marie in court. A cruel smile crossed her lips. It was difficult to think angrily of the ambassador for long. He was so pathetic. Linda remembered his puny body with his hands held out in front of him to cover his little embarrassment. And he'd thought he'd be able to sleep with her? The egos of such men ran so far ahead of reality.

Linda was sufficiently self-aware to realise her haste to visit the ambassador that evening hadn't been about concern for her duty to France but her personal interests. When she'd been summoned she thought they might have word about the fate of Sir Everard Digby. She needed to know if he'd been killed in Ireland. Her own recall to Paris at some stage was inevitable, only the timing was in question but she wouldn't leave London until she knew Digby was dead.

#

Digby couldn't remember being openly spat at in the street before but in the last half mile this had happened twice. Virtually every person he passed hurled abuse in his direction. From his clothing most people in the area of the new town of Belfast assumed he was Irish, and they didn't take kindly to seeing a Catholic walking through their streets as if he had every right to be there. All they saw a man who needed a lesson in manners.

The atmosphere around him was becoming increasingly unpleasant. Perhaps the stories Conn had told him weren't made up after all. As he continued to stride towards the centre of town, Digby wondered what could possibly turn hard-working God-fearing folk into a potential lynch mob. The men and women around him stared at him, eyes, heads and hearts filled with hatred. It was the most unnerving thing he'd ever experienced.

By the time he'd entered the main street, a small crowd had formed around him. People began to bar his path, jostling and pushing him back when he tried to pass them. Digby moved

156

this way and that to avoid them and carry on but almost inevitably the rumpus drew even more attention. A small number of men armed with wooden batons arrived. Digby didn't know where they'd appeared from but he realised he'd have to do something soon or feel the weight of their combined Protestant wrath. He had to speak out before someone did him serious damage.

'Hold! Stand back!' he shouted. 'I'm an agent of the crown. I must see Sir Arthur Chichester as soon as possible. It is a matter of some urgency. In the name of Queen Elizabeth, I demand you lead me to him immediately.'

Digby selected his words carefully and adopted the clipped English accent he'd used long ago during his visits to the royal court. He hoped this show of confidence and bluster would serve him well. His experience of the past seven days, and before that, his time in the Americas had removed some of his in-bred arrogance, but he needed it back now. They must believe who he was - an English gentleman, a knight of the realm.

How he wished he'd carried his own clothes in the sack with him across Ulster rather than whatever it was Conn had him carry. He could have changed back into them. It was obvious his appearance marked him down as an Irishman who needed to be dealt with but he was still surprised that simply walking through town could mark a man out as a trouble-maker.

The thugs with the batons approached him. The rest of the crowd withdrew a few feet. One of the potential bruisers bounced a club on the palm of his hand, as if unsure whether to unleash it or not. Another made up his mind. He approached Digby from behind and shoved him in the back. The mob murmured in anticipation of a spectacle. Some of them liked a good beating. The crowd then became hushed.

Four of the men formed a fighting ring, with Digby in the middle. They began to swish their sticks through the air but they didn't strike him yet. The coming moments would be crucial. Digby turned to face the man who'd pushed him. As he did so another man prodded him with his own baton. A third took a step back to take a swing. Digby turned and unleashed his fury on him.

'You dare to take me on? Did you not hear what I said?'

The man held his stick in the air but did not bring it down onto Digby's head.

'I am an agent of the English crown and government, here in Ireland as a special envoy of Queen Elizabeth herself. It

157

is imperative I see Sir Arthur Chichester at once. The very future of everything you hold dear in Ireland could depend upon it. Interfere with my mission and it will be the last thing you do. Now put that club down before I wrench it from your arm.'

Slowly the man lowered his stick. The others stood off a little. The crowd hushed into total silence. The bully boys looked like they no longer had the nerve to go through with the attack. Digby was getting through to them. They just needed a figure from the local population with some authority to tell them what they should do. They weren't used to thinking for themselves. It appeared unseemly to back down but surely no Irishman could talk like this.

'In the name of the Good Lord himself,' said Digby, 'get me some decent English clothes and clean water. If I stay in this Irish muck for another hour, I swear I'll smell this way forever.'

The crowd liked that. There was a small cheer. Hearing this, Digby continued his way along the street towards the more important looking buildings near the river. As the people parted to make way for him, he picked up a few snatches of conversation from those who'd flocked to the scene. They indicated they believed he was somebody important. One woman told her husband she'd never seen a spy before. He shook his head and said neither had he.

One of the thugs, now holding his stick behind his back almost apologetically, volunteered, 'Sir Arthur's most likely to be in his office, over there. It's that large stone building on the waterfront.' The baton now pointed towards where the masts of a ship rose above the rooftops. 'He's usually there this time of day.'

Another spoke up, emboldened by his mate, 'What are you doing here anyway? We haven't seen anyone from London for months.'

Digby ignored the question and began walking towards the masts. Some of his new entourage followed, fascinated by what the newcomer might be up to. Others stayed behind and stared, as if they still didn't quite know what to make of him.

As the group reached the administrative centre of the town, Digby threw off the thick woollen cloak he'd been wearing for the best part of a week. He'd grown warm from walking and from the rush of blood before the altercation. When he reached the riverside he removed another layer of wool from his back and thew it into the water. For a moment he stood on the raised planks used for mooring. The river looked lovely and clear. He could see fish swimming beneath the surface. The crowd watched in anticipation.

Digby tossed his purse to a young boy. 'Protect this with your life, lad,' he told him with a wink.

He removed the remainder of his clothing, apart from a pair of woollen under-hose and dived headlong into the water. The shock of the cold made the blood rush through his body. As he swam for a length underwater his skin tingled with exhilaration. A shoal of fish zig-zagged away from him but some of the others in ones or twos carried on about their business around him. The weeds on the bottom waved gently with the tide and he could see crabs and shrimps scuttling amongst the pebbles.

For the first time in a week Digby felt clean and in proper control of his destiny. He was a strong swimmer and was more than twenty feet from the quayside when his head finally broke the surface of the water. He took in a deep breath and involuntarily thanked the Lord for his salvation. Old habits die hard.

As he trod water with a contented look on his face, there was a second cheer from the crowd. They'd never seen anything like this before.

'What a man!'

'Washing that Irish muck off himself.'

'He swims like the fishes.'

'He's a government agent alright.'

'Aye, I bet he knows the Queen, herself.'

After swimming on his back for a few more moments Digby swam over to the ladder at the edge of the planking. A woman rushed forward with a blanket to cover his modesty and allow him to stay warm. He thanked her, took the purse from the lad and gave him and the woman a few coins.

'Now, good people, where can I get some new clothes?' asked Digby. 'You can burn that Irish stuff.' He pointed at the items he'd discarded on his way to the water. 'And do you have a barbershop, for I am in need of a shave and a trim of my beard and hair?'

Two hours later, his appearance quite different, he sat in the office of Sir Arthur Chichester ready for their first meeting in the newly constructed castle of Belfast.

Chapter XXI

'Please take a seat, Sir Everard,' said Sir Arthur Chichester. 'What a pleasant surprise. I was told you were dead, murdered in the bad lands beyond the walls of Dundalk. How did you ever survive and make it all the way to Belfast?'

Ever since he'd hauled himself out of the refreshing water of the River Lagan, Digby had been attempting to work out what'd he say when he first met Arthur Chichester. Initially he'd planned to speak his mind to the former Deputy Lord but the more he heard the Belfast townsfolk talk, the less he considered it a good idea. There wasn't just mistrust and dislike of the Irish, there was complete and utter hatred.

It appeared some had good reason for their extreme views. Most knew of friends, family members or neighbours who'd been robbed by the Irish at knife point. A few had lost loved ones in the war, or in the so-called peace which followed. In recent years the situation had deteriorated, in line with the progress of plantation, speculated Digby. Men were picked off in the fields or on their way between armed strongholds. The barber spoke with venom about the cold-blooded murder of his own son, a lad of seventeen. It appeared there were two sides to every story.

To tell Sir Arthur he'd walked across Ireland with a sworn enemy didn't appear to be a good opening gambit. Equally was it right and proper to mislead this man who was also a knight of the realm? This appeared a dishonourable course of action and Digby prided himself in being a man of honour. But pride, he noted, was also one of the seven deadly sins.

Digby knew he'd done bad things down the years but his motivations weren't drawn from spite or malice. His intentions had been noble. He'd not acted out of greed nor for personal advancement. His self image of a chivalrous knight went to the core of his being. In the end though, he also believed lies were acceptable if the intentions behind them were good. And he considered his were.

'I did indeed have a near death experience close to Dundalk,' replied Digby. 'But unlike my guide, a planter named Hamilton, I survived this unprovoked attack. I realised I wouldn't live long in my English gentleman's clothing and replaced this with garments stolen from an Irishman. Since then I've been trying to avoid attention and make my way here to see you.'

'Astounding,' said Chichester. 'But what did you eat? Where did you sleep at night?'

'I lived off the land. A few times I bought bread and meat from people who must have considered me rude or dumb or both. I was careful not to speak as my words would give me away as an Englishman. In the evenings I'd find an isolated barn or outhouse and bed down there. It was not the style of life I've become accustomed to in England but thanks to your river, tailor, and barber I feel like my old self again.'

There, thought Digby, it wasn't all an outright lie.

'But why have you come to see me? What is your mission here in Ireland? And what does Her Majesty's Irish Parliament in Dublin know of this?'

'I am the special envoy of the Earl of Suffolk and Queen Elizabeth. They tasked me with gaining a fuller understanding of what is happening in Ireland. Foolishly, I believed the best way to do this would be to see the country for myself.'

'And now you've seen the error of your ways?'

Digby nodded his head. Chichester shook his. 'You should have come to me in the first place,' he said. 'When you've lived here as long as I have, you begin to understand this land and its people.'

'Your insight and advice would be most valuable, Sir Arthur.'

'Of course,' said Chichester. 'But I'm sure you must know I'm no longer the Deputy Lord Lieutenant of Ireland. My constitution is not as strong as it was and the constant need to travel between Dublin, Ulster and England wasn't helping my health. I mainly stay here in Belfast and Carrickfergus these days. Perhaps you should travel to Dublin to visit my successor, Sir Oliver St John, or meet with him at his home in County Longford in the middle lands?'

'A fine idea,' replied Digby. 'But you come so well recommended from London, Sir Arthur. I was keen to speak to you first.'

'It's wonderful to know I am still remembered,' said a smiling Chichester. 'And, Sir Everard, it is good to see you in my new town of Belfast. There is something I must show you in the dining hall.'

They rose from the chairs. Digby followed Chichester out of the study. They walked along a not very well lit corridor. The walls were lined with darkly painted portraits and landscape paintings, many of which depicted Ireland. There were a few larger battle scenes, dominated front and centre by dashing Englishmen. Dead and dying Irish were scattered at their feet and around the margins. Digby recalled what Northumberland had told him about Chichester. In the war he'd made a reputation as a military commander who favoured starvation and scorched earth to pitched battles. Unsurprisingly Digby saw no depiction of starving people and burning buildings on the walls.

At the end of the passage one of Chichester's servants opened a large double door. The two men entered a grand dining hall, a place where families and friends dined and afterwards the women would leave and the men talk about business and plans to complete the plantation of Ireland. Once again paintings covered the walls. Even with an untrained eye, Digby recognised quite a few. Surely they were not all originals? If so, the room had a finer collection than many of the royal palaces of Europe.

'A room of the finest art in the world,' said Chichester. 'I have works by virtually all the great artists. Around these walls you can see the genius of Caravaggio, Titian, Rubens and many others. Of course, as you may also recognise they're all imitations but still they are fabulous works of art. What do you think, Sir Everard?'

Most of the near side of the room was filled with scenes from the Bible. There were storms and angels, multiple versions of Jesus and Mary and more than one Last Supper. In contrast the far end of the room near the head of the table was dedicated to sailors and explorers, English ones at that. As they walked around the dining chairs to get to that side, Digby could see the defeat of the Armada, Sir Walter Raleigh and two different views of Drake on his circumnavigation of the earth aboard the Golden Hind.

And then he saw it. A copy of the painting by Nicholas Hilliard. There were Hudson and himself shaking hands across the river but as he got closer, he could see it wasn't an exact copy. The native people were in the same positions, sitting in their canoes and standing on the riverbank but their attitudes had changed profoundly. Hilliard had portrayed them as handsome, brave and happy. In this stylised interpretation they appeared to be angry and mischievous. Digby suspected this came as part of a specific instruction accompanying the commission. The result was a scene not of racial harmony but of conquerors and conquered.

'What do you think, Sir Everard?' beamed Chichester.

162

'I must admit it is a good likeness of Hudson and myself,' he replied. 'But I've always felt it not quite right to have an opinion when I'm part of the scene depicted.' It was the best evasive answer he could think of in the few seconds he had to make it.

'Ah well, I'm happy anyway,' said Chichester. 'This is the first time I've had one of the subjects standing next to one of my paintings. At least since Sir Walter Raleigh visited me some years ago, although that was in Carrickfergus Castle, not here. This reminds me, Sir Everard. That is exactly where we're going. I'm planning to dine with another gentleman, a fellow planter, and sleep over at Carrickfergus tonight. I'd be delighted for you to join us. We can talk of the woes and opportunities in Ireland in my carriage and review the topic over supper. How does this fit with your plans and timescales?'

'Perfectly,' replied Digby.

#

'You can't really think you're suitable to be an earl,' said the man in the language of the Irish.

'Why not?' asked Conn. He looked hurt.

'Because you give a shite about ordinary folk like us. You carry that bag around with you and give what's in it to the people, rather than take from us like everybody else. You're more a saint than an earl.'

Conn didn't reply but he was moved by the words.

'And you mustn't forget,' added the man, 'that there's hundreds of people around here, perhaps even thousands of us, who'll rise up, fight and die for you if we have to do. We may live in groups of fives and tens but put us all together and we'll create an army you'd be proud of.'

'I'm proud enough already.' said Conn. 'And I don't want to see anyone fighting and dying. Least of all you, Donal. Now, won't you get me something to eat? The smell of that mutton broth your good lady is cooking is driving me to distraction.'

Donal laughed and nodded to the woman of the cottage. She came over and ladled lumps of the stew onto one of the rough rounded bowls and passed it to Conn along with the largest of the dumplings. After serving her husband, she shared out what was left equally between herself and the four children. Every one of them sat as close as they could to the small peat fire and ate their food with their bowls on their knees.

To Conn this was what Ireland was about. The people and landscape. Warmth from the fire, bravery and good men and women, some living in green havens and others in barren, windswept spots. The sunshine, high winds, crashing seas, the rain, he loved it all. Who'd want to sit at a table in Rome in the heat, drink wine and talk of things you'd never do if you could sit here where it really mattered.

Conn O'Neill was the real Earl of Tyrone and these were his people. He'd die for them if he had to but he'd didn't want them to die for him. Sitting there with a bowl of mutton stew on his lap he swore to himself he'd never betray them.

#

Sir Arthur Chichester smiled at Digby. The other's man eyes looked heavy. His whole body seemed tired. They'd not been in the coach for more than half a mile when Digby began to drift off. The rhythmic motion of the wheels and the rutted tracks saw to that. The movement was uncomfortable but soothing at the same time. For once the needs of the body took precedence over the mind. Chichester spoke but he knew Digby wasn't taking in what he said. The man's brain was shutting down and consciousness overcoming him.

When Digby fell into what appeared to be a deep and dreamless sleep, Chichester shook his head. He wasn't surprised the man was exhausted. Coming back from the dead took some doing. And twice at that. He was aware of the attempted sinking of Digby's ship and knew snippets of what had followed. The former Lord Lieutenant of Ireland realised he had a delicate challenge on his hands - how to solve a problem like Digby?

The letter he'd received from his friend on the Privy Council had alerted him to the threat. The soft brained axis of do-gooders made up of the Queen and her advisors, Suffolk and Northumberland, was at last turning its attention towards Ireland. Since the King's death, Chichester had had a free hand on this side of the Irish Sea. As long as he kept things quiet and didn't ask for too much money, they left him alone. London's focus had been elsewhere and so the plans for plantation had progressed despite contradicting the new tolerance laws on the mainland.

It was unbelievable really. Catholics killed the King and how were they punished? Not by their destruction, apart from for a few of the ringleaders, but by allowing them to practice their faith without fear of fine or imprisonment. For the men who'd fought the Nine Years War against the Papist Catholics of Ireland, these new laws were a betrayal.

So many things mixed up in people's minds. Religion, nationality, politics, but to Sir Arthur Chichester, it was simple. There could be no peace. The Irish had killed his brother, they

164

were robbers and murderers. Once the plantations were established and the Irish displaced, there could be no going back. The Protestants in Ireland had to get on with their work and make progress quickly.

During the last few weeks Chichester had arranged meetings with many of the other plantation leaders. His message to each had been straight forward - accelerate and they can not fail, dilly-dally and everything they'd worked so hard for could be taken away from them. If they were not careful, the land they owned and worked would be returned to the murderous bastards who they'd forced into the wilderness.

Sir Arthur looked at the hedgerows on either side of the track. With armed men to protect the carriage he should be safe but they were out there somewhere even now. Men like Conn O'Neill, the self-styled Earl of Tyrone. Did the man think he was some sort of Robin Hood? Even if O'Neill had heard the stories of the outlaw from Nottinghamshire didn't he realise that's all they were? Stories. Tales of a bandit with ideas above his station. The Irish were bandits alright, bandits waiting for the chance to slaughter every God-fearing Protestant in Ireland and kick their decapitated heads around the sheep folds and pig fields. Just as they'd done with his brother. He'd never forgive them.

Chichester's mind went back to Digby. If only he'd entered Belfast quietly and nobody knew he was there. That's how spies were supposed to behave. One of his men could have slipped a dagger into his back and bundled him onto the floor of the coach. Chichester would have happily tossed his body into the sea on his way to Carrickfergus himself. Confound the man for wanting to be the centre of attention and entering the town in the style he had. Discarding his clothes and diving into the river! Who did he think he was, Sir Francis Drake?

Too many people knew he was here. As a consequence it was going to be difficult to dispose of him but Chichester had an idea. If he could persuade Digby to travel with him to meet the new Deputy St John in Longford, it would be a simple task to stage his murder by some desperate Irishman. They could even point the finger at Conn O'Neill. What would Queen Busy Lizzie think then? Her man in Ireland murdered by the Irish. It might frighten her enough to focus on what she should be doing, which everyone in their right mind knew was finding a husband, getting wed and having babies. Sir Arthur decided he would confer with his dinner guest in private later that evening.

#

An early October dusk was beginning to fall when they reached Carrickfergus Castle. As the carriage pulled up at the iron gates in front of the building, Chichester was careful not to disturb Digby from his slumber. He opened and closed the wooden door carefully and walked off into the impressive buildings. A short time later Digby stirred and attempted to shake the sleep from his head. He stepped down from the vehicle and looked around. Two guards stood next to the coach. They nodded good evening as Digby enjoyed the view from the castle.

The incoming tide had already reached the rocks beneath. He took in the sounds of the waves, smell of the sea and taste of the salt in the air. The ocean always reminded him of different places, some faraway, some nearer to home. Blueish grey waves crashed down and surged forward before receding back in a much repeated pattern. The sea wall was blackened as if by flames, whilst sea gulls hovered overhead hoping to spot food amongst the to-ing and fro-ing.

The castle stood at the water's edge. Half of its perimeter was surrounded by water. This provided the fortress with natural protection from attack on two sides. The high walls provided vantage points over the adjacent land. Until recently Carrickfergus Castle had been the main fortification in the area but that was before Chichester had brought forward his plans for Belfast.

Digby knew that Scotland was only about twenty miles away from Ulster at its nearest point. He'd walked further than that in the past few days. It was obvious Chichester intended Belfast as a new gateway into Ireland, one which he personally controlled. If he could create a monopoly on customs and excise for goods coming in and out through the port, he'd earn himself and his descendants a great deal of money.

The freshness of the ocean breeze felt good on Digby's face. It whipped through his hair and slapped his cheeks, returning him quickly to full consciousness. He'd made a mistake by letting his guard down and falling asleep but he'd been exhausted and the rest had done him good. Luckily he'd not been murdered before he woke, and for once he hadn't dreamed either. He remained thankful for both non-events.

Overhead a few stars were glinting. He recognised the planets of Jupiter and Venus. They were in close alignment. Even as a man with no time for astrology he wondered what this meant for his future. To the north the moon was rising also, pushing itself above the cliffs of the headland. The skies were clear and there would likely be a frost, the first of the season. It would be a cold few hours for those who lived in the crofts and cottages. Digby wondered where Conn O'Neill was hiding that evening.

An armed guard stood by the gate. The man held a pike against the wall in one hand and a lantern in the other. When Digby approached, the lantern pointed to the door. Digby was observed through the spy hole and the door opened. Once he'd walked through, a thick bar was placed across the entrance to keep it shut. He acknowledged the man on the gate and walked to the centre of the keep. Digby was now beyond the high stone walls and inside the castle's ramparts. When he reached a second door another man assisted his entry.

Once inside this door he was within the main accommodation and living quarters. A footman accompanied Digby through a gloomy but roomy hallway towards the centre of the building. The two men walked down a corridor and then stepped up a set of winding stairs until they reached the first floor where Digby was shown into a guest bedchamber.

Before leaving him, the footman looked at Digby sideways and lengthways. Digby felt the man's eyes scan him slowly from head to toe.

'Are you an undertaker, man?' Digby asking indignantly.

'Why no, sir,' the footman replied. 'I'm not taking your coffin measurements. My master asked me to estimate your size, so I can find you some suitable gentleman's clothing to wear at dinner.'

After living roughly in the same garments for over a week, the sight of fresh bedsheets and opportunity to wear two sets of clean clothes in one day appeared to Digby to be the height of luxury. He was shortly informed the master was busy for the time being but would be ready for supper in approximately an hour's time. One of the castle's staff would be along to collect Digby when it was time to dine.

Some time later a set of evening clothes arrived. Digby put these on and for the first time for some days he felt the gentle massage of a ruff around his throat. A further period of time passed and there was a knock on the door. Shortly afterwards he was led to the castle's dining hall. This was smaller and more intimate than the huge room in Chichester's building in Belfast.

By now it was dark outside and the room was illuminated by a series of tall candles set in holders. These were positioned on the table and in a number of recesses built into the thick stone walls. A large log fire crackled and threw out heat from

167

one side of the room. The walls weren't adorned with paintings but a series of large animal heads were on show as hunting trophies. Digby inspected the staring eyes of the poor slain creatures. He concluded they were originals rather than faked imitations. He'd only witnessed the art of the taxidermist once before, and was suitably impressed.

The fine oak table was set for three people. One place was at the head of table. This was at the opposite end of the room to the glowing heat of the fire. The other two settings were positioned facing each other adjacent to the table's end. For a few moments Digby stood in the room alone but it wasn't long before a second door opened, enabling him to peer into a small study beyond. A beaming Sir Arthur Chichester interrupted his view and walked into the dining room. In his hand he held an expensive glass goblet with ruby red liquid inside.

Behind Chichester stood a second man. Chichester introduced Digby and the man to each other. The second dinner guest was announced as none other than Michael Obins. Digby attempted to hide the rush of surprise at meeting the planter he'd clashed with and only just escaped from near Portadown.

There was no hint of recognition or surprise in Obins's eyes as he shook Digby firmly by the hand. Obins was a thick-set man, with the handshake some men use to impose themselves onto others. When it was over, they took their places at the table. Digby subtly flexed his fingers behind his back in an attempt to get the circulation flowing once more.

'It's very good to meet you, Sir Everard,' said Obins as he sat down. 'But I feel I already know you.'

'How is that?' asked Digby. He masked his concern with a smile and looked into the eyes of the man sitting opposite him.

'From the painting in Belfast, of course. Where you discovered Hudson and saved him from the hands of those savages. It was quite a remarkable feat. Do they really slice men's scalps right off their heads?'

'I've heard such stories,' replied Digby. 'But never seen it myself. Many of the natives are good men. You'd be surprised how much like us they are.'

'Surely not?' said Chichester joining in with the conversation.

Obins' eyes remained on Digby's face as the other man spoke.

'What I mean,' Digby said, 'is there are good natives and bad natives. Some are our friends. Others are allied with the French and our enemies. A few of the tribes shun any contact with Europeans, perceiving us as alien invaders from another world.'

'But they're all heathens, aren't they?' asked Obins. 'Worse than the Papists. At least they know of God and Jesus despite their fascinations with all things Latin and Pope-ish.'

Digby wondered if he was being deliberately needled. He speculated whether the men knew he was a Catholic, even a lapsed one. He was about to speak of the work of others to convert some of the native Americans to Christianity when Chichester stepped in and diverted the conversation into a different direction.

'My wife, who unfortunately cannot join us this evening,' said Chichester, 'asked me to ask you about the latest fashions in London. She has heard men of the court no longer wear ruffs but prefer whisk collars. If this correct? If so I must apologise for my man's choice of clothes for you, but over here in Ulster we like to keep traditions alive.'

'You must forgive me, Sir Arthur,' replied Digby. 'I know little about fashion. I fear I have spent too much time away at sea and in the Americas.'

'Not to worry,' said Chichester. 'I think there's one thing both Michael and I would be interested in. Have you met the Queen?'

'Aye, I have,' replied Digby, wondering where Chichester was going with this.

'Is she as beautiful as people say? I once saw her when I was visiting London but she was only a girl then. She must be a woman now.'

'I've seen her a few times these past few months,' said Digby. 'I was a guest at her Majesty's twenty-first birthday celebrations. She looked quite splendid.'

'Because she is,' said Obins. 'She is the Queen of England and Ireland after all. God save the Queen!'

He pushed back his chair, scratching the stone floor, and stood to attention. The others followed suit. The servants waiting on the table behind them each took a step back

'God save the Queen!' said Chichester and they all raised their glasses.

'God save the Queen!' This time all three men said the words together and took a drink.

When they sat down the conversation became less strained. Chichester led the way, talking and listening with interest as if he was a father pleased to have his favourite sons back at home. The meal was superb. If Digby's diet had lacked protein for the last few days, the chicken, venison, lamb and beef he consumed over the next two hours made up for it. The goblet in his hand was frequently refreshed and the conversation flowed.

'The war was a nasty business,' said Chichester, 'I was glad I only took part in the final third. The things some of those Irishmen did.'

'And the idiocy is they've been rewarded for it,' added Obins. 'When the peace came, King James was far too generous to the losers. Some land was granted to the veterans of the war but much initially was retained by the Irish. A lot more than any loser should expect to receive. And still they wouldn't be happy, Their leaders continued to fight amongst themselves, and plot and pick on the English and Scots who lived with them in Ireland at every opportunity.'

'In Ulster,' Chichester remarked, 'I oversaw the peace myself. Minor rebellions and uprisings popped up all the time but we quickly repulsed them. Even though their leaders had abandoned them, the Irish people still keep up with their feisty behaviour. This being the case, they shouldn't be surprised when their lands are taken from them.'

Digby kept his counsel, deliberately allowing his dinner guests to dominate the conversation.

'At the end of the day, the Irish have a victim culture, Sir Everard,' said Chichester summing up. 'They act in ways which encourage their subjugation and then complain about it. It's astonishing really but I've talked enough. We should get Master Obins's views. Michael, do share with us your personal experiences over there in Portadown.'

'There's little to add to what we've already spoken of, Sir Arthur,' said Obins. 'I bought the lands around Portadown in good faith. I was the third English owner there. I wasn't responsible for any of the confiscations but the Irish appear to view me as the Devil incarnate. They pull down my fences, steal my cattle and attack my men. All this despite the fact I give them a good income and homes to live in. Without my charity, many of them would starve.

'They work for me in the fields and farms or on the construction of houses for the good English families I've brought with me from across the water. I've allowed the Irish to rent out cottages and crofts, as long as they're not too near my own people's lodgings. But the status quo cannot go on. We can't live in constant fear for our lives. My view is we shall soon reach a position where we'll have imported sufficient planters and will then need to move the Irish on.'

'Where to?' asked Digby.

'To the wilder lands to the west,' replied Obins. 'The Atlantic coast. They can live there. They'll be out of our way. Of course they can build new homes to live in, we can sell them grain and sheep so they won't starve and perhaps provide troops to police them and save them from themselves.'

'It's a wonderful idea,' said Chichester. 'Such a humane solution to the Irish problem. I hear the new Lord Deputy is keen on this approach too. What did he call the special places they would live in, Michael?'

'Reservations,' replied Obins.

'That's right,' said Chichester. 'Reservations. What do you think of this idea, Sir Everard? It is something you can recommend to your queen when you return to London?'

Digby hoped the colour in his face from the wine and food hadn't completely left his complexion. He suddenly felt drained. On some points during the evening the two men may have been correct. In his view the Irish didn't always help themselves or act as they should have but if his lands had been taken from him, he would have reacted badly too. The ideas they were now proposing were an abomination. What these men wished to achieve was evil.

What was even worse to Digby was he could see the approach used in Ireland being repeated elsewhere. Perhaps beginning with his beloved Americas. The natives would be exploited, worked, marginalised and the few who survived the treatment and diseases introduced by the Europeans would be moved on as soon as they were no longer of use to the settlers, the planters of America. The reservations these men talked of were prison camps in the people's own lands.

'It is an interesting idea,' he said. 'But I fear I am getting too tired to share my opinion. This last week has taken some of the vigour out of me. I must thank you, Sir Arthur, for your wonderful hospitality, and you both for the excellent conversation. It has been a fine meal and a fascinating evening but I think I should bid you both goodnight and retire to my bedchamber.

'Very understandable,' said Sir Arthur. 'But we do have one further suggestion for you.'

'Oh yes?' said Digby.

'Michael is leaving us on Wednesday to return with supplies to Portadown,' said Sir Arthur. 'From there he has a

171

need to take a journey over to Longford. We both think it would be a splendid idea if you could accompany him and meet up with the Lord Deputy St John on his estate. Michael will take you to his door and escort you back to Belfast. You can rest up tomorrow before the trip. What do you think?'

'I think it's a splendid idea,' said Digby. 'But I need to return to England to make my report to the Earl of Suffolk and the Queen, so I don't think it will be possible.'

'Oh, come on man,' interjected Obins. 'It will be a fast journey. We have strong wagons or you can ride. I understand you are a powerful horseman. It won't be slow like your walk from Dundalk and it will give you a chance to better understand Ireland. Is that not a key element of your mission?'

'It is,' said Digby. 'How can I refuse such a generous offer? It would be splendid to see more of the country and hold a conference with Lord Deputy St John.'

Chapter XXII

'No, yes, yes, yes, no, yes, yes, yes, no, yes, definitely not. Can't we halt this for a time?' asked Elizabeth. 'I'm getting tired.'

'I suppose so,' replied her mother.

The two women had been reviewing a list of potential invitees to the masque the Queen Mother was planning to hold in a month's time. She'd told her daughter that numbers needed to be confirmed and invitations issued. People had to make plans. Anne loved helping her writer Ben Jonson prepare for his productions.

'There are so many things to do,' said Anne to herself. 'It's a nightmare at times.'

'No, Mother,' said her daughter. 'It's not a nightmare. Alliances between the Spanish and French, the failure of the grain harvest, Puritans rioting against the tolerance laws, outbreaks of plague. These are nightmares. What you talk of is but a daydream in the garden. You must remember that.'

They sat alone in a small room at one side of the Queen's main chambers in Whitehall Palace. Elizabeth had come to London to spend a few days at the royal court. Her mother wanted her to listen to petitions, dine at the royal table and generally be seen by her people. Elizabeth hated these aspects of her royal duty. They appeared to be trivial in a world where there was so much to be done.

Anne was spending a little time with her daughter before the day's session in court in the hope Elizabeth would take out her frustrations on herself rather than her courtiers. The Queen Mother knew it wasn't easy to bear the strains of monarchy. They'd always been a mixed blessing. She'd seen it with her husband, James. In Scotland his royal responsibilities were the making of him. In England they'd led to his death and that of her sons too. A day didn't go by when she didn't think about Henry and little Charles.

There was a knock on the door. Anne Dudley waited patiently outside until asked to enter. She'd brought a message from the earls of Suffolk and Northumberland. They'd arrived together to see the Queen, apparently with news from Ireland. Elizabeth rose to her feet and left the room immediately. She walked along the beautifully decorated and furnished corridors in the company of four palace guards and three ladies-in-waiting to a side meeting room. As she entered she recognised the look of bad news and saw the aura of death on the faces of her closest advisers.

Their mood was sober. The two men held their hats in their hands and looked at their feet. Both knew how much the mission meant to Elizabeth. She'd wanted to achieve something historic in Ireland. It appeared her first attempt had failed. The Queen thought of the smiling face of Digby depicted in Hilliard's picture. He shouldn't have been in the painting but it was so very good. The man her father had knighted early on in his reign had wanted nothing more than to return to the Americas but she'd wiped that smile off his face and ordered him to Ireland.

'It's Digby, isn't it?' she said. 'How did he die?'

'We believe he was murdered by Irish bandits, Your Majesty,' replied Suffolk. 'Perhaps they were tipped off by their fellow Catholics, the Jesuits, or the French. At the moment we don't know. He was ambushed with his Scots guide in the fields outside Dundalk. The body of the guide Hamilton was found at the bottom of a well, stabbed in the back. The Dundalk militia have found Digby's clothes covered in blood stains but not yet his body. The search continues but there can be little doubt. I'm sorry.'

Elizabeth held her face straight, determined to prevent any tears. This was no time for emotion. She didn't want the men in front of her to mistake her feelings for female weakness. She had to be strong.

'Very well,' she said. 'He knew the risks. Put in place a pension for his family. Write a letter to his wife. Say that he died bravely in the service of queen and country, you know the sort of thing. I have duties in court for the rest of the week but the three of us should get together early next week to verify who to send next. When will Raleigh be back from El Dorado? My plans for Ireland will succeed. That is all. You are dismissed.'

Suffolk couldn't remember the Queen acting in such a brusque manner before. He left the chamber beside Northumberland without speaking. It was obvious she'd taken the news badly. Suffolk regretted telling Her Majesty she was sending Digby on a suicide mission. The Queen's mind had already been made up, and it would have been better not to inform her of the risks she took with the man's life. Two men's lives. They shouldn't forget Hamilton. He'd ensure Hamilton's next of kin, if he had one, would be contacted and offered a pension too.

When they left the room, Elizabeth beckoned Anne Dudley to come inside and close the door. Once her friend was with her, the Queen buried her face into her chest and cried quietly, not to be heard from outside. Anne held Elizabeth close, stroking her hair as a comfort. She'd done the same when they were young, when the Scots princess was sent away by her father to live in the Midlands with the Dudley family in her own embryonic royal household.

Elizabeth had no special feelings for Digby, although he'd appeared a decent man. The tears she cried weren't for him. They were for herself and the vision she'd created in her mind from Hilliard's painting. A happy coming together of her people and the natives they encountered on their adventures. A different way to create an empire, one which integrated nations rather than enslaved them.

After a few moments she stopped crying and wiped the tears from her face. This dream wouldn't die with Digby. She'd try again. They'd find another envoy and send him instead. And they'd do it again and again until they succeeded. And they would succeed. In years to come it was this determination which would change the direction of her nation and eventually the world.

#

'Of course Digby is still alive,' said Button to one of his officers. 'The man's a survivor. He's spent time on a naval vessel, just like you and me, and what's more, the stupid sod is as 'ard as nails when he needs to be. Did I tell you about the time he wrestled with a snowy white bear to save my life?'

Button paused to check his men were listening. 'Our boat was stuck in the ice pack and a few of us went off to search for signs of land. We camped overnight on the ice and this white monster attacked our tents. I was knocked clean out by the beast's first blow. I didn't have a clue what was going on but Digby fought the bear off and it ran away. The thing must 'ave weighed a ton by all accounts. 'illiard could have painted that, with me as the 'ero fighting off the bear and Digby fast asleep. Then we'd have been quits.'

Button laughed his loudest Welsh laugh. The *Sixth of November* was anchored off the Irish coast near Larne close-to but invisible from Carrickfergus. A few moments ago Button gave orders to sail. He wanted to get in and out of the harbour as quickly as possible and hopefully with at least two of the men he'd been tasked to pick up.

He'd heard the news about the death of Digby and the discovery of Hamilton's body but there was still no evidence of Digby's corpse. Until there was proof, Button remained confident. He'd pick up the Englishman and an Irishman from Carrickfergus and that Englishman would be Digby. He was sure of it. An Irishman, an Englishman and a Welshman, all on a boat off the coast of Ulster. There was a joke in there somewhere, he thought, but it would have to wait.

Digby was always getting himself into scrapes but he could get out of them too, thought Button, especially when he was on his own and didn't have Button around to save him. If Button wasn't about, Digby had no choice. He had to make an effort. In those circumstances Button was confident he could look after himself. You daft English idiot, thought Button, stay alive.

#

Conn gifted his clothes to a poor Irish family. He was now wearing a suit of planter's attire. He'd been told the man who used to wear it was a bruiser who had no further use for the clothing. He pulled the tunic down a little further to cover up the dark purple patch of dried blood as he walked past the small rough-looking buildings outside the town. These were the homes of the Irish workers.

As he passed unchallenged through the open gates into the little town of Carrickfergus, he whistled a Scots folk song to fit it with the locals. He couldn't believe he'd got away with walking into Dundalk to meet Digby and now he was doing the same again. Crossing his fingers, he hoped his luck would hold out for a second time.

The town was quiet that morning. Within the walls were a number of densely populated, multi-storey houses and a few terraced single-floor homes. The streets were dotted with businesses and services; Conn walked past two taverns and an ironmonger's shop. Each street had a narrow waste channel to one side running downhill to the sea, where the debris from human life washed away or rotted. In the quieter spots, the odd rat or gull sorted through the rubbish in search of something to eat.

To Conn's right there was a row of detached cottages. They were larger than the other dwellings, as each belonged to one of the wealthier families, but even these were within a stone's throw of their poorer neighbours' lodgings. There wasn't much space within the township walls, everything was packed tightly inside.

176

A small dock and harbour ran alongside the narrow sea front. Conn could see why Chichester had wanted to expand into Belfast. There was insufficient capacity here for what he wanted to do. Small fishing boats rocked up and down in their moorings as they mirrored the rhythm of the sea. There wasn't much space for bigger ships.

The far harbour wall was where he'd arranged to meet Digby. At least the Englishman had managed to slip out of Belfast alive. He'd been seen by Conn's watchers stepping into the carriage alongside Sir Arthur Chichester, two days before.

Conn's task now was to find somewhere unobtrusive to wait. He knew it must be around eleven o'clock. Before long there should be a bigger boat coming into port. He'd never been to England and wondered what it would be like. For a brief moment it hit him, he was going away again. He was leaving Ireland. Was this his own little Flight of the Earls? But then he relaxed. He was not going far or for long. He'd say what needed to be said to the English Queen, make the right negotiations, and return home.

#

Digby had spent the previous day looking out to sea thinking and sleeping in equal turns. Chichester and Obins had been busy with their work and he'd dined alone at twelve and more surprisingly been on his own for supper at seven that evening. Perhaps they couldn't face speaking further with a man they planned to kill. Perhaps they were genuinely busy. A few messages came to him in the bedchamber or as he strolled around the castle grounds. All was well. He should be ready by eleven in the morning. That sort of thing.

This gave him an hour to prevaricate before the boat arrived. His mind searched for excuses of why he had to miss the trip to Longford with Obins. He believed if he went he wouldn't get anywhere near the Irish Midlands. They'd attempt to do him in somewhere between Belfast and Portadown. He shivered, Perhaps they'd already dug a shallow grave for his body.

There was a knock on the bedroom door.

'Sir Everard, the carriage has arrived.'

Digby opened the door. One of Chichester's men stood waiting for him.

'Where is Sir Arthur?' asked Digby.

'The master has sent you a message from Belfast, sir,' said the servant. 'He apologises but his business has kept him in town. He wishes you well for your journey and asks if he doesn't

177

see you again before you set sail for England, you pass his personal regards onto the Queen when you return to London.'

It appeared Chichester was already distancing himself from Digby's departure.

'Excellent,' said Digby. 'Most kind. Please pass a message back to your master assuring him I will fully apprise the Queen of his work in Ireland.'

'Very good, sir.'

'By the way, where is Master Obins?' asked Digby.

'He is in the carriage, sir, along with three of his men. You can't be too careful these days,' replied the servant. 'He says you must depart immediately in case the good weather changes and rain slows the wagon's progress.'

Digby turned towards the room but realised he had no bag to collect. His only possessions were the purse in his pocket and the clothes on his back. Even those weren't his own. He accompanied the servant to the ground floor. They walked through the hallway and then went out through the door of the keep into the sunshine. From there they crossed the courtyard and passed through the thick walls through the gate to where the carriage was waiting.

Obins stood outside the coach with two guards. The third sat at the front ready to drive the horses. Digby fancied he recognised one of the men as the one he'd punched in the kidneys to prevent him beating Conn.

'Ah, good. There you are, Sir Everard,' said Obins. 'Jump in. We must be off as soon as possible.'

'I'm afraid I can't come with you,' said Digby. 'I must speak to Sir Arthur about something important before I leave. I'd hoped I would see him yesterday or earlier this morning, but now I'm told he is in Belfast. I shall have to wait here until he returns. I must apologise. Please don't let me delay your departure.'

'Not at all,' replied Obins. 'If you need to see Sir Arthur, we can take you to Belfast Castle on the way. Most of the road is en route anyway. It's not a problem, jump in.'

'What a good idea,' said Digby.

Reluctantly, he climbed up the side and stepped into the interior of the vehicle. When he sat down he was facing forwards. The three other men joined him. Obins sat directly opposite. There was only a single door to Digby's far side and the two guards took their places between this and their master and his guest. The driver released the brake, shook the reins and slowly they set off. The rhythm of wheels on the track was as it had been on the way over from Belfast but there was no way in the world Digby would fall asleep this time.

The carriage negotiated the entrance wall at the side of the castle with a series of slight bumps and jerks. With the sea to their left the coach pulled out along the harbour road and entered the town. Digby looked past the guards and through the unglazed window of the door. The sky and sea were the colour of sparkling blue. In the distance Digby was sure he could see a tiny sail. It could be Button's ship. Next to the harbour stood a man who appeared to be a planter with brown hair. To Digby's surprise, when the man turned, he recognised Conn. Unfortunately the surprised look on his face alerted the guard who was sitting next to Obins.

'There's the Irish bastard who broke Davey's ribs,' shouted the guard pointing towards Conn. 'Master, we must get him.'

The driver heard the shouting and began to slow the wagon down. Obins looked at Conn and considered his position. 'No,' he said. 'Drive on!'

'But, master.'

'I said no.'

At this point, Conn began to run, crossing the square diagonally towards the gate. Digby suspected his friend had seen him in the carriage.

'Faster!' instructed Obins.

As Obins was on the opposite side to the window, the driver couldn't hear what was said. He slowed the carriage further in direct contradiction to his master's orders. Obins's thinking was clear to Digby - he'd like to get Conn O'Neill but his priority was to ensure that he, Digby, didn't return to London. They could kill Conn another time.

'I said faster, you idiot!' he shouted in a louder voice still. This time the driver understood.

Digby noticed the guard next to him was staring at his face with malice. He wondered if the bruises on the man's back were aching badly and he felt every jolt the wheels made on the cobbles. He hoped so. The man pulled out a knife but he was a fraction too late. Digby had already swung away himself across the carriage towards Obins. Despite Obins's strength, Digby pushed, elbowed and manoevoured himself behind him until he held him by the throat.

'One wrong move and I'll twist his neck until it breaks,' he said, catching his breath.

The only flaw in his plan was he was now even further away from the door, but at least he'd developed an advantage.

'Get off me!' screamed Obins, as he attempted to wrestle his body free. 'Have you gone mad, Sir Everard? What are you doing?'

'Have you heard the sound of a neck as it breaks, Michael?' asked Digby quietly. 'I have.'

Obins ceased struggling.

'Sir Everard, I must again ask what are you doing. This is not the behaviour of an English gentleman.'

'He's no gentleman,' sneered the guard who'd pulled the blade.

'Shut up!' ordered Obins. 'Sir Everard, explain yourself.'

'Halt the coach,' said Digby, 'or God help me, I'll break your neck, here and now. You'd put me in the ground soon enough, given half a chance. Now, halt the coach.'

Digby tightened his grip.

'Call the driver,' Obins hissed to his men.

'Driver, slow down,' shouted one.

The carriage slowed as it neared the end of the square. This was just before it reached the terraced streets which led to the town's main gates, the only entrance wide enough for a large wheeled vehicle to exit. Having pulled back the reins, the driver applied the brake further. As the coach steadied, Conn appeared alongside the carriage door. Standing on tip-toes he observed the stand-off inside. The driver turned and recognised the Irishman.

'Sir, it's one of the O'Neills,' he shouted from the front of the coach, unaware of what was happening inside.

'We know that, you idiot,' said the guard who'd been bruised in Portadown.

'Now, this is what's going to happen, boys,' said Digby to the two guards inside who by now were both holding knives. 'You're going to get out and behave yourselves and not touch the Irishman.'

Obins nodded but his eyes flashed wildly left to right. Digby's guard wasn't sure what this meant but the other understood. As the door opened, Digby shouted to Conn.

'Get back to the harbour, Conn. Get us a small boat and I'll join you shortly.'

Conn turned and jogged his way back across the square. There weren't many people mulling around Carrickfergus but the few who were stared at the coach. Still gripping Obins, Digby moved his body around so he was now sat to the door side of

180

the planters' leader. He reached his left hand to the window's opening and pulled the door shut. As he did so he spotted one of the guards but not the other.

'Driver,' called Digby. 'Take the carriage back around the square to the gangplank by the harbour wall.'

The coach didn't move. Digby tightened and then loosened his grip on Obins's throat.

'Do it!' Obins hissed.

They heard the brakes release. The coach lurched forward. The mechanism of the wheels creaked slowly as the vehicle progressed. When they were half way across the square a bell started ringing. It was the town's warning bell used to highlight threats of attack. Men would be coming from every direction. Leaning forward, Digby could see the man ringing it was one of Obins's guards. He'd understood his master's signal.

Obins used the movement to free himself. With his head released, he tried to butt Digby's face. Digby reacted quickly. The rest in the castle had done him good. His forearm blocked the attack. With a right hook, he struck Obins in the midriff. Shaking off the blow, in his rage the planter raised his thumbs to gouge Digby's eyes but Digby punched him again. This time he threw a right, which hit home hard. Both men heard Obins's jaw break apart. His head rocked backwards. The fight was over.

The wagon was now two thirds of the way across the square. Digby swung the door open and jumped onto the road. One of the guards was waiting for him there. The man dived forward to prevent Digby's escape. Digby fell, and the guard followed through. Digby shifted to his left, whilst the guard's momentum carried him forward. They both hit the cobbles. Digby used the guard's shoulder to break his fall. The guard tumbled, and his head bounced with blood spurting out. He rolled over senseless.

The second guard stopped ringing the bell and charged towards them. Having heard the alarm, other men came forward. The coachman twisted the direction of the horses and turned the coach through a narrow circle. With the wheels half spinning, sparks flew into the air, as the rims ran on their edges for a few seconds as the carriage turned.

The driver aimed the horses at Digby's running body. Another man was about to catch him. Digby dodged and threw himself across the road. The coach missed him, but one of the horses knocked over his pursuer. The man was dragged under. Multiple hooves struck him. Two cartwheels struck his prone body. After this the horses panicked, and the driver frantically

181

attempted to apply the brakes. The coach span madly around the square.

Digby saw his chance and dashed for the harbour wall. Five men were chasing him now, including the bell-ringing guard but they were some way behind. Digby raced along the gangplank to reach Conn, but he groaned when he realised Conn didn't have a way with knots. He hadn't been able to get a boat free. Abandoning the idea of a boat, both men accelerated along the planking towards the open sea at the end of the boarding. Digby discarded his tunic and cloak as he ran. When they reached the edge of the water he pulled off his boots, but Conn waited and remained fully clothed. With their pursuers just yards behind them the Irishman looked at the water nervously.

A blade came close to Digby's face. He stepped sideways. In a deliberate act he pushed Conn backwards. Both men tumbled over and hit the water simultaneously, their bodies making a large and inelegant splash. At least they were out of reach of the knives. When he surfaced, Digby looked around but he couldn't see Conn.

Digby pushed his face back into the water. The sea beneath him was disturbed by the Irishman's flailing arms. Conn was being dragged to the depths by his waterlogged boots. Realising it would take an effort to reach him, Digby lifted his head and took a deep breath before dipping once more beneath the surface. Pushing himself down, he reached out for Conn. There was panic in his friend's eyes. Digby pointed to his feet but Conn shook his head wildly. His mouth was open and it appeared he was taking in water.

With bursting lungs Digby forced his body lower. He pulled himself down Conn's legs until he reached his ankles. It wasn't easy but somehow he managed to extract first the left and then the right boot. The drag on the Irishman was greatly reduced. Once this was done, Digby kicked his feet and hauled his friend back up to the surface. When their heads broke water, Conn coughed and spluttered but took in air. Digby pulled off Conn's outer clothes.

The pair had been lucky. The outgoing tide had taken their bodies further away from the land. By now Conn had enough buoyancy to float on his own. Digby scanned the scene as they drifted further out to sea. A crowd was gathering on the quayside, including Obins. Despite his broken jaw, he shouted furiously at the men around him.

A few things alarmed Digby. A second group of Protestants were walking along the gangplank carrying fishing gaffs and pikes. They were selecting a boat but there was an even more immediate danger at the end of the pier. Two men were kneeling down, carefully loading a pair of matchlock firearms brought from the town's arsenal. When they'd finished loading their guns they would light the fuses which enabled the mechanisms to fire.

'Come on, Conn,' said Digby. 'We have to swim further out.'

'That's easy for you to say,' coughed Conn. 'Further out? I can't swim at all. I've not been in the water before and I can't say I like it that much.'

'You're doing fine,' said Digby encouragingly. 'Like an Irish duck to water. You've been floating here with no trouble at all. You just need to kick out so we can move along.'

A loud bang sounded. This was followed by a fizz in the air and a splash. A patch of water bubbled up too close to their bodies for comfort. The first musket-man had missed but the second was already raising the gun to his shoulder to take aim.

'I don't like that much either,' said Conn. 'I'll give it a go, so I will.'

Bang, fizzle. The second splash was even closer but there was an audible groan from the harbour when it missed. It would take the men time to reload. Digby took a loose hold of one of Conn's arms to aid his confidence and the two men swam slowly away from the land. When a third and eventually fourth shot fell far short of the men in the water, the firearms were abandoned.

All focus was now on the boat. When this was launched it was too heavy in the water, almost sinking due to the weight of the men on board. Obins arrived at the scene and ordered several of the would-be sailors off the vessel to make the boat navigable and create enough room for he himself to board. He took hold of a fishing pole.

Obins stood at the bow of the boat, and adopted a pose not unlike Hilliard's depiction of Digby. On his orders the men behind started to row. The boat moved in the direction of Conn and Digby, too rapidly for then to swim away from it. As the vessel neared, several men raised their pikes and gaffs in anticipation. It wouldn't be long before the two men in the water would be within their reach.

Several of the men snarled and sneered at the swimmers. It was like the lynch mob in Belfast all over again, thought Digby, but this time he wouldn't be able to bluff his way past them. He considered his options. It might be possible to

183

escape several attacks and frustrate them by submerging and swimming underwater but this wouldn't work for Conn. He'd be an easy target.

'Have I ever told you about the time me and my friend were followed by a wolf in the mountains in Spain?' said Conn.

'What? No,' said Digby as he pulled at the water whilst watching the boat come nearer.

'I told the other guy I was going to put my boots on,' Conn continued. 'He told me not to be stupid, I'd never outrun a wolf. I said that was true but I could probably outrun him.'

'It's an old joke,' said Digby. 'And I've heard it before. What's your point?' He was impressed by how well Conn was swimming considering it was his first time. He was a fast learner but it wouldn't be enough.

'You know what I'm saying,' said Conn. 'You can't out-swim that boat but you can out-swim me. If they go for me alone, it'll buy you some time.'

Digby understood but he shook his head.

'You know another old saying?' asked Digby.

'Which one?'

Before he could answer a mighty blast shook the water around them. Even as the small boat approached a much larger vessel was coming in from the port bow. It was still some way off but it had made its intentions clear by firing a warning shot from one of its cannons.

'Button,' said Digby.

He realised his friend wouldn't be able to see who was being attacked in the water but he'd be able to hazard a guess. Damn the man, thought Digby, he's saved me again.

From their spot in the sea water, Digby and Conn watched as Obins ordered his men to retreat to the shore.

'He'll have no wish to be blown out of the water,' said Conn.

'Nor be caught red-handed trying to kill an agent of the Queen,' agreed Digby. 'He'll be working on his excuses already. He'll probably say when it became obvious I was collaborating with the infamous outlaw O'Neill, they thought I must be an imposter. But my likeness to the main in Hilliard's painting alone should be enough to hang him.'

'What painting?' said Conn, confused.

'Never mind about that,' laughed Digby, 'but whatever you do, don't mention it to Button.'

With one hand gripping each other's shoulder, they began swimming towards the incoming naval vessel. A few

184

minutes later they were hauled onto the deck of the *Sixth of November*. Digby wasn't at all surprised when they were greeted by the sound of Button's booming laughter.

'I know, I know,' said Digby. 'You don't have to go on about it but at least it was more than a few moments this time.' He wrapped himself in a by now all too familiar ship's blanket.

Button bowed. 'Is there anything else we can do for you, Sir Everard?'

Digby shook his head but smiled. 'Just set sail for England will you, you old Welsh bastard. I think I've had my fill of Ireland for now.'

Conn looked longingly back towards the castle, cliffs and coast behind them. Digby frowned for a moment. He understood what the Irishman was thinking, Conn was leaving his beloved Ireland to travel to England. Was it the right thing to do, or was just another fleeing Irish earl?

Chapter XXIII

The watchers outside the French spies' house on Love Lane noticed movement. Linda Blanchet and two of her male counterparts were leaving the house by the main entrance. They walked together and headed along the road in the direction of Thames Street. Carr decided to follow them and took three of the men with him. Two others were left behind to watch the house.

Carr suspected Linda was well aware the house was being watched; none of those inside had travelled far that week. When they'd ventured outside they'd been followed but not once had they visited a place of interest, unless they were involved in a conspiracy centred around butchers, bakers, candle-stick makers and the like.

For the last few days Linda remained in the house. Carr wondered what she was planning, this attractive woman who worked in a deadly trade. With her back in his sights he acted quickly and split his team into two. Each man would take a turn to follow closer up and then back off in the hope it would limit the chance of recognition. Carr and the man he considered to be his apprentice, John Fletcher, walked at the back behind the others.

Linda and the two Frenchmen turned left onto Thames Street. The road took them east in the direction of the Tower but they didn't stay on the street for very long. Instead, they took a sharp right into Billingsgate. This was the busiest landing place in the whole of London for fish, shellfish and much else besides. The place was a hive of activity, crowded with people buying, selling and moving between the dockside trading houses.

Carr was intrigued. Why would Madam Blanchet visit Billingsgate? It wasn't a place where ordinary people bought goods but a wholesale market where buyers and sellers traded commodities. In the centre there was a huge open area, populated with a myriad of stalls where catches and harvests were put on display before being sold and boxed for transport. The morning was the busiest time of the day. The smell of fish and the noise from the traders and barrow boys as they swirled around threatened to overload Carr's senses.

Maybe she had come this way to meet a contact or make a trade, thought Carr. Or perhaps this was the place where secret messages were delivered to French agents in London. Fresh secrets twice a week, all the way from Paris. He considered how convenient it would be to bring messages in by boat to a location not half a mile from where she and her spies lived and worked. For a moment Carr dared to dream they'd stumbled onto something important.

Apart from the river, there was only one way in or out. Carr nodded at the two men ahead to continue, and held a quick conference with Fletcher to agree what to do next. Once this was done they positioned themselves subtly inside two doorways, not quite opposite each other on either side of the entry point into the market area from Thames Street, near the entrance to St Mary's Hill.

Linda smiled, but she was almost disappointed. It was all too easy. She'd expected more of a challenge from the Englishmen. The three spies strode through the stalls and pushed people aside to get nearer to the quayside and the river.

Linda didn't shrink from the stares and leers she sometimes received in the street. She enjoyed them, as long as men didn't touch her. She made one man leap back and almost fall over when she pretended to bite him when he got too close. Men. So much bluster but most of them were just timid fools. At times like this she missed her husband the most. He was gone but she would never allow herself to become a widow people felt sorry for. Linda was more than capable of surviving in a man's world.

When they'd almost reached the quayside, Linda nodded her head sideways to the right. One of the men joined her. The pair of them jinked down out of sight and entered a tented area hidden from the outside world, erected to protect oranges and other fruit from the London frosts.

The rich citrus aroma inside the tarpaulin was intoxicating and a world away from the fish stink of Billingsgate or the street sewage of London. The air filled with unworldly delicate fragrance. When she retired, Linda decided she'd move to a chateau in the countryside in France and have an orangery of her own. It would be worth it, even if she had to marry a rich bastard to make it work. She smiled. It would be easy enough to make herself a widow not too long after the wedding if she deemed it necessary.

After a few moments the man who'd come with her left the tent. Linda remained. When he returned there was blood on his knife. He nodded. She smiled. There was a scream from the direction of the quay. Heavy footsteps pounded across the cobbles outside and a flood of people came rushing past the tent. The crowd was obviously getting larger.

A shout went up. 'Murder!'

'Here, quickly! Two men are dead!'

'There goes one of the killers.'

'He's heading to Somar's Quay.'

'Stop that boat - it's leaving.'

'Stop him!'

Carr despatched Fletcher to the quayside. He pushed his way through the crowd, ignoring all the swearing and shoving. His face joined fifty others in a moat of fascination around two dead bodies. Fletcher immediately recognised his colleagues. They'd been stabbed in the back. They were too close together, he thought. If they'd remained spread out perhaps one would still be alive. But nobody could teach them spy-craft now.

Fletcher reversed himself and forced his way out of the throng. A dozen people pointed and shouted at the river. He followed their gaze. One of the Frenchmen was standing at the stern of a small boat, as bold as brass as if he wanted to be seen. Fletcher couldn't see the woman or the other man but assumed they must be on board. The best thing he could do now was to report back to Carr, he thought, but then he thought again. Carr had taught him well. Instead of going back to his leader, he made a show of asking people what they'd seen and what the attackers of the two men looked like.

After a short time Linda was satisfied that any watchers who'd previously followed them would have shown themselves when they'd heard the shouting and seen the bodies of their colleagues. As she peeped through a rip in the tent fabric she could see there was only one of them out there and he was asking questions of the crowd.

She put her arm in the arm of her remaining colleague. They slipped out of the orange tent on the far side and walked boldly back through the stalls and onto Thames Street in the manner of a married couple. As they walked up the road they carefully checked each doorway and alcove and subtly swept the streets behind and ahead with their eyes. All appeared to be clear.

As they walked away from Love Lane, eventually they turned into Harper Street. After navigating a series of corners and making several abrupt turns, they stepped onto Marte Lane. Linda and the Frenchman approached the top half of the street, and with one last glance the pair entered the door of an inn. Carr watched from afar and waited.

Inside the inn, the Frenchman asked for a room for his wife and himself, on as a high floor as possible. The top room was vacant and so he paid to secure it for the next week. The innkeeper asked why they had no bags. The Frenchman said they'd be bringing them later. They took their key and went to the room. After watching for a few minutes Carr grabbed a boy off the street and gave him a coin, with the promise of another, if he would go to Love Lane and give a message to his men.

#

The Earl of Suffolk sat at his desk in his familiar office in Whitehall. Will Carr sat on the other side. Both men watched as the Earl of Northumberland stood by the window and looked down onto the courtyard. Finally he turned to face the others.

'So, you think the Blanchet woman is holed up with one of her men in this inn in Marte Lane?' he asked.

'Yes, my lord,' said Carr, turning to face him. 'I saw them enter the building myself. We've moved the watching operation over from Love Lane. Both the henchman and Madam Blanchet have been seen at a window in one of the attic rooms.'

'This time with her clothes on, I hope?'

'Aye, my lord,' replied Carr. 'Fully dressed, all in black.'

'What do you think she's playing at?' he asked.

'I believe Madam Blanchet became aware of the watch on the house in Love Lane and decided to make a run for it,' said Carr. 'We think in normal circumstances she would have left London by now, but it's possible she's waiting for orders or for something to happen. But what that might be we just don't know.'

'Do you think she knows we're still watching her?' asked Northumberland.

'I don't think so, my lord,' said Carr. 'There's more cover on Marte Lane and the watchers are well hidden. Blanchet and her accomplice have not left the building, so they haven't had the chance to spot anybody following them. Fletcher, the man leading the operation, is very good.'

'What do you think we should do?' asked Northumberland.

'Wait, my lord. Let's see what they do. We may flush out even more French spies,' said Carr. 'And find out what they're up to.'

'I'm afraid I disagree,' replied Northumberland tersely. 'We've waited long enough. I think we should go in there without delay and detain them. They're killers, after all. What do you think, Thomas?'

'Yes, the time for waiting is over,' agreed Suffolk. 'Blast the French and their plots against us. Carr, I want you to personally lead the raid. Go in there at first light and bring Madam Blanchet and her associate out. I want them taken to the Tower, dead or alive.'

'Very well, my lord,' said Carr, even though he felt they were making a mistake.

#

It was dark in Marte Lane. With no inside man to gain entry, they'd have to pick a lock or break the doors down. They'd try the former first. Crouched alongside Carr in the shadows at the back of the inn was a seasoned professional of the criminal variety. Unluckily for this lock picker, he'd been caught once too often. His liberty now depended on the occasional unorthodox job like this one.

Carr glanced at the windows in the walls of the inn above. Everything was black. All was quiet, but Carr was frustrated. The work on the lock was taking too long. They should have had the door open by now. The locksmith continued to twist his wrist back and forth without success. Carr wondered how long their luck would hold out.

There was movement in the alley behind them. A sack of vegetable peelings fell over. Carr turned. He couldn't see anything but he heard the scratching sound of a rat scurrying away, whilst on the roof above birds had already begun to chirp a pre-dawn chorus. The animal kingdom was waking. It would be the humans next.

Carr hoped they wouldn't have to force the doors. Fletcher was stationed across the road with six armed men and a battering log. Discounting the lock-picker, Carr had four more, and another group of soldiers had taken positions further up and down the street.

The burglar reached for something inside his bag, careful not to jangle his tools. This time he appeared happier. Despite the dim light, Carr recognised the makings of a smile. There was a click and then another. The tiny noises appeared deafening in the quiet but the lock was sprung.

Gently Carr lifted himself to his feet and raised the latch. He pushed the door gently. There was no resistance, the back door wasn't bolted. Inside there was nothing but darkness and the smell of yesterday's cooking. Carr crept into the hallway and beckoned his men to follow. The lock man's job was done. He picked up his bag and slipped away.

The five men edged along the corridor, feeling their way as they went. They passed a set of double doors to the kitchen and an open entrance to the dining room. The dark shapes and shadows within all remained still. After this there were two bed chamber rooms with closed doors. And then the main stairs which led to the rooms above. He didn't know which room the landlord stayed in, or which rooms had paying guests.

A set of hurried words broke the silence. Carr and his men froze. They listened. The sounds came from behind one of the bedroom doors. One of the soldiers raised his weapon. The noise repeated itself, only more loudly this time. But then it stopped and was gone. The men strained their ears. They could almost hear the hush of the darkness around them. For a few seconds there was a sensory vacuum. Nothing could be seen, felt or heard.

Every nerve in Carr's body strained. He could feel his heart beating. He listened. The silence was broken as a voice spoke out. Muttering, rambling, incoherent words. Angry at first but then increasingly sad until the words petered out. The conversation ceased. All was calm again. Quieter then louder. The pattern repeated itself, and the noises became recognisable as a man dreaming. The group moved on.

They passed two corners as they moved along the corridor and finally reached a second much steeper stairwell. Carr believed this led to the attic rooms. Everything appeared to be quiet. While his men waited, Carr pressed on. He reached the front door of the building and drew back two long iron bolts built into the sturdy door. As he did so he pulled the door inwards gently to limit the scraping sounds of metal on wood but the door didn't move.

He felt with his hand along the wall and hoped he was right. Yes! There was a hook. He liberated a keyring. Thankfully there was a single key attached to it. After three blind attempts he prodded the key directly into its hole. Two turns and a click later and the door was unlocked. All was ready for Fletcher and his men to enter when the time was right.

The four soldiers and Carr crept up the stairs. Their main weaponry were short stabbing swords. Pikes were too unwieldy and firearms would take too long to load and reload in the limited space. Carr knew his men with him were being as quiet as they could but each stair seemed to loudly creak, as every tiny noise became exaggerated by the stillness of the dawn.

When they reached the top step, Carr couldn't see the men but they needed no telling. Their orders were clear. They breached both doors and two men charged into each of the rooms. One was empty. There were shouts from the other. Two loud bangs were heard in quick succession. In the cramped space the noise was deafening. Carr's brain reverberated around his skull.

After the initial commotion, Fletcher's men charged into the inn. Carr's protege led two of them up the stairs holding lamps. In the first room there was nothing. In the doorway of the second bed chamber a soldier could be seen lying on the floor with his eyes open, shot and stabbed. A long fine blade was still imbedded in his chest. He was clearly dead. Carr stepped over him. The atmosphere was thick with gun smoke, twisting in the air.

At the back of the room the male French spy lay bleeding to death with two smoking pistols on the floor in front of him, and the second soldier's sword imbedded in his torso. The soldier, himself, was also wounded. He held a bloody left shoulder but when he saw Carr he forced a grimaced smile and nodded to the window. It was open.

The smoke from the gunshots swirled in the draught. Carr stuck his head through the window and looked at the street below. There was pandemonium on Marte Lane. People had heard the gunshots and poured out of their homes to see what was going on in the dim light. Carr knew the men outside would be creating a cordon and blocking the entry and exit points around the inn.

From the corner of his eye he fancied he caught a movement along the rooftops. There was definitely something there. He looked again. Nothing moved. As he continued to scan, his eyes became more accustomed to the poor light. He made out a crouching figure, trying to remain small and still so not to be seen. The shape was dressed all in black. When it realised it was seen, the figure leapt up and began moving away.

'Fletcher!' shouted Carr, as he pulled himself onto the window ledge. 'I think Madam Blanchet's crossing the rooftops. I'm going out there after her. Get your men's matchlocks trained on the ledges along the road but for God's sake make sure they don't shoot me.'

Fletcher launched himself down the stairs to ready his men. At the same time Carr edged out onto the rafters. He took a first step across the angled rooftop. The surface was wet with dew. His foot slipped, and his body wobbled for a moment in the air. He tried to steady himself but he'd already lost his balance and began to fall. An empty feeling filled his stomach. Dropping to the street below would surely kill him.

It wasn't Will Carr's time to die. The man behind him leant through the window, and grabbed his tunic. Somehow it didn't tear and Carr ceased to fall. He jammed his foot into the wooden guttering and pulled himself up.

Without turning he issued his thanks and tried again. From then on Carr was much more careful. Once he'd realised his folly in attempting to walk on the wet and uneven surface, he crouched down on his hands and knees. The nails in the rafters provided secure footholds to push against.

The skyline of the buildings to the east was now a silhouette. It would soon be daylight. As Carr looked ahead, there was a scraping and a black on black movement. Linda Blanchet was out there ahead of him. As he recognised her shape, she jumped from one rooftop to the next.

Carr realised he was making too limited progress and Linda was getting away. The Frenchwoman was prepared to risk anything, but Carr had a wife and children. He wanted to live. Linda had nothing and nobody apart from herself. He wasn't a coward but he wasn't a fool either. Falling from the roof by forcing the pace wouldn't help anybody, but neither would Madam Blanchet getting away.

He had to give up the chase or throw caution to the wind. The memory of the soldier's blood-soaked body came back to him. His heart beat increased swiftly as he moved across the ridges and skipped over the tiles and clumps of thatch until he'd cut Linda's lead down by half. He hadn't fallen. He was still alive. He was getting closer.

The Frenchwoman looked over her shoulder, saw him and increased her pace. It was a risky call for both of them. Other than an occasional blur of movement, Carr couldn't see Linda Blanchet very clearly yet. He wondered how she managed to cross the roofs so freely. He reasoned her movement would be constrained by her feminine clothing. He didn't realise she was better dressed for the skyline pursuit than he.

Above her undergarments Linda wore a man's shirt, tunic and hose. She'd worn the same attire during the last few days in the inn. At night she'd kept the window ajar in case they needed to make a hasty exit. The foresight had served her well. She knew she'd need to be mobile if she had to take to her heels across the roofs. The selection of the attic rooms was deliberate. Linda recognised an escape route when she saw one.

193

The attack on the inn had been a surprise but equally she prided herself on her speed of reaction. Unlike her man Francois, she preferred not to use pistols. They were heavy and unwieldy. She preferred the quick response of a blade. She hadn't expected the English to pursue her over the rooftops. There was only one of them but she realised he was beginning to gain ground. She needed to speed up. It would be interesting to meet him, this man who was risking his life to catch her. Perhaps he wasn't like the other Englishmen. But he probably was. So dull and ordinary.

Above the corner of Marte Lane and Hart Street, Linda looked across the way. The road below caused a natural break in the roofline. She had no choice but to turn to the right. The gap was a fraction too big to leap across. Suddenly there was noise. A loud bang came from the street. Above Linda's head a chimney pot shattered. There was a groan of disappointment from the road below.

One of the soldiers had shot at her. Linda hesitated and leapt from the house she'd been standing on to the roofline across the way. Carr followed. Linda heard rather than saw him as he landed close behind her. She doubled her speed. It wasn't long before she reached another gap. This was the junction between Hart Street and Seething Lane. Without thinking she accelerated and hurled herself across the abyss. From her vantage point in midair she looked at the cobbles on the road. If she didn't make it the rounded stones would surely smash her.

On the other side Linda's body hit a patch of bristly thatch. It scratched at her arms and face but she gripped onto the thicker husks for all she was worth. Once she'd landed she hauled herself upwards. This time she wanted to go over to the far side of the houses to shield herself from the weaponry below. To do this she knew she'd be putting herself in danger. For a few moments she'd be in the line of fire. She trusted in the unreliability of English marksmen's weapons and hoped they'd miss. When she neared the top of the roofing two more loud booms rang out, and the thatch to her right shook with their impact.

She heard a man on the ground order the others to cease firing in case they hit the wrong target. Linda reached the apex of the roof and clambered over. She'd didn't look back. As she crossed the next roof she descended two levels, taking advantage of the slope and uneven designs of the buildings. With relief, she realised she was out of sight of the road below. It was time to drop to the ground and make her escape on foot.

There was one last set of tiles to clamber over. She felt the movement of the Englishman in pursuit.

Blood pumped through Carr's body. He didn't believe he would make the leap to Seething Lane but he had. He'd scratched his neck badly on the thatch and droplets of blood trailed behind him. When he'd heard the second and third gunshots ring out in he thought he might die but the shooting had stopped. Fletcher was a good man, he thought, but there was now a chance she'd get away.

He watched Linda as she clambered over the top of the roof and then crawled and pulled himself up the thatch towards her. Only once did his footing slip again. He fell thigh deep into the roofing, one leg trailing into a void of nothingness. He gripped the top thatch and hauled himself back up. He was unhurt but he'd lost too much time.

When he reached the top, he saw Linda. She'd used the slope to increase her lead over him and was now lowering herself onto the ground. She clambered down until she hung from the edge of the roof and allowed herself to drop to the garden below. Her body fell the final ten feet. She landed on a suitably soft pile of grass cuttings and compost. As she stood up, Carr saw her closely for the first time. He was clearly surprised by her male attire. Linda shook herself down, and began sprinting through an orchard.

The building ahead looked like a priory but Linda knew in England these were dissolved and their spoils shared by money grabbing Protestants. This one appeared no different. The high walls were complete but the roof was gone, but wooden rails and row upon row of small window panes protected the inside from the worst of the weather. Linda heard the barking of dogs in the distance. She tried a door handle. It was unlocked. She entered the building.

The air inside was warm and humid. The place was a glass house for growing plants not suited to the English climate. Linda had never seen anything like it before. The interior was laid out in a set of intricately linked corridors with raised beds, stacking and tables housing thousands of twisting green plants. England was a land of gardeners, she thought, the glass in the roof must have cost a fortune. Linda didn't have green fingers but she recognised the room gave her cover. If her pursuer hadn't seen her enter it would be a good place to hide.

Carr lost sight of Linda as she dodged through the apple and pear trees, but instinctively he followed her route. On the way down from the rooftops he too had landed on the compost and brushed away the rotting turnips and grass from his feet and legs. Where was she? He knew she'd come this way but had she rounded the next building or entered it? If she'd passed on he may have lost her. If she was inside he still had a chance. He had to go in.

The glass house was isolated from the main street. From the sound of the growling dogs at the fence beyond he surmised Linda had probably not gone that way. With only a slight hesitation he put his hand onto the greenhouse door. What was he worried about? She was only a woman, but Carr remembered the lifeless staring eyes from the dead soldier in the attic.

Linda edged further across the ground along one of the passageways. She twisted and turned into another. The route eventually split into two. From where she was she knew she couldn't be seen from the main entrance. She was surrounded by green leaves. The sounds made by the moving irrigation channels were everywhere. Water dripped from pipes along the ground and overhead like ticking clocks.

The door to the glasshouse opened. Linda wondered if or how she would get out of this place and whether she could do it without confronting the Englishman. Crawling further along she saw a second entrance in the far wall. This was attached to the exterior of one of the adjacent houses. She moved towards it. Gently she reached up her hand and tried the handle. The door was locked from the other side.

Linda crouched again. She could see the arches of the window holes in the old priory above. The wind was whistling through these where painted lead-glass panes had been. Which English Protestant noble had robbed the Church of these, she wondered. There was a creak behind her. The Englishman was moving towards her position, but not stealthily enough, she thought.

Carr dipped down low. As he moved along he glanced up each passageway. It was gloomy but the light levels were increasing. At first he saw no evidence of human movement, just hanging tendrils, greenery and shoots from a dozen types of succulent plants. But he kept searching for the smallest sign. And then he found one, a scrape mark from a foot in a heap of soil.

He looked more keenly. Upon closer inspection he saw the surface of the soil was slightly dry but the sides of the scrape were damp like the rest of the earth around him. The mark had been made recently and the footprint was small. The person who'd made it had a small foott. A woman's foot, a deadly woman's foot. He reached for his belt but jolted. His dagger was gone. He was no longer armed. During the chase he must have misplaced his knife.

Linda decided not to try to force the second door but wait for the man to come to her. She no longer had her usual blade but a jagged piece of broken glass fitted comfortably enough in the palm of her hand. One sharp strike at the man's throat and he'd be gone. She knew the exact location of the body's weak points as well as any physician.

For a second Carr stopped. He thought of his wife and children. Was he taking unnecessary risks with his life? Margaret wouldn't be able to cope on her own. William would be alright but not Sophia. She needed his help to find a place in a household where she'd be safe and not mistreated. For a moment a jumble of different pictures filled his imagination. The dead soldier upstairs, the watchers in Billingsgate, the bodies taken from the Thames, their throats gutted like fish. He tried to push these thoughts from his mind.

Chapter XXIV

Button oversaw the change of watch on the deck of the *Sixth of November*. He'd decided not to put Digby and Conn O'Neill ashore on the coast of Wales, Northern England or even Bristol. Instead he wanted to take the two men directly to London. It would take a little longer but he was convinced it was the best way to guarantee their safety.

They'd been at sea for almost a week. Unfavourable winds had limited their initial progress but they were now making good time travelling along the Kentish coast. At first light the look-out sighted the white cliffs of Dover and the crew gave a cheer.

For the first few days on board Digby and Conn hadn't talked very much. Perhaps they'd spent enough time in each other's company crossing Ulster but for the last twenty-four hours Digby had begun to brief Conn on the ways of English politics. Both men realised Conn may be in for a rough ride in England where Irishmen weren't popular.

The Irish were seen as people to put down rather than negotiate with. Digby hoped Elizabeth's vision of a modern and different future for the seventeenth century would be shared by others as well as himself. The policies of plantation, marginalisation and reservation were flawed. He could see this but were there so many vested interests to change

Conn knew he'd have to compromise. There would be things he'd need to accept which he disagreed with, for the good of his people. Acceptance of English, British, or whatever they were going to call it, law might be one. But if they could use that law to protect the Irish as much as the planters and if they could be given sufficient land and rights. If, if, if… He hoped something might be possible.

He knew he'd have to answer to those who questioned his very right to negotiate on behalf of Ireland. He wasn't officially the Earl of Tyrone and he wasn't even the only Conn O'Neill. What would the other Irish leaders say? Even if he could gain support and make progress, the whole thing could take years.

But what if he didn't? Accelerated plantation, decades of persecution and armed conflict. Perhaps one day they could achieve an independent Ireland but at what cost? How many of his people might starve or be forced to leave in the meantime? If there was a chance to make Ireland a better place for the people who lived there, he'd dedicate his life to making it happen.

#

The Queen sat up in bed. 'He's alive. I know it,' she said.

Elizabeth pulled a shawl around her shoulders and ran from her inner bed chamber. Outside her large dressing room were a series of smaller rooms where her ladies-in-waiting slept. Anne Dudley had a room of her own. It was the closest to the Queen's. Elizabeth knocked on the door and burst in. Anne woke immediately.

'What is it, Your Majesty?' Anne asked.

'Digby!' said Elizabeth. 'He's alive. I know it.'

'But how, Your Majesty?' asked Anne. 'Has there been a messenger? Is there news from Ireland?'

'No,' said Elizabeth. 'I've just had a dream. He was on a boat, just like the one in the picture from the Americas and this time it really was him. On the far side of the boat was a man wearing green who must be from Ireland.'

Anne wondered how she was going to break it gently to Elizabeth that this was just a dream. Digby was dead. Everybody said so. She'd console her again when they received confirmation. Anne knew Elizabeth was troubled by what had happened in the last few weeks but to say everything was well because of a dream was almost madness. She checked her thinking, such thoughts were treason.

'Come on, Anne,' said Elizabeth. 'Don't look at me like that. I know what you're thinking. It's just a dream. Yes, but it was so real and, and, and, I wasn't sure whether to tell you or not but he spoke to me.'

'Who did?' asked Anne, still sitting on the bed with the Queen beside her.

A few of the other ladies had been disturbed by the excited talk and stood in the doorway but Anne's was the only opinion Elizabeth cared about. She only kept the others on because of her mother's concerns about tradition. Elizabeth reassured them everything was alright. They should go back to bed. She closed the door and sat back down next to Anne.

'Digby, Sir Everard Digby. He spoke to me.'

'What did he say?'

'He was in the picture, standing on the boat shaking the Irishman's hand, when all of a sudden the picture came alive. Digby turned his head, looked at me and said *Don't worry, my*

199

queen, I've had a few scrapes but I'm fine. As I expected, you were right about Ireland and I've found a man we can do business with.' but the funny thing is, and this is me talking now rather than Digby, I couldn't see the other man's face. So we'll have to wait and see what he looks like when they get here. I had to tell you, Anne, so the dream wouldn't fade away. Now I've spoken about it I can still see them both. Digby and the man in green. What do you think?'

'If it's true then it's marvellous but, as you say, we'll have to wait and see.'

Elizabeth shook her head. 'It's alright, Anne, I know you don't believe a word of it and I probably wouldn't in your place but it was so lifelike. I think it must be true.'

#

Will Carr edged along the greenhouse passageway. He found a brick and held it tightly in his hand. Carefully he stepped forward. He tried to tread as lightly as possible. Every now and then he bent down to the ground and scanned for signs of movement beneath the tables. As he stared through the trailing leaves, he was conscious of the location of both doors. He didn't want Linda to sneak past him and begin the chase again.

Meanwhile Linda had moved to a new hiding place, not far from the inner doorway into the buildings beyond. Hidden in a corner she remained in a crouching position. Concealed by a stack of wooden trays she was ready to move at a moment's notice.

Linda's viewing angle was limited but she could see the building's high walls towering over the surrounding houses and gardens. Ten or twelve feet from the floor, an intricate grid of wooden beams had been constructed and inserted into the framework of the building. These held hundreds of narrow glass frames which sheltered the greenhouse and plants below. Only the English could close down a place of worship and replace it with a plant nursery, she thought.

On closer inspection, it was clear the myriad of glazed panels above her head had seen better days. A number of the beams sagged. In some places whole rows of the windows bent inwards. Some of the panes were cracked and one or two were broken. The priory had been built to last millennia, it would easily outlive the greenhouse within its walls. One big storm, thought Linda, and the whole glass house would come crashing down.

There was a scrape. Fifteen feet from her hiding place Carr gently pushed aside a box of soil. He peeped beneath the tables. If the Frenchwoman was there she was well hidden.

200

Perhaps she was sitting tight for him to come close, so she could strike. Did she have a knife, he wondered?

From her unseen position Linda appreciated the Englishman was being thorough in his search. He appeared to be exploring each alcove and passageway. From the small sounds she calculated he was checking every potential hiding place before moving on. Maybe he was the one who'd discovered Francois and herself in Marte Lane? If so, how had he done it, she wondered.

Carr approached from the left. He moved slowly towards her. Another dour Englishman. If he moved and checked the far side to her right it might be possible to get past him without confrontation. The thing that mattered most was to stay alive long enough to be sure Digby was dead.

There was another noise. This wasn't good. The man was close. It would more likely be fight than flight now. She caressed the glass in her hand. The jagged edge would cut deep. She'd go for his neck. The blunter side of the shard fitted neatly into the palm of her hand. If she was careful and held it correctly, she wouldn't injure herself when she struck.

There would be no time to watch him die. She'd work out the best route to avoid the dogs and leave the place quickly. The streets would be crawling with soldiers by now. As if to prove the point there was a rattle behind the door and a shout.

'Is anybody on the other side of this door?' called a voice.

'Fletcher, is that you?' replied Carr.

'Yes, sir. I have two soldiers with me. What's going on?'

'I'm behind the door, inside a large glass house. I believe Madam Blanchet is here too but she's hiding. I think she may be close to the door in front of you. Give me a moment, and I'll return to the entrance to the gardens so she can't escape. Get your men to load their matchlocks and come in.'

'The door is locked, sir.'

'Break it down if you have to. I want the three of you to spread out and look for her. If you can catch her alive that's good but shoot her dead if you have too. She's dangerous. Don't take any risks. After everything that's happened, we can't allow her to escape. Do you understand?'

'Yes, sir,' said Fletcher. 'Hold on.'

Carr backtracked through the greenery towards the other door. As he did so, he called out to the Frenchwoman.

'Madam Blanchet! Escape is impossible. If you stand up and raise your hands, we'll arrest you. You'll not be harmed. I give you my word. This is your last chance. My men are coming and they saw what you did to their comrades. They'll fire on you without blinking.'

Do your worst, thought Linda. She remained hidden.

A key could not be found for the door so the soldiers kicked it in with their boots. The rows of window panes and fragile roof timbers above Linda's head shook with each blow. Finally the wooden panelled entrance gave way and the three men stepped into the glass house. The two soldiers moved forward with Fletcher behind them. He remained in front of the doorway to ensure she couldn't get past.

'One of you go down each corridor,' Carr shouted over to them. 'Fletcher, you make sure you guard that door.'

As Carr had suspected, Linda's hiding place was near to the door of the buildings. The first soldier didn't have to take a dozen steps to reach her. Linda leapt out and surprised him. He lifted his gun to shoot. She knocked the barrel upwards. He fired. The second soldier let loose with his own firearm. He shot wildly above the table tops. The combined noise of the two blasts in the confined space was deafening.

The low ceiling shook. The first shot flared up and struck the rafters, the only things holding the glass above their heads. The world stood still. Gun smoke hovered. For a heartbeat it appeared the roof would hold. Fletcher stepped forwards. Carr watched on. They heard a crack. Everyone looked up. The ceiling began to crack. Strips of timber splintered, fractured and concertinaed. The window panes broke. Thousands of pieces of glass shattered onto the ground.

The noise was tremendous. The roof caved in. Wave after wave of window panes rose up and then crashed to earth. The rafters rippled like wooden blocks on a xylophone. Carr stepped back and moved behind the door. As he did so the ground in front of him filled with deadly shards. The sound of crashing glass was everywhere. It was almost musical. The soldiers took the brunt. Fletcher was hit by a piece of falling wood which knocked him backwards through the door unconscious. If he'd fallen forward he'd have died.

Linda dived beneath the body of the first soldier, and held him close for all she was worth. He died saving her life. The noise stopped. She pushed the corpse aside, rose and fled. Leaving the mayhem behind she stepped past Fletcher and ran into the interior of the house. Carr could only watch. She'd taken a few steps across the glass filled floor. He'd have to take fifty paces to pursue her by which time, despite his boots, his feet would be cut to shreds. Two more men were dead. Another was injured. Linda Blanchet was gone.

Chapter XXV

'These plans aren't just good, Master Jones,' said the Queen Mother. 'They're a master piece. The Queen's House in Greenwich will be the building you'll be famous for, for all eternity. See this project through to fruition and you'll be remembered as an architect of the greatest distinction. Don't you agree, my dear?'

The Queen's mind was elsewhere. As they walked through the grounds of Greenwich Palace surrounded by guards, footmen and ladies-in-waiting, the spectre of Ireland clouded her thoughts. Even Inigo Jones couldn't cheer her up.

Jones and the Queen Mother continued their conversation. Elizabeth heard a few individual words - *classical, Roman, cube-shaped, Palladian, helical stairs, Renaissance* - but nothing in between. None of it made sense. She held Anne Dudley's hand, pleased her friend was with her. They'd said nothing more about the dream. It had come to nothing.

A cannon boomed in the air from a passing ship. They sometimes did this when passing Greenwich Palace as a show of respect for the monarch. Elizabeth wished they wouldn't. It was far too loud.

There was a flurry of boots behind the group, and Jones, the two Annes and Elizabeth turned to see what was causing the commotion. An officer from the Queen's guard ran towards them. As he approached the royal party he interrupted their stroll.

'Your Majesty.' He bowed. 'Ladies, Master Jones. I have no wish to alarm you but the ship which fired just now has issued a rowing boat which is coming ashore on this side of the river. As you know, this is strictly forbidden. I've dispatched a squad of men to the riverside to intercept them. I'm sure it will come to nothing but I respectfully request Your Majesty accompanies myself and my men to the fortified section of the palace.'

Due to recent rumours and problems with the Puritans, French and Jesuits, the Queen's guard was on high alert. The officer appeared doubly keen to ensure nothing went amiss on his watch. The Queen, the other women and Jones did what was asked of them and followed the officer to the palace. Once inside, they were taken to a suite of comfortable rooms, strategically positioned within the stronghold area.

The officer locked the doors. He inspected the guards. It would take a small army to get past them. Once he was satisfied he relaxed a little. All they had to do now was wait and watch events unfold.

#

'I keep telling you, my name is Admiral Button,' Button repeated again.

He was sitting in the rowing boat he'd launched from the side of the *Sixth of November* a few minutes earlier. A row of troops watched him through gun positions and arrow slits. They viewed Button and his companions with suspicion. Each of the three men in the boat was being carefully lined up in the sights of multiple firearms. The gun barrels had to constantly move up and down in time with the ebb and flow of the water. On-shore cannon were aimed and ready to fire at the larger vessel in the middle of the deep river channel behind them.

'Look at my ship,' said Button. 'You can see it's an English naval vessel. I fly the royal ensign and bring official visitors for the Queen herself.'

The *Sixth of November* had already begun to leave the scene. Button watched with pride. Not many deep-hulled vessels could get this far up the river. He'd managed to exploit an agreeably high tide. Button had inherited a skilled and experienced crew. They were just about managing to manoeuvre the boat around without running it aground. The vessel was turning seaward. He'd given his crew orders to navigate back up the channel to Woolwich docks and wait for him there.

'You're lucky we didn't fire our cannon and sink you,' replied the second officer of the day. 'You can't land here like this. It's not allowed.'

'I understand that,' said Button. 'But you must let us come ashore. I bring two special envoys who must see the Queen.'

'I won't permit it,' cried the officer.

The plushly uniformed man stood on the special ramparts which had been built above the riverside. They were designed for defence against waterborne attack but nobody had expected they'd need to use them in anger. The navy would stop any enemy vessel long before it got this far up the Thames but the boat which faced them now was one of their own.

Digby stood up. He waved to the officer, with something in his hand.

'Please see Her Majesty receives this letter at once. I am her agent. I work for the Queen and for the Earls of Suffolk and Northumberland.'

The officer could see the man had a letter in his hand. Interesting he should mention Suffolk and Northumberland. They were both due at the palace for meetings later in the day. Perhaps, he should see what his commander had to say on the matter. If he passed the letter on, the responsibility for making a decision might pass along with it.

'Come closer,' he said. 'Continue to watch them, men.'

Button steered the rowing boat to the side until the wooden planking of the little vessel collided gently with the stone wall built into the riverside. The officer reached through a gun slit and took the letter. He dispatched one of his men to take it and ask for advice from his superior. Once this was done, the officer instructed Button to row back away from the wall and maintain his previous position in the river. Button did this. After a while he began to feel the strain on his arms and shoulders from having to row simply to stand still against the tide.

A short while later they heard a flurry of excitement from behind the ramparts. Half a dozen soldiers whispered or exclaimed 'Her Majesty!'. A head peered over the ramparts and looked down at the scene. The face lit up for a moment when its owner saw the occupants of the boat, but after this Elizabeth's countenance became calm and dignified. She was a queen of twenty one years of age after all, not some giddy girl.

'Sir Everard,' she said elegantly. 'We've received reports of your death. Do I understand, in fact, you are alive?'

'Very much so, Your Majesty.'

'Excellent,' said Elizabeth. 'I'll send word to London immediately.'

'Yes, Your Majesty, I agree. It would be beneficial if we can hold a conference with yourself and the Earls of Suffolk and Northumberland as soon as possible.'

'No,' she said. 'I didn't mean that. In any case they're already on their way. I want to send a message to Master Hilliard,' she replied. 'We must make another commission for him. But tell me, why have you returned to London in such an unorthodox manner? Do you simply like posing for paintings?'

Button pushed Digby aside for a moment.

'Your Majesty.' He bowed. 'I am afraid this is all my fault. I wanted to deliver Digby and this other fellow to you quietly and discretely.'

'It's Admiral Button, isn't it?' said the Queen. 'I'm afraid you have failed in your attempt, Admiral. Unless, of course, you consider causing alarm and the issuing of reinforcements to the palace to be discrete?'

Elizabeth beamed down at the men from behind the protection of the fortified position above the river. She was struggling to contain her elation but there was somebody else down there too. She looked at the back of the boat. Yes, there was a third man. A little jaded and wild looking. He wasn't dressed in green but he must be Irish, surely? This must be the man who'd been selected to speak on behalf of his people in the coming talks. As she observed the man she detected a glint in his eye as he looked back up at her.

'And who is this other fellow with you?' she asked.

'A very good friend of mine and a nobleman from Ireland, Your Majesty,' said Digby.

'Then the three of you had better land your boat, come ashore and enter the palace,' said Elizabeth. 'I've no idea why you've stayed out there treading water for so long. I tried rowing on the Thames near Windsor once. It was hard work. Admiral Button, your arms must be killing you by now. For goodness sake, come ashore.'

The boat was hauled in. By the time the trio had crossed the ramparts the Queen had already departed. She wanted to find a quiet room, get Anne Dudley in there and squeal as loudly as she could with delight. Her dream had come true after all. Digby was alive and he'd brought back an Irish leader to do business with.

Button, Digby and Conn O'Neill trailed along the grass. The second officer of the watch led the way, flanked on both sides by half a dozen soldiers. Each man carried a pike on his shoulder. Digby nodded to Conn.

'Welcome to England.'

'Thanks,' said Conn. 'Are things always this entertaining when you and Button get together?'

#

After the gunshots, collapsing glass and mayhem surrounding her escape, Linda had intended to abandon the city but the glass splinters in her feet were giving her too much trouble. As she approached a row of ramshackle houses she felt herself slowing down considerably. It was time to weigh up her options.

She was just few yards from the entrance to the city walls at Aldgate. This area was a conundrum. In some places there were the fine buildings of the rich and in others jumbles of rundown abodes such as the ones she now faced.

An old man emerged from a door and came onto the street from the second house. As he did so he saw Linda struggling towards him. Out of kindness and charity he asked what was wrong. Linda stopped, looked around and hopped over towards him.

With a slight surprise he realised Linda was a woman and not a man as he'd assumed. There was definitely something different about her, he thought. As she approached his doorway Linda took a second glance up and down the street. Seeing all was clear and no-one was watching, she pushed the elderly fellow inside and quickly followed. With a sigh of relief, she closed the door behind them.

The elderly man was taken aback. Within another minute he was dead. Linda could see from the state of the room the man lived alone. No woman, she reasoned, would live in a hovel like this. If he'd once had a wife she was long gone. She dragged the man's body to the back of the room and placed two old sacks over him.

For the next few minutes she searched his belongings for anything of value or practical use. There was little else Linda could do for now. She found and pocketed a few coins the dead man had hidden away. She bundled the rest of his belongings together and heaped them over his body.

Her stomach rumbled. She was hungry. It would be good to go for a walk and get some food but she daren't risk it. In any case her feet hurt too much. There wasn't much food in the house but she ate the remains of yesterday's bread, smeared with butter and the man's last few lumps of cheese. There was no wine but she found an almost full keg of ale and a small half bottle of some spirit or other.

Linda cleaned out a wooden drinking vessel with her fingers and poured spirit into it. A pleasing warming sensation hit her stomach. She followed this with a larger drink of beer and checked her feet. Carefully she removed a slither of glass. Blood dripped from the wound. Linda hoped this was what had hampered her walking. She trickled spirit onto the sole of each foot. There was pain but she figured it would do her good.

A few hours cooped up in a hovel like this would be enough for anyone but she needed to stay hidden, and spent the rest of the day dreaming of her return to France. The hours dragged by but eventually darkness came as it always did and she slept, bedded down on a shelf which served as seat and bed, covered with a reasonably clean blanket.

The next morning Linda remembered was Friday. She would go out and buy some fish. It was unlikely they'd still be searching for her in this area with no obvious French connections. Later on she'd cook the fish on the fire. What a ridiculous superstition it was that people thought Friday the 13th was unlucky. It was just another day. Linda wasn't superstitious and she deserved a little fish. Unlucky for the fish but lucky for her, she thought. She ate fish every Friday, whether it was the 13th or not. She wondered if the old man had liked fish.

The nearby doorways would need to be clear when she left. She didn't want to attract attention. If she could avoid the neighbours she'd be safe. No English spy would search for her here, living the life of an urban peasant. She wouldn't stay for long but how long would that be? It would be good to return to France and enjoy proper wine, good food and decent conversation. She just needed to confirm Digby was dead.

#

The initial meetings went better than they could have imagined, except perhaps for Elizabeth. For her the unlikely future of Ireland they talked of was meant to be. Digby had opened the discussion by describing his epic walk across Ulster with Conn O'Neill. He spoke of the environs of Dundalk, Portadown, Belfast and the beautiful countryside in between.

Eloquently he positioned the plight of the Irish, contrasting this with the ambition and ruthlessness of the planters. For balance he put over the Protestant settlers' side of the story and spoke of the genuine reasons behind their fear and distrust, highlighting the fate of Hamilton as an act of savagery which Conn had been powerless to prevent.

Conn agreed with many of the points being made but didn't speak, even when he disagreed with Digby or viewed things in a different light. They trusted each other and this was the approach they'd agreed upon during their final hours aboard the *Sixth of November*. Digby completed his outline with the latest attempt on his life. Although this was carried out by Obins, he said, the sponsorship for it surely came from the former Lord Deputy Chichester.

Digby praised Conn O'Neill as a prime example of a noble Irishman. Here was a man, he said, who'd saved his life on numerous occasions during the week. He also praised

Button's pivotal role at the start and the end of their Irish adventure. Without these men, he said, he would be as dead as they'd all believed him to be. All apart from one, thought Elizabeth.

He saved his last words to make the case for the bigger picture. England and Elizabeth's new Britain, he said, were about to start on a great adventure around the globe. As it did so, it must learn from the mistakes made in Ireland. Surely empires aren't simply about conquest and slavery? They should focus on creating economic benefits for the Queen and her subjects but also enlightenment and empowerment for those they encountered. Digby concluded by saying there were better ways than plantation - both in Ireland and further afield.

Conn took to the floor. He spoke passionately of the intolerable impositions placed upon the Irish by one-sided English law. He asked how anybody, even a queen, could justify the land grabs, the wages, the food prices. Every day they placed an ever-increasing squeeze upon his people.

Bowing his head for a moment, he apologised personally for what had happened to Hamilton. After this he admitted some of the Irish had been guilty of crimes and wrong-doing but was there not murder and robbery in England? There was in every country, he said, but it was always worse where the people of a land were driven to desperate straits.

Elizabeth listened, mostly in silence. A number of times she was clearly aghast at news of crimes committed in the name of her crown. She barely spoke at all for the first few hours, although Suffolk and Northumberland asking pertinent questions during the discourse on her behalf. The earls grilled Digby and Conn whenever they felt the two men strayed too far from the facts or offered personal opinions. They expertly probed the words of the knight and the Irish fellow, teasing out additional information where they could.

The Irishman spoke as highly of Digby as the Englishman had of himself. He talked of times his own life had been saved. Once from the beating by Obins' men near Portadown and the other when drowning in the sea in Carrickfergus harbour. He praised the Queen and the two Earls for having the wit and wisdom to investigate the truth and use Digby as their envoy. Equally he castigated the Earls of Tyrconnell and Tyrone, even though he claimed one was his father, for abandoning their people.

Conn concluded by making two points. The first was he should be given the title of the Earl of Tyrone. He said he needed the title, not for his vanity but to give his place at the negotiating table legitimacy. Northumberland, as a learned man and an expert on such things, interjected here. After the flight of the earls to the lands of England's enemies, he said, both earls had been declared traitors and their earldoms withdrawn. There was no longer a title to give to Conn or anybody else. Never again would there be an Earl of Tyrone.

Conn O'Neill's second point was a plea for his people. There would be no peace in Ireland, he said, without a political solution and this needed equal participation from both sides of the divide. He was willing to stand up for his people and offer compromise if those who fought against them, even in peacetime, would do the same. When he finished, the Queen and two English earls nodded. Yes, thought Elizabeth, here is a man we can do business with. If he needs a title I shall give him one.

Digby asked one question near the end of the day. He wanted to know how much land in Ireland was still the property of the crown. Northumberland and Suffolk saw the reason behind his enquiry immediately. If there was to be a fairer settlement where land could be traded for commitments to peace and order, the land would have to come from somewhere.

There would be a need for tribunals, perhaps held over a number of years, overseen by judges as independent as they could make them. No doubt some planter leaders and Irishmen would be found guilty of crimes against each other. An approach would be needed to determine who should be punished and who should be pardoned. There could be no room for the worst of the planters, nor the worst of the Irish. People on both sides would face exile or worse. Others would need to be forgiven for their crimes and escape scot-free for the sake of peace.

This would free up some land for re-distribution but if they were not to impose an unfair settlement on the planters and incite their wrath, they'd need more. If the lands of the crown were significant and could be fairly re-distributed, perhaps the peace process had a chance. All knew, whatever happened, there would be serious difficulties along the way. It would need strong and fair-minded leaders on all sides.

By midnight virtually everything which could be said on this historical first day had been said, but Digby wished to raise one more topic. He voiced his concerns for the Americas. He'd seen first hand the folly and bloodshed caused by the policies of plantation in Ireland. He'd heard of plans to move whole populations and create reservations. If these mistakes were repeated in the Americas, one day his people would not be remembered for their great discoveries but for the intolerable suffering they caused to men, women and children. If this was the way things were to be, he said, he wanted no part.

For the first time Elizabeth spoke. She extolled the virtues of Hilliard's stylised view. The world she wanted, she said, was one where her nation explored, discovered and found new sources of wealth but in a way which would benefit her people, who'd suffered from hunger, disease and poor government in the past, and the peoples they encountered.

'The nation,' said Elizabeth, 'and my family at its head have suffered much over the years from intolerance and injustice. My grandmother Mary was beheaded by my namesake Queen Elizabeth, due to her Catholic faith. My father was assassinated because he was a Protestant who mistreated Catholics. I have no wish to suffer the same fate as my forebears nor impose such hardships onto others, simply because of where they come from or what they believe.'

She looked at the five men in the room in front of her.

'We've just spent the day here discussing how we can create a better future and we are right. The people of these islands have learned. We are better than we were. The future will be different. Yes, we shall explore the world but we shall do it in a different way. The days of plantation are numbered. We shall make Ireland a better place, and then we shall take the lessons learned and share these in the Americas and beyond. Gentlemen, there are great days ahead and you each have your part to play in them.'

Elizabeth smiled and looked up. 'This is God's will,' she said. 'He gave man the freedom to make mistakes and although we've made too many, it's time we learned from them. A better future starts today.'

The five men in the room were spellbound. They hailed from different backgrounds and held diverse beliefs. Three were born in England, one in Wales and one in Ireland. Two were Protestant, two were Catholic and one in truth doubted the existence of an all powerful God. But they all listened to the Queen speak. Elizabeth was born in Scotland, raised in England and the monarch of four nations.

None of them had ever heard a man, let alone a woman, speak like this. Each was mesmerised. Elizabeth's words, her emotions, her passions were clear. Her coronation had been some years ago but this was the day she really became their queen. It was clear she believed every word she said and the men in the room believed her too. Different and similar thoughts flickered through their heads. Each decided they would gladly die for her.

One of the Englishmen, the least religious of them all, crossed himself and made thanks to God if God existed that he hadn't kidnapped Elizabeth when she'd been just a nine year old princess. One of the others fell in love with her there and then. It was a love which would never leave him, no matter what happened in the future. He simply knew he would love that woman until the day he died.

Chapter XXVI

The next three weeks flew by. Button returned to the *Sixth of November* and sailed back to his mission around Ireland. Before he left he enjoyed an afternoon sitting for Hilliard, during which the artist sketched him from almost every conceivable angle. The Queen had commissioned her favourite painter to create a new work entitled *To Greenwich from Ireland.*

The painting once finished would depict the arrival of the three men at the Queen's palace. They were to be shown standing on the rowing boat with the Queen waving regally from the shore standing between the Earls of Suffolk and Northumberland. Elizabeth had given Button categorical assurance he'd feature in the centre of the painting.

#

The Lord Deputy of Ireland, Sir Oliver St John, was recalled to London. Michael Obins, Sir Arthur Chichester and several other prominent planters were arrested. Obins and Chichester were charged with the attempted murder of Sir Everard Digby and placed in separate cells in the Tower of London.

#

Digby and Conn O'Neill worked tirelessly alongside Northumberland and Suffolk on the initial plans for a new start in Ireland. All four men recognised many people would need to be involved as the topic was complex but they had to start somewhere. Their early focus was on the creation of new laws to be announced by the Secretary of State during the opening of Parliament.

On November 6th 1617 Queen Elizabeth lit a bonfire and gave the annual King James Night address. She talked of her vision of a United Kingdom encompassing all four nations of her islands and many others around the world.

Elizabeth carried on in the same vein the next morning when she opened Parliament. Her Secretary of State, the Earl of Suffolk, followed the Queen's lead. He outlined plans to develop a *"new start"* in Ireland focused on benefiting all the people who lived there and announced a special conference which would bring together for the first time the English, Scots and Irish Parliaments in the new year of 1618.

This would be a historic moment. Following much discussion, diplomacy and promises beforehand there was consensus for this in each of the three Parliaments. Of course there were dissenters. There always are when historic changes of direction are being made.

For many in the country, the highlight of the session wasn't the fine speeches but the fact that the state opening of Parliament was held in the newly rebuilt Parliamentary buildings in Westminster. A huge final effort had been made and the buildings made ready just in time for the ceremony.

A new tradition was also created that day. A ceremonial search was carried out before Parliament opened. The buildings were swept above and beneath ground in search of strangers and explosives. Thankfully none were found during the formalities on the 7th November1617, nor in the more extensive security operation in the days before. Nobody who'd lived through that time would ever forget what had happened to the previous Parliament House twelve years before.

#

In the intervening weeks Will Carr spent much time interviewing Digby about many topics, including Linda Blanchet. Digby recounted what had happened in the Americas. His story confirmed Carr's suspicions about the Frenchwoman's motivations. Additional guards were placed on Digby and around Greenwich Palace, as the ongoing potential threat from the French, Jesuits and Puritans was taken very seriously.

Carr and his watchers continued to search for Madam Blanchet but they failed to find her. Some thought she'd killed herself rather than be taken. Others believed she'd returned to France, although Suffolk's spies across the channel found no evidence of this.

During this time Carr was made aware of a series of unsolved murders around London's city walls. The victims were single people who lived alone, their bodies discovered inside their houses where little or nothing had been stolen. There were no witnesses to any of these killings but Carr had a feeling the Frenchwoman was behind them. She was out there still, he believed, moving stealthily from place to place. If these thoughts were true, she remained a step ahead of her pursuers.

#

Following a successful but exhausting day, filled with pomp and ceremony in Westminster, all that remained for many people was attendance at the evening's celebratory events in Greenwich Palace. Ben Jonson's new masque was to be performed under the patronage of the Queen Mother. Anne was extremely excited about what was to come but Elizabeth had three more meetings to endure before she could finally go to the ballroom and take her place on stage as Queen of the Stars. The first two sessions were interviews with potential suitors. The third centred on other state business.

The first conference was now in progress. In the room were Elizabeth, the Earl of Suffolk, Archduke Ferdinand of Austria, a translator and lead lady-in-waiting Anne Dudley.

'Your Majesty,' said the translator, 'my master wishes to convey to you he controls much of Austria but later this year he'll also become the King of all Bohemia,' said the translator.

Ferdinand spoke again and the translator listened intently, nodding occasionally. Elizabeth looked at Ferdinand and he looked back at her. He wasn't bad looking and not that ancient either. She'd been told he was thirty nine years old. The translator spoke again.

'My master says it is the future which is most important. My master's brother, Matthias, is Holy Roman Emperor and King of Germany. As such he's one of the most powerful rulers in the whole of Europe. However, the health of Matthias is failing and his marriage is sadly childless. My master says if Matthias dies, as many expect, he'll naturally assume his brother's titles to add to his own. Together you could achieve the most powerful alliance in Europe, stronger than either the Spanish or French. England would be safe forever from the fear of invasion.'

The translator halted and Ferdinand spoke again. His face became more expressive now and he twice touched the tunic beneath his ruff in the area of his heart.

'My master pledges,' said the translator, 'that he will be a faithful husband to you, as he was to his first wife, Maria Anna, until she was tragically taken from him. He says Maria Anna was a fine woman and bore him seven fine children but he believes it is time he loved again. If you accept this proposal of marriage and alliance, he'll remain faithful to you, as it is the word of God that once together, no man and wife should become apart.'

Elizabeth knew Ferdinand was devoutly Catholic. She suspected once the proposal was agreed his first action would be to attempt to convert her to Catholicism ahead of the marriage. As they gazed at each other, she also worried his second step would be the swift removal of the tolerance laws, although it would not be the Catholics who would be persecuted this time but the majority Protestant population.

At that moment Ferdinand harboured happy thoughts along the same lines. The Protestants would be taught the error of their ways. They had to be punished, and not just here but right across Europe. Even if this meant thirty years of war, he would make it so. His smile turned into a beam towards Elizabeth. She was an attractive young woman. Perhaps they could make seven more children.

'The words of your master on his fidelity are comforting indeed,' said Elizabeth. 'But what are his views on marrying a member of the Protestant faith?'

The colour drained a little from the translator's face. He hesitated.

'Ask him, please,' said Elizabeth.

There was a flurry of discussion between Archduke Ferdinand and the translator. Words were spoken, some not intended for direct translation.

'My master says this is something which the two of you should discuss once his proposal is accepted,' said the translator diplomatically.

'I see,' said Elizabeth.

The regal smile had vanished from Ferdinand's face. He blurted out angry words to the man alongside him. The translator's eyes widened further. He appeared a little flustered and embarrassed.

'My master says you have a beautiful smile, Your majesty. It is a smile which would light up any room. He asks for you to smile at him once more.'

'I don't believe you,' said Elizabeth. She didn't look at Ferdinand. 'What did he say?'

'P-please, Your majesty,' stammered the translator. 'You put me in a very difficult position.'

'You will answer me truthfully and swiftly if you wish to leave England alive. Do not forget I am the Queen of England, Wales, Scotland and Ireland. What did he say?'

'He said he would like to see your teeth, Your majesty. I am sorry but he said he has heard the English do not have very good teeth.'

'Oh, why didn't you say so?' said Elizabeth. 'That's fine. We'll do an exchange. Tell the Archduke he can see my teeth if I can smell his feet. I hear the Austrians have odorous feet - and very small manhoods but I'm happy to wait to address that one until after the marriage proposal is accepted.'

'Your Majesty, please no!' exclaimed the transistor.

Suffolk coughed and spoke up. 'I believe what her Majesty is saying is that it has been a long and tiring day and she has several more meetings scheduled before this evening's entertainment. She thanks the Archduke for his time and will carefully consider his proposal.'

'Thank you, my Lord,' said the translator gratefully.

He spoke quickly to the Archduke, who was determined to find out what had really been said once they were out of the room. If she accepted his proposal there were going to be some changes around this place, he thought. With a flourish of bows and formality the guests left the room.

There was an awkward moment in the corridor as Archduke Ferdinand came face to face with Elizabeth's next visitor. This was the Protestant Germanic noble Frederick of Palatine. Their eyes met. There was a look of intense dislike between the two men. It was the type of dislike which could easily spill over into hatred and bloodshed between their peoples and religions.

In the moments before Frederick's entry, Elizabeth admonished Suffolk. There would be no more meetings with foreign leaders unless they had a translator of their own, she said. Better still, they should make use of a hidden interpreter and pretend they had no idea of what was being said. Carr would have been proud of her, thought Suffolk to himself. What's more, said Elizabeth, she was not going to marry the Austrian. She was tolerant of other faiths and religions but this was going too far. She wouldn't marry a bully and a bigot.

The meeting with Frederick was brief. No translator was needed as Frederick spoke excellent English. For this meeting, there were only four people in the room, Frederick, Elizabeth, Suffolk and once again in the shadows, Anne Dudley.

'Your Majesty, you look as majestic as ever,' said Frederick, once the footman had closed the door with a grand bow.

Elizabeth smiled. There was an inward sigh too. Frederick was a man she could have married. Perhaps if her father and brothers had not been killed and she'd remained a Princess she would have done so. They would have made a fine couple but it wasn't to be. She was a queen and he was only a minor noble. Time was a great healer though. She no longer felt the same sadness she had in the summer. Elizabeth had decided to listen to his proposal, feign regret and as politely as possible decline his offer. And that would be the end of that.

'Your Majesty,' said Frederick. 'I am soon to be a king. The people of Bohemia are tired of the oppression of the Catholics of Austria. They've asked me to be their king in place of Archduke Ferdinand. This must remain a secret for now but soon I will have my own lands and power. I will be a king, and as such a suitable man for a woman to marry and I would like to begin my reign as King of Bohemia with a suitable queen on the throne beside me. I believe I have found that queen and wish to make her my wife. I have come here, Your Majesty...'

For a moment Frederick hesitated. Anne Dudley looked at the floor, her face as white as a sheet. Here we go, thought Elizabeth. This is good but Bohemia's still too small. She'd need to reject him but she felt uneasy. He was back to being the Freddie she liked, perhaps could even have come to love. She didn't want to spoil his dreams but she'd have to.

'I have come here, Your Majesty,' he repeated, 'to ask for your permission to marry your lady-in-waiting, Anne Dudley. Anne's father, Lord Dudley, has accepted my request on condition you are also supportive of the match. I would like to make Anne my wife and when I am King see her crowned my Queen of Bohemia. She is the daughter of an English Lord, the favourite of the English queen. She is right for me and my people will love her. Please Queen Elizabeth, will you permit this?'

He bent down on one knee in front of Elizabeth and put his eyes to the ground. For a moment, she was taken aback. This wasn't the proposal she'd been expecting to politely decline.

'Arise, Frederick,' she said. 'Please, please, stand up.'

He stood and faced her in her chair, the mini throne. Anne couldn't bear to look.

'Of course I approve,' said Elizabeth. 'You'll make a wonderful King and Anne...' Elizabeth looked at her best friend. The girl who had always been there for her, virtually all her life. Tears were streaming down both their cheeks. Anne rose and came to Elizabeth and they embraced. Frederick and Suffolk looked on from a respectful distance.

'Anne, I am so happy for you,' said Elizabeth. 'Now, we can both be queens. You will return to England to see me from time to time, won't you?'

Anne stepped back slightly. 'Of course, of course,' she said. 'And once things are settled in Bohemia we would be so happy to receive royal visitors from England. Frederick has told me so much about his land and the Rhine and also about Prague. He says it's one of the most beautiful cities in the world.'

For the next few moments there were more tears and smiles. Frederick left and then after a short interval, to allow a respectful gap between them, Anne Dudley departed from the room too.

There was just one more meeting before Elizabeth would need to be made up and helped into her costume for the masque. This one had been requested by Conn O'Neill, the newly titled Earl of Ulster. Whilst Elizabeth and Suffolk had remained ever present in the series of meetings, this time they were joined by Conn and the Earl of Northumberland.

Conn bowed and when invited to do so kissed the Queen's hand. Not for the first time he wondered what his friends in Ireland would have made of this. But he was sure he was doing the right thing. With the help of this woman he could transform the lives of his people. Yes, it would take time. There would be hurdles along the way but Conn was a convert to diplomacy. In his heart he'd begun to believe words could really be as powerful as the sword.

What's more, this Queen of England beguiled him. Since the moment she'd spoken so eloquently on his first night on English soil he'd loved her. Nobody knew of this, not even Digby. It was a secret which could do no good, so he kept it to himself.

'Lord O'Neill, I'm afraid we don't have much time before the masque,' said Elizabeth. 'The Earl of Northumberland tells me you have something of importance you wish to discuss with only the four of us present. What is it? What do you want?'

'It is a delicate matter,' said Conn. 'It's about the position of Lord Deputy of Ireland, now vacant since the removal of St John from the role.'

'I'm sorry,' interjected Suffolk. 'But you must know we can't possibly give you the position. None of the planters, not even the moderate ones, would stand for it. We need somebody who can be viewed as an independent figure.'

'That's exactly the issue,' said Northumberland. 'We need to choose someone who didn't fight in the war on either side. If we go for a veteran like Chichester or St John again, the Irish won't support it and we'll be back to square one.'

'I agree,' said Conn. 'I'm not after the job.'

'Then who?' said Suffolk.

Elizabeth knew where Conn was going with this. 'Digby,' she said.

220

'Digby?' said Northumberland. 'But we promised him, if he was successful in Ireland he could return to the Americas.'

'He learned more about my country in a week than Chichester did in twenty years,' replied Conn. 'He's the only man I'd ever trust to be impartial. The only one I would accept an instruction from if it went against my way because I knew he'd be doing things not because somebody told him to but because it was right.'

'I agree,' said Suffolk. 'If we can distance Digby from your recent difficulties in Ulster, he would make the ideal candidate. He's an English Catholic for heavens sake, with no connections with the war or the troubles. It might just work.'

'But we promised him,' said Northumberland. 'His heart is in America.'

'Matters of the heart can quickly change,' replied Elizabeth tersely.

'What do you mean?' asked Conn.

'Nothing,' she said.

They all went quiet for a moment.

'My goodness,' said Elizabeth. 'I shall have to put a move on, or you'll be arresting my mother for assassinating the Queen. If I miss my role in this masque, she'll surely murder me for all the preparation she's put into it.'

For once nobody laughed at the Queen's joke. There were enough threats on her life already, real and imagined.

Chapter XXVII

Ben Jonson prowled around the rehearsal area in a panic. The performers watched him nervously. They peeped through the curtains of their cubicles and wondered who he'd bellow at next for some minor misdemeanour. The final moments were always like this. The non-appearance of the Queen hadn't helped Jonson's anxieties. It was a great relief for him when Anne Dudley appeared back-stage to confirm Elizabeth would be arriving shortly at the special make-up closet Jonson's dresser had created for her.

As he risked a peep through the curtain, and saw the evening's audience for the first time as swiftly as the dark mood had descended it was replaced by light. This was brilliant, what he lived for. There was nothing like live theatre and a first night premiere was very special.

The theatre room at Greenwich Palace was packed to the rafters. Inigo Jones had completed the extension work to the room a decade earlier. Jonson's sometime partner sat in the front row looking pleased with himself. Probably making a critique of my set designs, thought Jonson. There were earls, lords, countesses, nobles, Members of Parliament and foreign dignitaries. Was that Archduke Ferdinand, he wondered?

Jonson watched as the Queen's leading lady-in-waiting returned from her visit backstage and sat herself down with her father and the Dudley family. Why did Lord Dudley and his daughter look so happy, he wondered as he closed the curtain.

At that moment Sir Everard Digby entered the room. As he made his way along the middle aisle towards his seat he was pleased to see Conn O'Neill was already there. Digby hoped he'd be ready to entertain him as usual with amusing stories of his life in Europe before he returned to Ireland.

As Digby neared his seat he saw her. There could be no mistaking that straight back. The world stood still. There was nobody else like her. Nobody in England. Nobody in Europe. Nobody in the world. Digby's heart missed a beat. The dark hair. The head held so high. The proud look. She had her back to him but he knew it was Chasquéme.

She was talking to a man Digby didn't recognise. Adrenaline raced through his body. He pressed forward through the masque-goers but Chasquéme hadn't seen him. She'd started to walk away with the stranger towards the back of the hall. Digby cut a path directly towards her. He sliced through the crowded room like Button's ship through the thin ice of the northern ocean.

The sudden rush of movement made her turn her head partly back towards him. Her shoulders swivelled. A few people wondered what was going on. The throng in the aisle parted for Digby as it had for Moses in the Red Sea. A channel opened between the two people who'd once been one. Digby's body floated towards her.

He was two feet away from her when he spoke. A single word. 'Chasquéme?'

She turned towards him. She was beautiful. But it wasn't her. When the woman looked into his eyes she saw disappointment. This wasn't Chasquéme. Her striking face was North American but it wasn't Chasquéme's.

Digby's heart slowed and almost ceased to beat. His lungs stopped taking in air. His legs almost gave way from under him but he forced himself to stand, gripping the back of a chair with both hands. She had been so real.

'Hello,' said the woman. 'I'm sorry. You look like you've seen a ghost. Do we know each other?'

'Chasquéme,' he whispered. It was all he could say.

'That's a beautiful name,' she said. 'It means maize or corn.'

'I know,' he replied gently.

'But I'm not Chasquéme,' she said. 'My name is Rebecca. I'm pleased to meet you, sir. My husband is over there, John Rolfe, the tobacco planter. Do you know him?'

'No.' The world had become a strange alien place.

The woman calling herself Rebecca laughed. 'Of course Rebecca wasn't my original name,' she said. 'I've had so many down the years. My mother called me Matoaka. Later my people called me Pocahontas but my Christian name and the name I answer to these days is Rebecca. It's quite a long story. Have you been to the Americas?'

'Yes.' Digby's voice was a whisper, almost inaudible.

'Yes, of course! It's you!' she said suddenly recognising Digby's face. 'The man in the painting! Sir Everard Digby. You're the man who found Hudson the explorer, aren't you?'

'Yes,' he repeated. 'That's me. I'm the man in the painting.'

'Who was Chasquéme?'

'A woman I knew,' he said. 'I met her in the Americas. From a distance she looks a lot like you but I've not seen her for some time.'

'What people was she from?'

'The Muhhekunneuw.'

'Oh, I'm sorry,' said Rebecca. 'Did the smallpox get her?'

'What do you mean?' asked Digby.

'One of John's tobacco shipments came in last week. The outbreaks of smallpox over there are getting worse. Many of the peoples have been affected, especially the ones living nearer the bigger rivers. I was told the villages of the Muhhekunneuw were hit badly. Some were wiped out. Many have died.'

'Are there survivors?' asked Digby. In his mind, he thought, please God, give me hope. Let there be hope.

'Some I think but not many,' she replied sadly. 'I'm sorry to pass on such bad news to you, Sir Everard. Chasquéme obviously meant a lot to you but you must forgive me. My husband is calling me over to be seated. The masque will be starting shortly. I wish you well.'

'Thank you,' he said. 'Tell me, do you plan to return to the Americas?'

'Yes, we'll go back there soon,' she replied. 'We're going to my husband's house in Gravesend tomorrow to begin plans to sail in the spring. We'll be travelling to my husband's planation but if I'm honest I don't like it much. My people are often treated badly and there is much sickness. Will you go back?'

'Yes,' he replied, 'I hope to go soon.'

With this Rebecca turned and was lost in the crowd. Digby was engulfed by a crush of people as they began to take their seats in preparation for the evening's performance. He moved slowly back to his own seat and sat down. A few times he glanced over towards where he thought Rebecca was seated but he couldn't see her through the crowds. The hall was dark and packed with people, all pleased to be invited to the evening's festivities.

Conn was already seated when Digby joined him. Digby could see Conn's mind was filled with his own thoughts. For once he wasn't talking. When the masque started neither man really took much detail in of the plot in the first half, although Conn observed it was a wonderful spectacle. Music played. Men and women acted. Figures and shapes danced. The moon had a major role as did the stars.

During the interval Digby remained in his seat. Conn stood up to stretch his legs. Standing next to his friend he asked him if he was alright. When Digby remarked quietly he was just tired Conn went off for a walk before returning for the second half. He could see from Digby's face his mind was disturbed, so he left him to it. Sometimes men didn't wish to be questioned.

There was a huge cheer as Queen Elizabeth took to the stage part way through the second half of the performance. For the final act she was carried shoulder height by Orion and his friends and placed upon the throne of the Queen of the Stars. From time to time she waved regally at her celestial subjects.

Digby looked at Conn and realised the Irishman couldn't take his eyes off Elizabeth. He was captivated by her. For a second Digby was diverted from his own troubles. He hoped this was a passing thing, it would be a dangerous attraction for his friend.

Elizabeth continued to wave politely. She had a fixed smile on her face as the moon, clouds and stars danced around her. Jonson stood up and waved his arms madly in an effort to encourage the members of the audience to get to their feet and dance and dance through the finale. It took a while to get them gong but when they did they created a wonderful celebratory chaos.

Conn swayed from side to side as much as the people around him. Digby appeared to be the only person still sitting down so the Irishman yanked him to his feet and spoke to him. He had to shout to be heard above the melee around them. 'Come on, you miserable so and so,' he said. 'I've never been to a masque before and it's grand. Everybody else is enjoying themselves. Give it a try.'

Conn joined in a huge round of applause. Digby stood but he didn't clap or dance. He had the look of a man whose mind was elsewhere.

'They're fantastic dancers aren't they?' called Conn. 'Every one of them apart from that scrawny lad over there. He'd got two left feet. Jonson must be seeing his old lady or something to give such a poor dancer a part in the production.'

Digby didn't care about what was going on but he looked in the direction of Conn's nodding head. The recognition was instantaneous. He knew the dancer. They'd rolled around together on the dewy evening grass of the Greenwich maze. The boy had been carried unconscious onto the burning deck of the *Tramonata* and after that Digby believed he'd wrestled with him in the Irish Sea. His mind reactivated. The Puritan assassin had to be stopped.

'That man's a killer,' shouted Digby as he came back to life. 'We must protect the Queen.'

Both men pushed forward but there were people dancing and singing all around them. The two men could hardly move through the crowd for merrymakers. A shapely blonde woman made a grab for Digby's waist. It was clear she wanted to dance with him. He pushed her away but the woman was insistent and tried again. Digby handed her off without even looking.

Conn was now ahead of him. Both men forced themselves towards the stage. The blonde woman followed and tried to pull Digby back towards her. Digby half turned to voice his rejections. The woman raised her right hand. A knife appeared. Her arm struck down. Digby was caught across the temple. Blood splattered out. A woman near to Digby saw this and screamed. The sound was lost in the mayhem of music and cheering. Nobody else appeared to notice.

As Digby stumbled the blonde woman saw her chance. She threw herself onto him ready to finish the job. As she raised her arm a second time Will Carr stepped forward. He'd suspected something like this might happen and had spent the entire evening watching Digby's back like a hawk.

Carr grabbed the woman's wrist and prevented the downward movement. In response she struggled madly. The woman's face filled with rage. Linda Blanchet wanted to sink the dagger into the heart of her husband's murderer. The English spy she remembered from the glass house stopped her. She attempted to free her knife-wielding hand but his grip was too firm. When this failed she punched and scratched at him with her other hand until he he was forced to clamp her second wrist. Once this was done he held her still.

A circle of people turned to view the commotion. They stared at Linda in wonder. She understood she was beaten and began cursing at Carr in French at the top of her voice. Her eyes were wild with fury. When she finished she spat in his face. Carr released her wrists for an instant and threw a punch. He caught Linda Blanchet's unconscious body before it hit the ground.

The altercation attracted the attention of more of the audience. From his stage director's position Jonson couldn't see what was happening. He assumed somebody was drunk or had fainted. In any case the show had to go on. He waved madly at the dancers and orchestral musicians to continue to dance and play as vigorously as they could.

Looking at the stage Jonson was annoyed. Who was that lad dancing in the grand finale? He might have a star on his back but he certainly wasn't one. And where was the excellent dancer who'd been in his place before the interval? If the fellow carried on it could affect Jonson's reputation. Only the best performers were selected for his productions.

The less than excellent dancer wasn't concerned about reviews or critics. At the end of the first half he'd attacked one of the dancers near his own size, taken his clothing and trussed him up. This would be his one and only stage performance. As he turned his attention from the audience, his left hand felt for the knife hidden in his costume. Deftly he extracted it and switched the blade to his right.

The Puritan assassin could no longer hear the music or see the dancing. His body and mind were focused only on his target. He turned towards Elizabeth and felt himself being pulled through a tunnel towards her. After a moment she saw him approach. From the throne she saw the knife glint. She looked around but nobody else saw it. She remembered the date. It was the 7th of November 1617.

The attacker's and victim's eyes met. Elizabeth thought of her sister Mary. She hoped she'd be alright. It would be difficult but given time Mary would make a fine queen. Other thoughts flashed through her mind. Her mother, plans to build an empire, Ireland and Conn O'Neill. How strange the Irishman should appear so large in her final thoughts.

The assassin stepped onto the lower threshold of the Queen of the Stars' throne. He looked at the Queen. She stared back at him defiantly but her body was frozen. She didn't attempt to call out. The heretic queen faces her death bravely, thought the assassin, good for her. The fact didn't alter his resolve. Once he struck her he'd be a dead man but he didn't care. His reward would be in heaven and hers in hell.

He took the two last steps to the throne until he stood above her. He raised his arm. The knife came down. He struck hard and twisted his hand. Flesh was pierced. Blood spurted out. There was an involuntary cry. Nobody heard it apart from the person making it and the woman behind him.

Conn's face contorted in pain. The assassin left his knife imbedded in the man before him. How had he been able to put his body in front of the Queen? It was a question for another time. People were staring at the stage and screaming.

The attacker dashed through the back-stage curtains. Two guards went after him. He struck the first with his fist. The second tripped over a curtain rope and broke a leg. The Puritan escaped. The place was in pandemonium. The Queen was rushed from the room surrounded by bodyguards. Soldiers and guards ran in all directions. The royal physician crouched over Conn's bleeding body. It was clear he was losing a lot of blood.

Many of the guests and dancers wanted to leave but every door was sealed. Will Carr led the search for signs of additional attackers. Linda Blanchet, her blonde wig removed, was led away accompanied by the Earl of Suffolk and a row of soldiers. Everybody else was questioned.

Digby stood on stage, a bloody scar across his temple but otherwise fine. He looked at Conn's face with compassion. The Irishman had lost consciousness and the surgeon was attempting to stem the loss of blood. It didn't look good.

Chapter XXVIII

Digby sat alone in the Whitehall office temporarily assigned to him by the Earl of Northumberland. It had been an eventful few days. The months to come would be even more challenging. His eyes felt sore from the strain of working in candle light until the early hours. He rubbed his temples and turned away from the charts and walked to the edge of the room.

Standing by the window he gazed outside at the rain as it fell heavily against the leaded panes and spattered down onto the rutted roadway and square below. Puddles were forming. The dusty ground created by the recent dry spell had turned to mud. Small groups of men scurried between the administrative buildings. As they did so they were pursued by a swirling wind, more reminiscent of winter than autumn. There was a rap on the door.

'Come in,' said Digby.

Will Carr pushed the wooden door open and entered the room. Digby welcomed him with a handshake and bid the Earl of Suffolk's spy to sit as he returned to his desk. Before he seated himself Digby carefully rolled away the detailed map of Ireland which had been spread out in front of him. A little earlier he'd retraced the route Conn O'Neill and he had taken as they'd journeyed across Ulster from Dundalk to Belfast. It was a troubled country but a beautiful one. The challenges of the island were no longer other people's problems. They were now his own.

'Good day to you, Lord Lieutenant,' said Carr. 'And many congratulations on your appointment.'

'A good day to you, Master Carr,' replied Digby. 'I'm glad you have come. In the commotion I haven't had a chance to thank you for saving my life.'

Carr smiled. 'It's all part of the service, my Lord.'

'What brings you to my new abode?'

'I'm here under the instructions of the Secretary of State,' replied Carr. 'He wanted me to give you an update on the future of Madam Blanchet. Following his recent conference with the French ambassador an agreement has been made that Madam Blanchet will no longer be detained in England. Instead she will be returned to France in exchange for ten Englishmen and two

Scots currently held by the French for their activities on the continent.'

Digby looked at Carr with interest. He knew relatively little about the woman who'd been hellbent on his destruction but she was obviously held in high esteem in France. One woman for twelve men was quite a bargain.

'When does she leave for France?'

'On the morrow. Would you like to see her before she departs?'

'No,' replied Digby. 'I don't think that would be a good idea. The truth is I am guilty of the crime she accuses me of, although as you know there were good reasons for my actions. I doubt there is anything I could say or do to placate her.'

Digby recalled the dead bodies in the burned out native village near the river and crawling through the mud of the tunnel into the French stockade. Briefly he remembered other nights and his time with Chasquéme. He knew these thoughts would do him no good. He wouldn't be returning to the Americas any time soon. Like Button for the time being his world revolved around Ireland.

Carr nodded thoughtfully. 'I should also inform you the Secretary of State made his agreement with the French Ambassador on two conditions.'

'Go on,' said Digby.

'The first stipulation was Madam Blanchet should never return to England. That was agreed upon.'

'And the second?'

'She desists from her interest in your demise.'

'And this condition was agreed to?' asked Digby.

'By the ambassador, yes,' replied Carr. 'But not by Madam Blanchet, and I don't think it ever will be. If I were you, I'd continue to watch my back, my lord.'

'I agree,' said Digby.

'At least there aren't many Frenchmen in Ireland,' added Carr.

Digby caressed his short beard. He wondered if Carr was aware of his role in the Powder Treason. Surely Robert Cecil had known. Digby studied the spy's face. The steady eyes betrayed little, fitting for someone who'd once been Cecil's right hand man. Carr may have saved Digby's life but a cautious wariness remained between the two men.

'Have the physicians formed an opinion on your friend, O'Neill? Will he recover?' asked Carr.

Digby smiled. 'You're one of Suffolk's spies so I'm sure you know as much as I do, if not more on that matter. But, yes, they think he'll be fine in the long run. He just needs rest and recuperation.'

Both men were aware of the events which had occurred since Friday evening. O'Neill had spent the first night close to death's door, attended to by the Queen's personal surgeons and constantly watched over by Elizabeth herself. The word was she'd not left his bedside since. Rumours were running rife in Westminster and Whitehall of the Queen's infatuation with the Irishman.

'Will he join you in the coming months on your mission to Ireland?' asked Carr.

'I'm quite sure he will,' replied Digby. 'I suspect your master and the Privy Council won't wish him to tarry too long in a bed in the royal suite in Greenwich Palace.'

Digby thought of the scandal which would be caused if the Queen really did fall in love with an Irishman. Surely a romantic liaison between the two was impossible? It would be even more unlikely than a union between the Queen and the lowly prince who'd left her table at the birthday celebrations in August. The idea was unthinkable. Every Englishman, even those who supported Elizabeth's more tolerant approach towards the Catholics, would view this as a step too far. In the extreme she could even lose her crown if the country took against her.

'There is one question I'd like to ask,' said Carr. 'Then I must be off.'

'Ask away,' replied Digby, a little warily.

Carr leaned back and opened his cloak. With his right hand he reached down into the interior pocket of the dark garment. Gently he extracted a rolled up parchment and began to untie the ribbon which bound it.

Digby wondered what on earth this could be. Surely not another letter like the one sent to Lord Monteagle warning of the Powder Treason? The spy placed the scroll onto the desk before them.

'We're looking to print two hundred copies of this document with a plan to place them on display in the most prominent public locations across London. Before we do, I wished to verify with yourself whether the artist has made a good likeness. It appears you've met the man more times than anyone else.'

231

Digby watched with fascination as Carr pressed the palms of his hands onto the two ends of the parchment until it was laid out flat in front of them. An artist's impression of the Queen's would-be assassin was sketched on the paper in grey and black. The resemblance to the youth with dark hair, staring eyes and no beard, the man who'd attempted to kill both Queen Elizabeth and Digby, was uncanny.

Beneath the picture the following words were written… *Wanted dead or alive! Cash reward for crimes against the state. Man known by the name of Oliver Cromwell.*

'Aye, that's him,' said Digby.

THE END

Printed in Great Britain
by Amazon